# Love Makes Things Happen

Written, Produced and Arranged by:

## *Jonathan P. Mance*

Written in Baltimore City/Harford County Maryland

Written in Concord, North Carolina

2016 The Black House Publications

Book Cover Illustration by: Jess Bastidas

Edited by: Charisse Williams

Managing Supervisor: April M. Perkins

Executive Producer: Cendra S. Clarke-Mance

The Black House Publishing Inc.

ISBN-13: 978-0-9972731-0-6

ISBN-10: 0-9972731-0-0

Library of Congress Cat. Num. in-pub.-Data

1-19K8Y65

PRINTED IN THE UNITED STATES OF AMERICA

The Black House Publishing Presents:

Love Makes Things Happen:

In today's world, all of us have friends of the opposite sex. For most of us they are just that, friends. Your family knows it, their family knows it and in your mind you know it. What happens when your souls know you two were meant to be more than friends? Despite your most valiant efforts to keep things neatly in the friends box. Despite your promises to others and yourself, that you would never do that. Sometimes love is so powerful, it will rearrange the universe to connect. That's when you find out, love makes things happen….and there is nothing you can do about it.

*This book is a work of fiction. Any similarities to any actual persons either living or dead is strictly coincidental and is based entirely on imagination and creative thoughts. While actual places, events and other circumstances may exist, they do not change the fact that the author drew upon his knowledge of such places or events and interlaced fictitious characters to make the story more intense and realistic.*

# Dedication

*To Janie Mance, for all you did, especially bestowing the gift of thinking
and writing on me...I will always love you. To Cendra, here's the book
boss lady. Love you to pieces. By far you are the smartest and prettiest
boss I've ever worked for. To Jonah and Kain Carter, To Carolyn V.
Mance, thank you for being you. You are a true black Queen and I will
always love and appreciate you. Ms. Valarie Mance-San Leandro, CA I
love you more than words can say. Ms. Geneva Vanderhorst Atlanta, Ga,
Ms. Jackie Mance Charlotte, NC, Ms. Pamela Mance, Baltimore, Md, I
love you all in a special way. Ms. Robin Harvin,(Fort Mill, SC) No matter
what, no one will ever occupy your space in my heart, I do love you from
here to eternity. To my super smart business partner Ms. April M. Perkins,
(Baltimore, Md ((the other boss lady)) I'm blessed to have such brilliant
business partner. Ms. Veronica Gee, (Baltimore Md.) Much love to you
beautiful lady. My brothers Justin, Lincoln, Rob and all of you on the side.
My other brother Joseph Bell EBRPS, My nephew Jarrad Woods NYC via
Oaktown, Lincoln Mance Jr. and my sweetheart neice Monie- Lacey, Wa.
LaShawn Michelle, (Charlotte, NC), You're so beautiful,...if only.... To all
of my great teachers whether you're still here or not. Especially those
from the Almighty Capitol Senior High Baton Rouge, La. Your impact on
our lives was tremendous. I personally want to say thank you to all of you.
Ms. Jonna Steward, Charlotte, NC. Hi beautiful. Ms. Myrtle Glover, What
can I say about what a beautiful person you are? Thank you for always
being so kind to me. You will always be precious to me. Love you with all
my heart. Ms. Tovondia Jones, you're still one of the greatest people I've
ever met. You know I love me some you. Neicy Briscoe, I hope I'm still
your Boo Boo, I love you. Launa Harcum, love you lady. Shanell Johnson,
what a classy and beautiful lady you are. I don't know if you knew this but
you impressed me. April Glover, You must have been born fine. Smile,
love you 29 times. To: Robin, Melissa, Karen, Sheena, N'Kenge (the
lifelines), I still love you. Thank you. All my blue family*

# Love Makes Things Happen

There is a difference between whom we love, whom we settle for and whom we were meant to be with.-Unknown

# Parental Discretion-
# Is Advised.

The Black House

Baltimore, Md.

Contact: For Book Signings and Appearances

BlackHousePublish@gmail.com

(443) 904-0649

Love Makes Things Happen

# The Name is Bond, Real Bond

They met through a mutual friend and had grown to become the best of friends. They were always there to talk to one another. To listen to the other's hopes, dreams and complaints. Or sometimes they could just talk about nothing for hours. Christopher and Angel were truly a unique pair. They had often noted, that on paper they shouldn't even like each other. Christopher was comedic, silly at times and not very open to meeting new people. However, once he got to know you, he would say just about anything that came to mind. He also took business serious when it was time to make a move to secure his future. He and Angel only had that in common.

Angel was more laid back on the personal side but constantly going about business. No matter what the two of them might be talking about. Angel would find some way to tie it to Accounting, taxes or investments. As a Certified Public Accountant and owner of her own business, this made perfect sense to her. Christopher was a retired Transit cop, Owner of a Private Security Firm and small real estate investor. Accounting only interested him at times. When he wasn't busy with his own business. Angel was the type to walk up to anybody at any time. She'd ask them about anything she saw them doing that even remotely interested her.

Christopher was also a sponge for information. His mind overflowed with trivial information on thousands of subjects. He sought his mostly by keeping informed of current events in the news. He also loved History, Science Literature and kept up on entertainment news. They had a huge difference on religious beliefs. Christopher believed that man had severely tampered with the Bible. Angel believed in religion and going to church. Christopher was not a fan of reality shows. He thought all of them were a waste of time. To his surprise, Angel who shunned most nonsense, would engage in watching a few of these shows.

He was well aware that he surprised her with some of the things that interested him as well. Angel Renee' Robinson and Christopher Paul Watson could not be more different. They also couldn't be more alike. Even if they had been able to ask God to make them that way. They were two oddballs that didn't fit in with the crowd but did fit with each other. Basically, on their core level, they were just two regular people. They'd worked hard to try to carve their own path to success. Often, Christopher thought about the context of their friendship and the complexities of it all.

On one hand, he saw her as this beautiful goddess. She was stunning as she was a well-built package. Always dressed professionally in business attire. Never showing off her body through revealing clothes. She carried herself with class and had the most beautiful face. She also had the sexiest pair of lips this side of Heaven. Yet she was his dearest friend. Someone he cherished like no other friend before. She knew all his thoughts, his ambitions, his pain and his hopes. He never wanted to mess that up by crossing the line with her.

So he just viewed her in what he called the middle passage. The middle passage is where he could acknowledge her remarkable beauty, and yet appreciate her as his wonderful friend. She was a friend for whom he would do just about anything. He also knew that Angel would be there for him if he ever needed her. They made great efforts to never give the other the appearance that their relationship was one sided.

They called each other often. If the recipient of the call was busy and could not talk, they always called each other back. Most of the time it was just to say, "I didn't want anything. I just called to say hello." Sometimes, Christopher wondered if Angel ever saw him in a different light, as he would sometimes see her. Sometimes, he would think she was flirting with him. At other times he would flirt with her. Yet, it was always routine for the one that was being flirted with to sit there like; "*what the hell are you doing?*"

Whatever small spark that may or may not have been there never manifested itself. At least not beyond playful name calling by their middle names. They both preferred no one to call them by their middle names except each other. Neither of them ever tried to show much in the way of public displays of affection. They would not always embrace upon seeing each other. They just understood that this person was very special to them. Words or actions were rarely needed to convey this in their minds. Angel purchased a home in Northern Virginia, just south of Washington, DC. Christopher purchased a home in Maryland, North of Baltimore. Angel is originally from Philadelphia, Pennsylvania and Christopher is from Baton Rouge, Louisiana. One being Northern and the other Southern never created any borders between them. While in Atlanta they both began job searches because they felt stagnant.

They were both offered jobs in the DMV (DC, Maryland and Virginia). As fate would have it, that put them in the same circles. They longed for a simpler life but felt they had to leave home and make their fortune. They both dreamed of someday moving to retire in the South. Or perhaps find a country in Africa and live happily ever after. That was about 20 years ago when they were both around 22. Once in the DMV, they both lived their own separate lives. While they were close enough to visit, they were not right around the corner from each other. It was just over an hour drive from one house to the other. So visits had to be coordinated whenever they did occur.

Every now and then, when they could find the time, they would grab a bite to eat together. Or maybe see a movie and always debate whose turn it was to pay. While hanging out together, they would talk about some of everything. From their plans, news stories to politics. Often they would disagree but would then agree to disagree. Never did those disagreements create any riffs between them. This was the most perfect of friendships Christopher would often think. The two of them could miss weeks of talking to each other, and pick up right where they left off.

They would sometimes buy each other small gifts. Things such as books or novelties for the home, to show how much they loved each other. Although they rarely uttered those three words "I love you" to each other. They knew it and didn't have to say it, Christopher rationalized. Angel was not big on showing affection. At least outside of her relationship with her immediate family. That was fine with Christopher. He was not quick to tell most people that he liked them either. He could not define his friendship with Angel. Other than to say, it was always there.

Whenever he needed to hear her voice or just be near her he could. Then he could feel it was okay to dream. They seemed to hold the utmost respect and love for each other.

Anyone outside of them was told instantly that this friend is very important to me. If you knew Christopher, you knew Angel. Even if you had never met her before or knew what she looked like. You knew her through Christopher.....that was a given. If you knew Angel, you knew Christopher, that was also a given.

There they were strolling down this middle passage. Both seemingly unaware they had built the most perfect type of relationship. It was the farthest thing from either of their minds. Or was it buried somewhere deep in their psychosis? Forever fearful that they may lose this perfect friendship. They took great pains to not cross the line and try to be more than friends. Angel had helped Christopher setting up his business and doing his taxes. She taught him much of what she knew about business. Now, he was at the point where he knew how to find and utilize tax laws for himself. He was so grateful to Angel for that.

Angel was all business but as her client she cared about you. Old, young, little money or lots she cared. That is why Christopher called her a goddess. She was built like one and blessed those she cared about like one. Angel was not without her flaws. Christopher knew he had more flaws than could be stored in cyberspace. They were not above giving each other advice on how to better deal with a situation. Most advice never caused any friction between them. Occasionally they would have heated debates. One of them would call afterwards to make sure that they were still good. They could never stay mad at each other, so they moved on. They would rather see what the other thought about the next topic.

They acknowledged each of them had a little zaniness about them. That it was part of the package. So, they accepted each other "*as is.*" They promised not to return one another to the store as damaged goods.  Angel and Christopher truly had a bond, a real bond.  This relationship existed for nearly two decades.  In that time these two had shared so many of life's joys.  Also disappointments, sorrows, goals, aspirations and silliness. They trusted that whatever confidential words were said between them, would always stay between them.  They trusted each other with the keys to their homes.  They entrusted their family secrets and anything else to one another.  They shared stories of whatever had happened to them good or bad.

Break Yourself Fool!

In every contact they had and in every thought, Christopher marveled at this woman. She was so intelligent, attractive and on many levels like-minded with him. One day they found time to go see a movie. One that Angel wanted to see about a religious topic. Christopher knew that he didn't particular care to see it. However it was a chance to spend some time with his dear friend, so he went.

Christopher picked Angel up at her house in his Escalade. Then they drove to a movie theater in Falls Church, VA. Christopher went in hating a Hollywood movie on religion and Egyptian Gods. However Angel was enjoying it. The more he sat and watched, the more Christopher hated this movie. Angel noticed that he was not paying attention and gave him a gentle elbow. As if to say, watch this. Christopher sat in silence and resolved to let his friend enjoy the movie. He couldn't wait to get out of there. Once they left the movie they were back in Christopher's truck. Angel asked him what he thought about the movie.

He made some general, negative comment and tried to be quiet. Angel kept prodding him for more commentary. Suddenly, a flat out argument had erupted. They had many disagreements before. Many heated discussions, but this was different. This was a different argument as in, "what is wrong with your black ass, to not like or to like this movie?" Their voices were loud. The look of contempt swept over their faces as they drove back to Angel's house. Once inside, the argument continued. Anger like they had never experienced with one another, for any reason.

They argued back and forth over their likes and dislikes about the movie. Angel sat at the formal dining table. Christopher sat a chair away from her. Clearly, this discussion was taking them down a road they had never before gone.

They made covert snide remarks to try to lightly insult the other. Never in the history of their friendship had either stooped to this level. It was scary for Christopher. He felt he was on the verge of losing his most cherished friend. He didn't want to say or do anything too disrespectful.

Still he knew if he felt Angel was trying to cut him with words, he may try to cut her deeper. That was one of his many flaws. They both searched frantically for words to argue their point. Yet without being too insulting to the other's view. Christopher could clearly see the anger in Angel's face. He was also sure his face was not beholding to a pleasant smile at that time. Somewhere in the back of his mind, he told himself that he had to end this argument. Before they did irreparable damage to their friendship but how?

Should he get up and leave? Should he tell Angel enough and that this argument is over. He knew that it may not be that easy, because Angel was angry. You can't just make her be silent when she has something to say. Should he lie and say I see your point, you were right and I was wrong? He knew that would not be convincing. So, what could he do to save their friendship? Angel looked like she wanted to slap the taste out of his mouth. In desperation to save them, he stood and walked over to her. He kissed her passionately on her beautiful lips as she was still speaking. She being stunned, tried to pull away and was really about to curse. Christopher held her firm. In seconds, she kissed him back. He took her hand and stood her up leading her to the sofa.

He kissed her again and then knelt in front of her. He began unbuttoning her pants. "What the hell are you doing;" she asked? "Break yourself fool, he thought to himself. Run home and never look back." Then, he said out loud; "I am going to worship you for the goddess that you are Angel Renee. The beautiful goddess that you are." With that, he pulled down her pants and panties. He marveled at the exquisite beauty of her body. He had imagined it many times over the years, but now he could see it standing before him. So chocolate, so lush, so curvy and so perfect.

He pushed her gently to sit. He removed her shoes and pulled her pants and panties completely off. He began to suck her toes and said, "I don't want to fight with you goddess. You should be worshipped and not fought with." He kissed her feet from top to bottom and then worked his way up her juicy legs. Angel flowed between relaxing in the moment and wanting to stop this immediately. Christopher knew he only had seconds to get past that point.

Christopher raced kisses up her left leg and inner thigh. Stopping just short of her treasure. Then he went back down to her right ankle. His mouth raced kisses up her right leg and thigh. Once he reached the top, he pushed her legs apart and began to lick slow, taunting circles just outside her lips. Lips he noticed were just as beautiful as the pair on her face. "What is that scent you're wearing;" he asked her? Angel mumbled, "Black Orchid by Tom Ford." Then she whispered; "Oh fuck" as he licked left, then downward and then back up on the right side. "Do you mind if I lick all of it off your body;" he asked? Angel could only open her legs wider to say yes. She was gasping for air as he inserted his finger inside of her.

Then he continued to attack her with kisses and licks that seemed to be coming from everywhere. Now, down the right side over to the left and back up. He found her clit and slowly but firmly licked it. Then grabbed it with his lips and gently pulled it in his mouth. Angel let out a moan of pleasure and he knew he was on the right course. He locked his arms behind her knees. Then pulled her legs so that her pussy was close to the edge of the sofa. He took his tongue placing it just under her vagina, as he pushed her knees to her chest.

He stiffened his tongue, as he licked slowly from the bottom of her vagina up to her clit. He began to kiss it, lick it and make love to it with his mouth. He felt her body squirming under his mouth. He assaulted her vagina with his tongue and he had no plans of stopping. He rammed his tongue inside of her while kissing her lips. He savored her juices as they poured into his mouth. "What a goddess you are Angel;" he mumbled. Quickly diving back in to lick, kiss and suck her vagina relentlessly.

He caressed her inner thighs. He paused briefly to kiss them, then going back to devour her pussy. It was so beautiful in the way it was shaped. Just the right amount of hair and surrounded by the most beautiful skin color. Christopher knew where her skin was darkest, it was rich in melanin. Those were her most sensitive parts. That was some of the massive trivial knowledge he acquired from reading so much. He being a sponge for information, retained a lot of it. He licked and sucked those dark areas with vengeance. "What would Angel say after this was over;" he thought? Would she be angry, would she never speak to him again? Would she blame herself for what Christopher had done and end their friendship?

He didn't know and he thought maybe he should stop this himself. Yet at that time, right in that moment. The only thing he wanted was for her to come in his mouth. He knew what a good-hearted person Angel is. She constantly has extended herself for others. She rarely had anyone do a selfless act on her behalf. Christopher wanted to give her what he felt she needed, an orgasm. "Do you like my tongue in your pussy Angel;" he asked? She moaned in approval. "I've wanted to do this for so very long;" he said. He gazed over her voluptuous skin and ran his hands everywhere he could touch.

Her skin was so silky soft and smooth. Her scent, especially her vagina was intoxicating to him. Angel was slightly taken aback with the way Christopher spoke. In all the time she had known him, he rarely used profane language. Now here he is removing her shirt and bra before standing to remove his clothes. Angel felt like she was in a daze. She had so many reasons not to allow this to happen. Christopher's fingers, mouth and tongue felt so nice circling he body. Slurping, sucking, licking, and making love to her pussy.

It was as if he had separated it, just to make love to it all by itself. Then found a way to make her feel so completely adored, worshipped and HOTTTTTT! She felt the lips of her vagina kiss him back. Her walls gripped his tongue as it stretched inside of her. She felt the smoothness of his freshly shaven face. She felt his bald head gliding between her soft, silky legs. She felt as if it belonged there. Hell the way he was kissing her so passionately, she knew he belonged there. So she grabbed the back of his head and she made sure at least for this moment.....he would stay. Oooh you handle her like a man; Angel said.

You turn me on so much Christopher. I'm going to call you "Mr. Man" every time you turn me on like this. He was relentlessly licking her pussy and sliding his fingers inside of her. He sucked and tugged on her clit with his lips. His fingers were driving deeper and deeper inside of her. He seemed to be ambidextrous as he touched her all over. He could begin to hear her breathing grow louder. Her hands grabbed his chocolate bald head and pulled it closer to her body. He prodded her to come for him as he continued his oral assault. He licked her clitoris and sucked her pussy lips. He rammed his tongue inside of her then replaced it with fingers. He flicked his tongue like a snake all over her clit repeatedly. Until he felt her explode and her juices squirted, poured and rained all over his face.

Her legs clenched his head tightly as he continued to lick and kiss her vagina. Meticulously he kissed her shaking body as she came down from her high. He found her juices running down her legs. He licked them up as her sweet nectar was a gift to him. "Angel;" he called to her. You are a goddess and I love worshipping your body. You have a gorgeous pussy and I could stay down here and lick it all night. But I want to do something else." "What's that;" she muttered breathlessly? He took her hand and led her to the bedroom. He put her on her knees in bed, then stood before her. She took him in her mouth.

# Intensive Care

The sight of those magnificent lips wrapped around his dick was everything. Add in those seductive brown eyes and it was almost too much to bear. Still, he fought to hold out. He knew he may not ever get this chance again. He wanted to savor every second. "Oh Angel;" he moaned as she took her tongue and licked the underside of his dick. Making him delirious with pleasure. "Would you lick my balls for me baby;" he moaned? Angel pulled him down onto the bed. She laid him on his back. She began licking his big set of balls and stroking his thick dick. Christopher was insane with delight. He knew not many men had ever before been taken on this pleasure trip with Angel.

For now, right at this very moment, she was all his. He motioned for her to turn. He wanted her in the 69 position. As soon as she straddled his face, he went to work. He wrapped his arms around her back and lowered her clit into his mouth. While she sucked on him, he spread her cheeks staring up at her. Knowing he was seeing one of the most beautiful views any man could ever see. He licked her all over because she was so beautiful in that moment.

He wanted every part of her. As his tongue played with her up and down, she squirmed and then moaned in delight. He could feel her mouth working to give him the type of pleasure she was now getting. Her breast brushed across his hips and he pumped his dick into her mouth. He licked to meet her strokes as she began to grind her pussy over his face. Angel had complete control over her orgasm in this position. She was determined to release again her lava all over his dark brown skin.

Angel rocked back and forth as Christopher stiffened his tongue out. Now she could just swipe her clit back and forth over it. He inserted his fingers inside of her again and he heard her breathing grow louder. Her hips rubbed harder against his face. He responded by spreading her labia with his hand. He wanted her to know it was okay to empty out all of that tension. Cum that was stored in there while he kissed and sucked on her pussy. "Call my name when you cum, Angel. Call my motherfucking name!" "I'm cum, I'm cum, I'm gonna cummmm, Chriiii---------stooopher!"

That was all he heard her say before she mashed her hips over his face. She grinded them as she let out a long scream of relief! She used his face as if it were made for her pussy to fuck and get her off. He didn't mind it one bit. After all this was the woman that he promised, he would do anything for. She dismounted and began sucking on Christopher again and he stopped her. She asked him was something wrong? He looked her right in her beautiful eyes. "Angel Renee' Robinson, I want to make love to you so bad;" he said.

He laid her down on the bed. He climbed on top and kissed her forehead. Then her eyes, nose and then beautiful lips. He wanted her to taste her own sweet juices that were covering his lips and face. He then began to kiss her neck working his way down to her breasts. He gave them some attention by sucking and licking her sensitive nipples. Then lifting each breast to lick the underside of them. Caressing them with his hands. Angel called his name; "Christopher". "Shhhhh, he replied, quiet as I worship this temple. I won't leave any marks as I give you this intensive care." He kissed her neck as he massaged her shoulders. Also sucking her breast and kissing her stomach all over.

He sat back and looked at her body, all of it. He thought what an amazing crafted beauty Angel is. She was a stallion and a true black beauty. All Christopher wanted to do was fuck her like there was no tomorrow. He placed himself in between her legs then lifted her legs over his arms. He then guided his dick inside of her pushing just the head of it in. He began a slow back and forth stroke with just the tip of him inside. He could feel Angel trying to get the rest of his love inside, but Christopher would not comply.

He started increasing the pace making love to her with just the tip of his penis. He was also kissing her feet that were suspended on the side of his face. Angel's body was moving, pushing upward to try and get him all in. He resisted her in every attempt. He teased her for several minutes with just the tip of his manhood. Then without warning Christopher slammed all of his dick inside of her. He was grinding his pubic bone across her clit and fucking her deep for about 50 seconds. Then he pulled out all of him but the head of his dick. He began making love to her like that again for several seconds. Then, he rammed his dick back inside of her with a fury.

He began a slow pace that quickly sped up. Just as he'd imagined, Angel's pussy was incredible. Angel's pussy felt so velvety smooth, warm, soft, golden, sensuous, delicious, exotic and so perfect. Christopher thought to himself; "If I died and went to Heaven, it would not compare to where I am right now." He looked down at the beautiful sight of seeing himself go in and out of Angel. Her beautiful legs were positioned perfectly over his shoulders. It was the sexiest pose he had ever seen. They both had made love to others before. Yet this feeling of making love to one they had a true mental connection with was beyond priceless.

"Damn! It feels so good inside of you Angel;" Christopher said. He was determined to fuck Angel so good that she would want to give him more. He took his hands moving her legs over his arms opening her wider. He then placed his hands under her ass cheeks. Lifting her hips off the mattress, he began pounding in her sweet pussy. Suspended in air, she was at his mercy. He begin fucking her with extreme intensity, pounding her air-lifted pussy in a passionate rage. He began to talk to her. "Oh my God Angel; he said. You have the sweetest pussy in the world and it feels so damn good.

I loved it when you sucked my dick. You made me want to cum in your mouth baby. I want to fuck you every way possible beautiful woman." Angel whispered; "Stick your finger in my ass." With her juices pouring out of her vagina, Christopher moisten his finger. He let his finger slide into her ass. "I'm going to fuck your pussy with my dick; he said. While my finger fucks your ass Angel. I'm fucking both holes at the same time." Angel wrapped her arms around him tighter as Christopher continued to pound in her pussy.

Their bodies moved in unison, much like their minds had done all those years as friends. He leaned in kissing her mouth. His dick drilled inside of her as if searching for oil. Their lips tightly clenched each other as their hips banged into each other. Pleasures were increasing and reaching a boiling point. That's when Christopher stopped. "What's wrong;" Angel asked? "Nothing sweetie. I just want to feel and watch your beautiful body as I fuck you from behind;" he replied. She turned to the doggy style position and he moved behind her. Once again, he found himself mesmerized. She was one of the most beautiful sights he felt had ever graced the universe.

"Angel, you are so damn beautiful, baby. I can't believe I never tried to have you long before now;" he said. He pressed her head down towards the pillow. He slid his dick up, down and across her slit. He found the entrance to her golden treasure. She arched her back and they both moaned as he entered. He grabbed her hips before beginning a rhythm that had them both feeling intense pleasure. All Christopher could do was stare at her body, which seemed to have perfect symmetry. As she moved, he basked in the aroma of her sweet smell that drifted under his nose.

Suddenly, he began ramming into her body. Almost as if trying to rattle her spine. Her pussy was feeling soooooo damn good. He took his thumb and moistened it with her juices. Gently he pressed it over her ass before letting it slide in. "Angel Renee' Robinson, I want to cum all over your asshole. Damn, you're so beautiful in every way. He kept fucking her for several moments and then suddenly stopped. He pulled out all of his dick except the head. He began fucking her like that for about 60 seconds. Then without warning, he slammed his dick balls deep inside of her. He banged his hairy balls on her clitoris until he could feel her moans get more intense. Then he slowed the pace.

"Not yet baby. I want to see your face when you cum again;" he said. He laid her back down and climbed into her. He moved her legs back over his arms, but not all the way over his shoulders. He started moving inside of her, while he kissed her mouth. Their tongues wrestled with each other as climaxes built up in both of them. Their hips moved faster and faster and faster. Christopher was grinding his pubic bone over her clit. Angel locked her arms around him. He locked his under her shoulders pulling her down towards his hips.

Their lips embraced as she wrapped her legs around him. Their eyes locked and they could feel eruption coming. "I'm going to cum in your pussy Angel; he said. I want to cum in you so bad. First, I need you to cum for me Angel. Give me that cum. Give it to me baby. Give it to me." He rammed into her as if trying to stamp his imprint on her pussy lips. Angel held him tightly and the glistening sweat between them made them glide in unison. "Fuck me Christopher. Oh hell yes! Fuck this pussy, baby. Tell me you love making love to me;" Angel commanded.

Christopher panting and trying to catch his breath repeated; "I love making love to you, Angel. I love your pussy and Angel, I love you. I want you to love me too Angel. So I'm going to write my name on your walls baby. Here it comes." He pounded balls deep inside of her. She felt the hot cream steam her walls. He shook her entire body with each stroke. Pounding 11 times he called each letter of his name spelling it inside her. C.H.R.I.S.T.O.P.H.E.R! He then collapsed on top of her but the show was far from over. He began wiping her forehead and kissing her pretty face.

She is so beautiful he thought, and far sexier than he ever imagined. He gently let her legs down from around his body. Angel stretched her legs out. He straddled his legs over her right one with his still hard dick inside her. He then wrapped his right ankle under her left ankle. He placed his hands on her hips. He motioned for her to move them in a grinding fashion. He pressed his pubic bone against her clitoris and stiffened his body. Angel now had her very own real life dildo. She quickly caught on and began working her clit. Soon reaching an explosive orgasm controlled completely by her. She used his body for her pleasure. He moved his mouth from her right to left ear talking dirty to her.

She was now fucking him. Each new sentence he said was spoken in a different ear. "Yes, Angel, fuck this dick. Grind that sweet pussy on this dick. Ooooh! You know how bad I've wanted to fuck you Angel. I've wanted your pussy for sooooooooooooo long. I wanted to feel your arms around my body. To feel those soft legs around my waist. I wanted to ride this pussy Angel. I wanted so long to feel your tongue lick my balls." Back and forth from ear to ear he continued. "I wanted so bad to feel this dick in your mouth.

Angel, your pussy must be made of sugar and spice. It is the sweetest thing I've ever had. Fuck me Angel. Make that pussy cum on this dick. Shoot that sweet juicy cum all over my balls. Wet these sheets, soak these sheets with your cum Angel. Give that pussy to me. Oooooh goddamn! Angel, give me this sweet ass and pussy. Do you want to suck this dick for me Angel? Do you want me to eat your pussy? Baby, just tell me what you want, and I'll do it for you." She bit his neck and scratched his back. Realizing just how powerful of a position she was in to make herself CUM. She moved as hard, as quickly and often as she wanted to right now.

She moved her pussy like she had just discovered the secret to making it work. She wanted to fuck him like a man but act like a lady. Angel came, and she came again and again. "OH FUCK! Christopher, you're my bitch now! Keep that dick right there. Don't move. No don't you move that dick, bitch! That's my dick now! Who's dick is it Christopher;" she demanded? "It's yours Angel. Anytime you want it. This dick is yours;" he replied. Angel quickly built up another eruption. Each one seemed to be more powerful than the last, but this one…this was Epic!

She pushed her body so hard clamping onto Christopher. He felt she might break his dick off. This position was physically challenging for a man. Still Christopher was determined to hold steady. He would let her have her orgasms and then some. She let out a scream that stung his eardrum. She came so violently with her body twitching and convulsing. She was shaking and sweating while she struggled to catch her breath. She kissed him like he had found her a gold mine, and that only made his dick hard again.

He knew this was her moment and just lay on her kissing her shoulders softly. He watched her as she came down from her high. Once she tried to speak he knew she was returning to earth. He began moving his dick inside of her. He knew her clit was super sensitive at this point. Any touching of it the right way would set it off. He moved slowly and deliberately inside of her because now he was on a different mission. She had her fun and this was to fulfill one of his fantasies with her. He pumped his dick inside of her basking in the exquisite pleasure that was Angel.

Pleasure he always believed was there and now he had irrefutable proof. He stroked inside of her as her soft body lay beneath him. He made love to her in a way that was not too strenuous for either of them. He could tell by her motions she too wanted him to cum again. She would do anything to make that happen. Just as he felt his orgasm building, he stroked her pussy with a bit more direction. He edged his orgasm to the brink and then quickly, he climbed up to her gorgeous face and lowered his dick to her. "Suck both of our juices off of this dick Angel;" he said.

She took his dick in her mouth and she tasted her own juices. Mixed with the sweet cum that was still lightly on him from when he had cum inside of her before. She sucked him like she was seducing his penis with her mouth. With the lips Angel has, it was the most incredible experience he had ever felt. If this woman told him to pack up and move with her right now he would go. To the Sahara, the moon, wherever without debate he would go. He was straddled over her shoulders as he fed his dick to her. He watched the sight of her gorgeous face and mouth. Angel made him feel he was with the most beautiful woman in the world.

After staring at those lips for a few more seconds he could no longer hold back. Releasing his all natural cream into her mouth. Angel made sure none of it escaped her lips as she drained him. No other woman would ever compare to her she thought. She was absolutely right as she was branding him. After she released him, he lay next to her and reached for her hand. They stared into each other's eyes. Once again without saying a word they told each other, I love you. Then Christopher spoke out loud, "I love you more. I love you, Angel Renee' Robinson."

Angel smiled and said; "I love you Christopher Paul Watson." He kissed each of her eyes, nose and beautiful lips. He kissed her chin, cheeks and ears, then he stared at her. "Angel oh my god, you are so beautiful;" he said. "Thank you, Paul;" she replied. "Only you can get away with that Angel;" he replied and smiled. "You know I do not like to be called by my middle name;" he continued. "I am aware of that Paul; she taunted. I also know you are never going to stay mad with me no matter what I do." Christopher smiled to acknowledge that he knew she was right on that too.

"What did we just do Angel;" he asked? "I think we just made love;" she replied. Christopher said, "I think that we did too but it was too quick." They turned onto their sides facing each other. He took his dick that she has nearly stiffened again, and rubbed it across her succulent lips between her legs. "Making love to you the right way takes a bit more time than this;" he said. I want to make love to you, Angel. I know we crossed the middle passage though;" "The what;" Angel asked?

# The Middle Passage

"The middle passage, commonly known as the trans-Atlantic Slave route; he said. However, tonight it's where we went from me seeing you as my attractive friend. To seeing you as the sexual goddess that you are. For me seeing you in this light was kind of middle of the road. I've always thought you were beautiful and sexy as my friend. Damn I'm way across the middle passage now. My God woman, your body is a work of art. Now, all I want to do is kiss and touch you. Lick you, make love to and fuck you." He kisses her again, and they reach out and touch each other as they savor this moment.

"You are sexy as hell Angel;" he said. "You think so, Christopher;" she replied? "I don't think, I know. I want to thank you for sharing all of this beautiful body with me woman; he said. I don't know how many more ways I can possibly love you than I already did. This will definitely transmogrify how often, but not how I think about you now. Can I get you something to drink Angel;" he asked? "Yes, I'll take a cold glass of Maple tea, if I have some in the fridge;" Angel responded. "If you don't have any, I will run up to Canada and get you some; he replied. I will do anything you ask me to do.

He got up and washed his hands and put on his pants. He brought her back some tea in a tall glass with ice. "Wow," Christopher uttered. "Wow what;" Angel asked? He replied; "I always knew that I loved you and I always knew you were an amazing woman. I think you have just turned me out Angel. And wait a minute, did you call me your bitch a lil while back?" Oh, you thought I forgot about that didn't you?"

"Is that what we're doing now, recording my statements; Angel laughed. That was in the heat of passion." "Heat of passion nothing; Christopher said. You're trying to pimp me but I will gladly be your bitch Angel." "Okay, don't be switching up on me when we have a disagreement about something;" Angel shot back. "If you're going to be my bitch, that's through good and bad times. When we agree and don't agree." Christopher responded; "Angel, if there is one thing you should know by now is I am in your life forever. In this world and beyond. No disagreement will ever tear us apart.

If you go to heaven, I'm going with you. Hopefully not at the same time though. That would mean one of us fucked up real bad. We would have had to be in an accident or something. He laughed and continued. If you go to hell, I am coming to rescue you. Even, if I got a ticket to heaven. I will be like, I need to switch my accommodations to be with Angel. The plan is however that we both go to the penthouse and not the basement." "So, you don't think what we did is wrong and might land us in the basement;" Angel asked? "No, I don't because what we did was born out of love. Not lust of I don't know this person but I want to sleep with them. Everybody that knows us knows we are special to each other.

Our dearest loved ones know it and God knows it. So nobody should be shocked that we shared our love. Love that Stevie Wonder and Ray Charles could see. I don't see anything wrong, with you and I making love Angel. I think our mental, physical and emotional connection is deeper than the Atlantic. Others may not be thrilled about it, but they will have to understand. We are two unique spirits that found each other." "I don't know; Angel said, but I liked where you had me grinding on you with my leg in between yours….Gee whiz…that was too awesome."

"Well, all I did was lay there Angel. You were grinding me and as I recalled. You called me your bitch while cumming all over me. I felt so used;" Christopher joked. "Well, I have to use you again like that sweetie. That was better than a Jack Rabbit;" Angel said. "What are you about to do now Christopher;" Angel asked? "Get in the shower, get us cleaned and give you a massage. Then I'll suck your clit and lick on your pussy from the back some more." Angel smiled. "Boy, you're so nasty." Christopher turned on the water in the shower. "It ain't my damn fault you're so sexy Angel; he replied.

Now come get in the shower with me. So I can adore your beautiful body soapy, soft and wet. Then I want to take you to dinner and just stare in those beautiful, brown eyes. Then I can think of what I would love to be doing to you all throughout our meal and conversation." Angel moved to get up, and Christopher walked back to the bed and stopped her. He kissed her lips as if to savor another special moment. He caressed her breast, kissing her neck, working down to suck her nipples. He worked his way down to her stomach and began a barrage of kisses all over it.

He then turned her over onto her stomach, so he could massage and kiss her back. He ran his tongue up and down her spine and back up to the back of her neck. He kissed the back of her neck tenderly in 3- second intervals and then ran his tongue back down her spine until he got to her juicy ass. He continued to run his tongue between her cheeks as this goddess was simply irresistible. Angel's body is enjoying the attention and then.......he said to her, "Angel, do you know what I want to do now?" "What's that?" she asked "I want to....."

# Guilty until proven innocent

Angel awoke in her bed the next morning soaking in the sunlight coming through her blinds. She glanced around the room, orienting to the reality of life. She looked at her exotic perfumes on her dresser. She noted the small pile of clothes in her sitting chair. She caught a glimpse of herself in her mirror, the complete look of happiness on her face. Damn she felt so good, and then felt instantly bad as she glanced at her nightstand. She saw the face of her husband's picture. Smiling, apparently at her. She was suddenly filled with the guilt and appreciation for the relationship they have.

Then, she thought of the night she just had with Christopher. She knew if her husband ever found out, he would be livid. She also felt very guilty because her husband was away on business. He had a small construction company that kept him busy. This was due to his connection with someone in the Governor's office. He was away working on a project for an office complex in Norfolk, Va. The betrayal she did was tearing at her soul. Yet, Christopher had made her feel oh so damn good. She had never had a man desire and please her like this. It wasn't just him desiring her that made her feel so good.

It was the fact that for so long Angel had felt uncomfortable with her looks. Her curves were very pronounced. They would make a NASCAR driver lose control. She never saw herself as any type of sex goddess. Yet last night she was loved and treated special. She was worshipped as the most high of the sex goddesses. All by a man she had never seen as more than just a friend. Oh, what a friend he was.

She was soon drifting off onto memory lane. Then she heard the intro music to "Take me with U" by Prince. That was her ringtone on her phone when her husband called. She purposely chose that ringtone as her husband had to regularly go on the road. She had been with this man for almost 15 years and married to him for 12 years. "Hey baby, she answered. "How are you;" the voice on the other end began the conversation. Angel smiled at his words and the comfort of knowing he was okay.

Somewhere deep in the back of her mind she had this constant dread. Someday one of David's friends would be using his phone to call. Telling her the most horrific news. She knew often accidents have happened in the construction business. Although she knew David always practiced safety on every job site, she often worried. She loved David and clearly being unfaithful was not in her plans. Listening to his reassuring voice she was at ease. Still she was wondering how this thing with Christopher happened?

How could an argument that almost tore their friendship apart give birth to that which was forbidden? It was taboo and guilt ridden. At that moment it has her searching her husband's voice. Searching for any hint that he might know what his wife was doing last night with another man. "Don't be silly Angel; she said to herself. How could he know? He's in another city. What if someone saw Christopher come to my house, called my husband and he's just waiting on me to lie? Wait. Who in that neighborhood even talks to my husband? Who would have his number to call? Get it together, Angel. Why do I feel so guilty? As far as he knows, I'm innocent. I miss you so much David;" she interrupted his words to say. I lay in bed and think about you all night.

Well that is true, most nights; she thought. It just wasn't true last night. David told her of all the hard work he was doing. He didn't want to cause too much worry so she'd have to call every hour. David was working on stabilizing a building that was crumbling. They both knew all too well the dangers. She knew each job was dangerous and that a mistake could be his last. How terrible she would feel, if God forbid, something had happened to him last night. How would she ever live that down? She couldn't. So, she knew what she had to do and that was to break it off with Christopher.

No if, ands or buts. This had to end and it had to end today. She told her husband how much she loved and missed him. How she couldn't wait until he got back home. "Oh, yeah, are you going to have something waiting for me when I get there;" David asked? "You best believe it; Angel said. I'm going to let you hammer on this body." "Oh, I like that baby;" David said. "I might let this building fall down and head back right now." "Well come on then; Angel teased. Sheeba and I will be waiting on you." "Oh, woman, let me get off this phone and get back to work. Before you have me walking around here with a hard on.

One of the guys may think it's for them;" David joked. They both laughed and Angel said; "You better tell all those guys, I've got papers on you. They better find their own man, if that's their thing." "It can be their thing but they better not try to bring it to me. That's not my thing;" David replied. Angel replied; "Well, if it ever is your thing, just let me know. I'll step out the way." "I'll be sure and do that baby but I wouldn't worry about that anytime soon;" David said.

"Okay baby, well you make sure you keep your hard hat on and be safe out; Angel said. I love you." "I love you too;" David replied. They hung up and she thought to herself how crazy she felt. Chastising David not to fool around, while she had done just that. She was going to get herself into a shower, put on her white jeans and crimson red blouse. Then go over to Christopher's house. I will let him know that this can never happen again. "I love my husband;" she thought. Besides, she knew that Christopher didn't love her. He probably only wanted her because she was safe as a married woman; she thought. "Yes sir, I am going to go right over there and let him know this is over.

I need him to forget this ever happened and not to bring it up again. We need to avoid this happening again and let's just go back to being friends." As she arrived at his house, she wondered if Christopher had been thinking similar thoughts. What if he had his fun and no longer wanted her anymore? Was he going to try and weasel out of their *"benefits package"*? She went to press his doorbell, but he opened the door before she could. "What? Did you see me drive up;" she asked? "Yes, I've been staring out the window hoping you would come by all morning;" he replied. "You're lying. If you wanted me to come, why didn't you call me;" Angel asked? "I did text you to see if you were awake. When I got no response, I figured you were sleeping Christopher said. I didn't want to wake you."

She grabbed her phone, "I didn't get a text from…." She looked at her phone and saw that Christopher did text her. While she was on the phone with David. "Oh, you must have texted me while I was talking to my mother. Damn, she thought to herself. Now I am lying to both my husband and my lover. "How low can you go Angel;" she thought.

Well, this is definitely it. I am going to tell him this thing is done. "Listen, Christopher, about last night…we shouldn't…." Christopher took a step towards her. He stared her right in her beautiful eyes and said to her; "Come here." "What;" she asked? "Come here;" he repeated. She drew to his voice like a moth to a flame. Feeling the heat that both consumed her and would ultimately burn her she felt. "What do you want;" she asked? "I want you;" he responded.

He pushed her back against the wall taking her hands into his. He lifted them over her head as he kissed her passionately. He told her with his tongue that she belonged to him. She kissed him back just as assertively. Now he understood that he belonged to her as well. Lust and desire quickly took over them. His hands slowly slid down her arms onto her body. They began to seek out every body part they could find. He grabbed her breast through her blouse. He was kissing her face, not just her mouth.

He kissed her neck being oh so careful not to leave any marks. Both understood they didn't want any knowledge of this, to somehow make it home to her husband. She quickly unbuttoned her blouse, exposing her bra. Christopher quickly ripped off her bra so that he could suck her breast. "Ahshhh," she gasped as he took her nipple into his mouth. He clasped it between his index and middle finger. Then began licking it while giving it a tight pinch between his fingers.

He rapidly descended to his knees and unbuttoned her white jeans. He unzipped them and tried to rip them to his carpet floor. She stepped each leg to help him get them off of her. "Oh My God;" he said. As he realized he was standing before her magnificent body. Her body was only covered in a pair of black panties.

He turned her around, so he could look at the beautiful shape of her very voluptuous ass. Instinct made him lick and kiss each cheek. He held her cheeks as he tried in vain to get his tongue all over her, but he felt the restriction of her panties. "These have to come off;" he said. With no resistance, she allowed him to peel her panties off. Her smooth round ass became exposed to him. He savored in the aroma of her scent. Everything about her smelled so seductive. He turned her gently around and began kissing the front of her thighs. She grabbed him by the back of his head and commanded; "Suck my clit!"

With that, she took her fingers and exposed her puffy clitoris. She gently cupped the back of his bald head with her left hand and pulled him close. He could offer no objection. He took her clit in his mouth like a small penis and he sucked it like a male prostitute. He licked her labia in firm stiff strokes before inserting his finger inside of her. She stood there with her legs spread to allow him full access to all of her glory. She maintained a firm grip on his head. She wanted to shove her small clitoris deep down his throat.

Oh how bad she wanted to cum in his mouth. She was determined to make him suck and lick her until she did. "Yeah! That's it. Suck it. Suck that clit boy; Angel ordered. Suck it like you want this pussy juice in your mouth." Christopher had never heard this side of Angel before. He wondered, what else could this quiet, reserved lady, be hiding. What kind of freaky stuff might she be into? She took her hand and pushed his broad shoulders down. Making sure he was low enough so that she could rub her pussy all over his face. Christopher had just shaven so his skin was really smooth. It felt good to her as she grinded and smeared her juice all over the top of his head and face.

Her life's mission at this time was to explode in his mouth and all over his face. It seemed to her that his life's mission was to get her there. Angel was grinding her hips and thrusting her clitoris deeper into his mouth. Christopher grabbed her soft firm round ass and let her use him. He made sure she stayed right there. He ate her pussy like it was a juicy peach. Angel's breathing became heavier and heavier as she looked down. Seeing this man kneeling before her fingering her pussy and sucking her clit. He looked up at her as he slid his tongue inside. Angel saw his brown bedroom eyes and lost all control.

She gripped his head with both hands. As if she was trying to smother him with her vagina. Her orgasm poured out of her body into his waiting mouth. She bent his head back so his face was looking towards her. She took her clit and fucked his chin up to his nostrils. Up and down his chocolate face her juices gushed out in waves. She slowly calmed then took his hands off her hips. Lifting him to his feet so that she could taste her juices on his face. While she kissed him, he slipped his fingers inside her vagina and began to finger fuck her. "I want you inside of me;" she said.

"Your wish is my command;" he told her and they walked to his bedroom. Angel sat on the edge of the bed, as Christopher took off his pajamas and t-shirt. He walked towards her so that his dick was just inches from her face and then he touched her shoulders. Laying her down and using his legs he spread hers even wider. He climbed on top of her and kissed her sweetly. Like she were the greatest prize in the world.

# Five Alarm Fire!!!

Angel knew then that this wasn't a man kissing her just because he wanted some pussy. She was special to him and he certainly knew how to show it. As his hands played with her breast, his dick found the entrance of her moisture. Like a heat seeking missile, he entered her. At that moment Christopher knew one thing. God had never created anything in the universe that felt as good as this woman. He quickly pulled her legs up over his shoulders. He wanted to drill his dick into the deepest depths of her. Angel was only overjoyed to feel him like this. The sounds of their bodies smashing into each other seemed to make the most beautiful sound.

Christopher looked down at Angel's face and was mesmerized. He could swear to Jesus that she was the most beautiful creature he had ever seen. She was so sexy when she made love to him. Christopher just wanted to make this moment last forever. "I want you from behind;" he muttered as he continued to pump her. He lowered her legs and Angel got into position. Christopher seemed amazed at the view before him. Her ass seemed perfectly sculptured and round. He just wanted to admire the view. He spread her cheeks and rubbed his dick up and down her slit, resting the tip of him on her asshole.

"I didn't say I was ready for all of that;" Angel gently protested. "Shhhh woman, he responded. I got this. I know what I am doing." He took his hand and pushed his dick so that the tip was now pressed against her pussy. He began to rub his finger across her clitoris to absorb some of her moisture. He then took his finger and pushed it slightly inside her ass until it was knuckle deep inside of her.

He then moved from behind her and went to his night stand and removed three items. "What did you just get;" Angel inquired? "Something for you sweetie;" he answered. "Something like what;" she inquired? "This is a blindfold, some lubricant and a wand; he answered. I don't think I want to use this wand right now. So, I will use this;" he said. "What is that;" Angel asked? "This is a little two-inch bullet;" Christopher told her. "What is that for;" she asked? "What are you Police? Asking all these questions;" Christopher sarcastically implied?

He slipped the blindfold on her eyes. He opened the packet and removed the bullet. He turned the slightly moist bullet on medium speed. He carefully pushed it into her anal cavity. He then guided his dick into her wet pussy and began to make love to her passionately. The sensations running through Angel at this time were spine tingling. They made her deranged with pleasure. Their passion was raging hotter than a five- alarm fire. No water from a fire hydrant could put it out. Christopher made his thrust come faster and harder. The waves from the bullet intensified her pleasure. Angel was literally losing her grip on reality.

Her entire body seemed to be shivering to one massive climax. The bullet filled her with electrifying pleasure waves. Waves that traveled from her ass to up her spine. Then to her brain and down to her breast. From there back to her clitoris. Simultaneously, his hard dick pounded inside her pussy. She was quivering with small multiple eruptions. "Ooooh! Damn you! Fuck me! Christopher! Fuck me! Oh fuck, this dick is sooooooo good. Oooh shhhhh!!.....Ah FUCK! I'M CUMMMMING, I'M FUCKING CUMMING!" The spasms caused by the bullet in her ass magnified her orgasm ten times. It had her bucking like a wild horse in a rodeo.

She never had an orgasm this intense and riveting. That was saying something considering what she had just experienced the previous night. Her entire body was tidal wave after tsunami of immense pleasure. Those waves swept over her like a hurricane making landfall. Her senses alternated from various pleasure. Both feeling Christopher's hard dick pounding inside and the good vibrations caused by the mini bullet. "Hoooan," her voice was low and deep. She tried to cope with the eruptions taking place all over her body. She almost sounded like a wounded animal as she clenched the sheets.

She felt his hands holding her hips steady, so he could fuck her for all he was worth. Her body never felt so alive and yet so helpless. She could not control the atomic actions going on deep inside her core. This was a feeling she had been chasing since her first sexual experience. Finally she found a man that could give it to her. The mystery of being blindfolded only added to her pleasure. Christopher looked down at her beautiful firm body as his dick went in and out of her.

He noticed the bullet had her anus contracting rapidly during her multiple orgasms. The thought of her orgasm only intensified his pleasure. Soon he began to lose control. "Ooooh god-damn Angel. I'm going to cum inside your pussy;" he moaned. "Ohhhh, baby! This is the sweetest pussy in the world. Oh yes Angel. Bounce that ass back to me." Angel made several thrust back. Christopher shot out his load with the force of a shotgun into her. They both were shaking with pleasure until they could catch their breath. Angel still felt the bullet vibrating, and she collapsed on the bed. Still feeling tingling sensations inside of her.

Her glistening body was spent after her orgasms had exhausted her. "Oh my God that was an experience; she said. Her breathing was heavy. Where did you learn that? Never mind, you freak;" Angel teased. Christopher lay next to her also breathing heavy and felt her breath as it cooled his face. "I know you're hungry aren't you woman;" he asked? "I am starving;" Angel said. "Okay cool, I will take a quick shower. Then run you a warm bath in the Jacuzzi and fix you breakfast;" he said. "What are we having;" asked Angel? "You ask too many questions beautiful woman; he said.

Just let me lie next to you for now. I'll get up in a few and take care of you like I'm supposed to do." Shortly Christopher left the bathroom. Angel prepared to soak in the bubble bath surrounded by candles. She heard the sound of Johnny Gill singing, "Let's just run away." She closed her eyes and lay her head on the Jacuzzi pillow. She took a nap while she waited on her breakfast. In about 35 minutes, Christopher came to get her. She had a plate filled with maple turkey bacon, waffles and a bowl of grits. A caramel latte', fresh cut melon, pineapple juice and lastly a veggie omelet made with cheddar cheese, tomatoes, green peppers and onions.

They ate without saying many words. They had both worked up an appetite. Christopher asked her if everything was okay. "It's delicious;" she said. "I'm black, you'll tell me anything;" Christopher joked. I'm black too; Angel said. After breakfast, Christopher cleared the table. Angel volunteered to wash the dishes. "No, Christopher said. I will take care of this. I need you to go get dressed. I have to make a run real quick and then we can hang out." Angel wanted to know where he had to go but decided not to ask. She knew he would never take her anyplace unsafe.

They pulled up at an old and vacant house in the Ashburton neighborhood. Angel looked befuddled. "Does somebody you know live here;" she asked? "No woman, we're going to look at it when my cousin Geneva gets here. I need to see what it looks like inside;" he said. "Oh, you're thinking about buying it and fixing it up;" she asked? "I may, it depends on what it looks like inside." Geneva pulled up shortly after they arrived and exited her car. "Oh you're early Christopher. How long have you been waiting;" Geneva asked?

"I thought I would beat you to an appointment for once;" he replied. "We just got here five minutes ago. We just happened to be out this way. Oh, by the way this is Angel;" Christopher said. Geneva extended her hand to shake Angel's and noticed the wedding ring on her finger. She knew Christopher was divorced, so she started adding two and two together. "You say you guys were already on this side of town huh? What part of town do you live Angel;" asked Geneva? "Oh I live in Alexandria;" Angel responded before realizing she had disclosed she was nowhere near her home. "Is that right; Geneva said. Well if you ever want to move into something up this way, you should call me.

I would love to be a real estate agent for you as well." They went inside and walked around the vacant house. Christopher took photos and wrote notes. 'Let me think on this Geneva. I will let you know by tomorrow at this time;" Christopher said. "Okay great, if you don't like this one, I have plenty more to show you; Geneva said. I am actually waiting for something to come online. I think would be perfect for you in Silver Spring. It's a duplex a bit closer to Alexandria." "I'm black, you'll try to sell me anything Geneva; he joked."

"We're all black my precious cousin; Geneva said. Angel I guess you know he's very militant and a comedian right? He's also very smart and a good person. I love him to pieces." "Oh yes I know Geneva;" Angel said. "Anyway; Geneva continued. That house may give you a reason to be closer to Virginia more often who knows?" "I am not fooling with you Geneva. Always trying to start some trouble;" Christopher laughed out loud. "Well, you call me later Mr. Christopher. I want to hear all about what you've been into lately;" Geneva said. "I love you Geneva;" Christopher said. "I love you too;" Geneva replied. They hugged and Geneva hugged Angel before driving off.

Christopher and Angel entered into his Escalade and he began to press the screen on his phone. "Now what;" Angel asked? "I am trying to find us some tickets if you must know;" Christopher responded. "Tickets to what;" Angel asked? "Well, I thought since it is a nice warm day, we could run up to New Jersey. Maybe go on one of those whale watching boats. We can take pictures of the dolphins and whales. Then, if you don't have my five dollars you owe me. I might throw you overboard;" Christopher said. "Really, Angel said with dismay. You would kill me over five dollars? Man, I tell you, damn Balti-Rouge men;" she joked. "Yes and I love you too Angel;" he replied.

# That's what friends are for

Out on the boat, there were about 50 other passengers. All jockeying for a position to see something in the water. Angel wandered aimlessly, waiting for someone to move away from the rails. Soon she found a spot near the rear of the boat on the starboard side. Christopher walked up behind her and wrapped his arms around her waist. He purposely pressed his groin against her ass. Her light sun dress seemed to be inviting him to come in even further.

She slightly arched her back to let him know he was welcomed to be there. He adored the scent of her perfume as it drifted off of her body and into the wind. He slightly kissed her neck. "What a beautiful life;" Christopher thought. Angel had her business that made her self-sufficient. He having retired early and being a real estate investor. That meant that they could pretty much spend their days however they saw fit. Angel grew up in not the best part of town in Philadelphia's West side. Christopher grew up in not the best part of East Baton Rouge. He joined the Marines after High School.

Angel relocated to Washington DC and attended Howard University. After she finished college and he got out of the Marine Corps they both looked for jobs. Chance landed both of them in Atlanta. It was at an outdoor Jazz concert held at Piedmont Park they met. A mutual friend named Melissa introduced them. They both had modest success in the ATL. Then, individually decided to move to the DMV area for greater opportunity. It wasn't planned as each of them thought they would be leaving the other behind. However fate had other ideas. That's when their bond really blossomed.

Now they ate at fine restaurants and took nice trips to exotic locations.  They bought whatever their hearts desired for the most part.  They just didn't do those things together often.  Both had gotten married after they moved to the DMV. Christopher was later divorced, but his friendship with Angel had only grown. Angel was still married, a fact that was not lost on either of them.  Several times they made plans to meet for coffee or hang out. Sometimes Angel would cancel. Mostly when David was in town so Christopher understood.  It was truly a great friendship.  Neither of them ever intended to cross the line and yet here they were.

"Hey look! There's a killer whale;" someone yelled! Angel and Christopher both turned to look in the direction in which the man was pointing.  The excitement of seeing the beautiful mammal got them caught up in the moment.  They tried to take pictures of the whale following the boat. Someone else blurted out; "There goes an entire pod."  The whales as if on cue, jumped out of the water.  They seemed to showcase their talent for the spectators. Everyone was delighted in the display.  Soon the boat came upon dolphins and tiger sharks.  "No great white sharks out here;" some lady asked?  "Nah, not with those killer whales around; a man said.

Those great whites don't want no parts of killer whales."  "I thought the great white was the meanest thing in the ocean;" a lady exclaimed.  "Not hardly, the man stated. The killer whales will ram into them in an ambush to stun them.  Then they turn them upside down and drown the sharks.  Apparently, if you hold sharks upside down, they will drown.  Killer whales are very smart. They figure out what weakness their prey has.  Then they know the best way to kill it.  They work together, so there is not much in the ocean they don't kill.  Including Great white sharks."

"Man, I should hire you as a tour guide, the boat's captain said. You seem to know your stuff." "I just watch a lot of NatGeo Wild and Discovery channel is all;" said the man. "Wow! What are those over there;" some lady asked? "That is a school of jellyfish. I am very thankful we are on this boat and not in the water;" the captain said. They seem harmless, but their sting can put a hurting on you. Well folks, we're coming up on the end of our two-hour tour, so it's about time we head back.

If you would've paid for the three- hour tour, I'd take you to Gilligan's Island. Maybe we could get shipwrecked." The crowd laughed at the dry humor. All continued to try to look for any last sights as the boat headed back to shore. Once back on land, Christopher took Angel's hand to help her step onto the pier. He didn't let go as they walked slowly toward the parking lot. "So, did you like that sweetie;" he asked? "Yes, that was really nice; Angel said. Different and really nice. How did you know I would like such a thing?" "Well, I didn't think you'd like to waste such a beautiful day. Trapped inside a dark movie theater seemed wrong.

Your feet stuck to a sticky floor. Watching Idris Elba or Denzel on screen. When you could be hanging out with me." "Wait, we could have gone to see Denzel or Idris? You got me out here looking at fish; Angel sarcastically asked? Man, Denzel wanted to see me." "Oh so you're playing me like that, big head woman; he asked? Next time I will take your ass to McDonald's. Get you an Ebony magazine with them in it to go with your Happy Meal. Then, we'll see how happy you are then;" Christopher said. "Oh, you know I am just kidding with you. Don't you Christopher; she asked?

I had the best time with you today; Angel said. Who are you calling big head woman, Baldy;" Angel demanded? "I didn't say big head woman. I said is Jed coming;" Christopher said. "Who the hell is Jed; Angel asked? So let me get clarity on this. We're lying now is that what we're doing; Angel asked? I've got to B-more careful about who I hang out with." "Woman, you are now rocking with the best and don't you forget it;" he said. No need to be careful, I'll protect you from most things.

"Now, if a telephone pole fell into my hands and hit you in the head, that's not my fault. That's call gravity and centripetal force. As you know, I do not control all that shit." "You are so damn silly boy;" Angel said laughing. "Hey, do you want to get something to eat;" Christopher asked? "Yeah, I could go for a little something, since you insist;" Angel joked. "I didn't insist on a damn thing for your greedy ass; Christopher joked. Look, only because you're so fine and beautiful, I am taking you to this special place. Don't think this will become a habit; Christopher warned.

You can have anything you want off the dollar menu. You just have a two-dollar limit so make this shit count. Don't order a drink either. I have bottled water in the back of the ride." "Man, you better quit playing with me; Angel said. You know I don't do no damn dollar menu. You better spend at least $5.00 on me or it's going to be a problem." "Oh shit! I don't want no problems with you Angel. So on that note, you can go anywhere you want to go;" Christopher relented. They drove up to Linden, N.J, to a quaint little restaurant called; "Beyond The C". "I really enjoyed this place when I was here before; Christopher said. I told myself I would come back. Then again, I'm black, I will tell myself anything." "You know you have no damn sense don't you; Angel laughed.

Angel was looking over the menu, while Christopher stared at her. "What are you looking at;" Angel inquired? "Your beautiful, brown eyes;" he replied. "Thank you;" Angel said with a blushing grin. "What about my eyes do you like?" "I like how pretty they are, and how they can't see to order anything but water. Look at these prices. Twenty dollars for this stuff;" Christopher exclaimed! "Man, you've been talking like you have no money forever; Angel teased.

You're going to spend $20 on me today or I may have to whip your behind, mister." "Yeah, that is an ass whipping I do not want to take; Christopher said. If I wasn't scared of you, I would have clocked you by now. I thought about it a many of times. You be getting on a nookas nerves sometimes." "When do I get on your nerves;" Angel asked? "The other day, when you were doing what you did, after I told you not to do it and you did it anyway, didn't you;" Christopher answered? "Shut up fool. I swear you are one silly ass man;" Angel smiled. "May I take your drink orders, please;" the waitress asked? "Do y'all have a layaway plan up in here; Christopher asked?

I mean can I pay like a nickel on our food today? Then mail you a nickel every month until I get the bill paid off?" "Don't pay any attention to him miss;" Angel said. I'll have a pitcher of tea. I'm going to send him out to the car to get a hot ass bottle of water." "Damn! Christopher said. You see how she treats me (he looks at her name tag), Kathy? Can you call Child Protective Services, please? She abuses me." "Aren't you a little old for Child Protective Services sir;" Kathy asked? "Oh, you're calling me old? Your tip just went from 80 to 20 cents. That will learn you to call me old;" he joked.

"Oh! I am so sorry sir;" Kathy smiled. "Can I bring you an extra water to at least get back up to 50 cents?" "Hell no! You ain't getting no 50 Cent from me. I'm not trying to find you in da club, bottle full of bub;" Christopher said. "Uhm...you got your hands full with this one ma'am;" Kathy said to Angel. "What do you want him to drink;" Kathy asked Angel? "Oh, now your tip is a dime; Christopher yelled out! Keep it up and you're going to owe me money." "No seriously, can I have a glass for tea too.

Kathy still laughing said; "You know we have a very good house lemonade." "Bring him a glass please, and can I get a glass of hot water to clean my silverware;" Angel asked Kathy? "Certainly ma'am;" Kathy replied as she walked away laughing. "Why are you so silly man;" Angel asked? "Because, I love to see you smile;" Christopher replied. "Awww," Angel responded. "Plus, it helps to keep me from crying looking at these prices on this menu. I just want a napkin;" Christopher said. "Man, you own a few houses; Angel said. An apartment complex, got your little retirement income, you've started your own security business and you're in an investment group.

I would say you can afford to spend a few dollars on food. Although I know this will not be as good as your cooking." "So, have you figured out what you want beautiful lady;" Christopher asked? "Yes, I will have the baked sea bass dinner." "So, are we ready to order;" Kathy asked? "Yes, this gorgeous lady is going to have your baked sea bass dinner. I will have the glazed salmon with garlic mashed potatoes. We will both have a garden salad with Italian dressing. I will take the New England corn chowder. I think she wants to try your seafood gumbo. Oh and let me get a fried chicken leg quarter."

"Those are excellent choices sir. I will get your order in right away;" Kathy said. "I see you're trying to get back up to that 80 cent tip but I am not impressed;" Christopher said. They all laughed. "Don't worry girl; Angel said. I will take his wallet and make sure you are taken care of." "Hold up! Did you just hear her threaten to rob me and commit a violent act;" Christopher asked? Kathy, can you give me the number to 911? I need the police up in here." "Nope, I didn't hear her threaten anybody. We ladies have to stick together;" Kathy said while winking at Angel.

"That is great news;" Christopher replied. "Both of you meet me in the outside. I'll take a stick and beat both of you with it together." "Oh no he didn't. I just heard that, he threatened us girlfriend; Kathy said to Angel. Do not make me go get my vicious dog. He is a wild poodle and will bite your thumb. If you put it close to his mouth; Kathy warned Christopher. I'm not messing with you anymore sir. Let me go get this food order in." Angel said; "I want you to know I am documenting all these threats. About hitting me with telephone poles and sticks.

They go straight from the recorder on my phone to the police station." "Man, ain't nobody listening to that; Christopher said. They probably put your call on hold. I hope they are not listening now. Never mind, I'll just wait to ask you about that dead body and cocaine in your car, Angel Renee' Robinson. "I'm about to have another dead body around here;" Angel said. "They're probably in the break room watching Sports highlights; Christopher said. Speaking of that, you need to eat fast. I need to get home and watch some pre-game show. Before San Antonio plays tonight;" Christopher said. "Man, that game doesn't come on until like 11 o'clock and it's only 3p.m;" Angel said.

"Yeah, I know but I have to shower and then I have to um. Umm, I have to organize my lettuce in the refrigerator. Um, um, and then I have to….oh yeah! I have to think about if I want to try to get that house we saw this morning;" Christopher said. "Really dude; Angel asked? How long will all of that take?" "Until I'm finished dammit;" Christopher said sarcastically! "If you don't stop playing, I will hit you with this bottle of ketchup;" Angel joked. "Oh see where I learn all this violent talk from; Christopher responded. Before I met you all I ever did was volunteer at the mission. Tried to do some good in the world and then you corrupted me.

To this day, I don't know why we get along. You're a bad influence on me Angel." "That's what friends are for;" Angel said slyly. "I use to go to church and sing in the choir. Now you got me dealing drugs and you are pimping me out to old ladies on the Usher board;" Christopher continued. "Oh my God! This man is so crazy; Angel laughed. Your ass couldn't sell a Tylenol to a woman with a migraine. Much less make it out on the streets. You're one of those uppity negroes." "Just like your ass is;" Christopher said. Angel replied; "You got that right. The streets ain't got nothing I want. I want to live in a house, to hell with the streets."

"You're a sexy mother shut yo mouth, when you get a little preachy;" Christopher interrupted. "I just want to…." "Here we go;" Kathy interrupted. She began placing their dishes on the table. "Now is there anything else you would like ma'am;" Kathy asked? "No thank you;" Angel said. "How about you sir, Mr. Comedian;" Kathy joked. "No we're good. I might raise you up to 55 cent depending on how I feel when I finish my food. Don't get your hopes up too high;" Christopher joked.

"Oooh weee! You may give me 55 cents? I will make sure I take a cruise around the world with that;" Kathy laughed. Christopher and Angel enjoyed their meal. Kathy promptly arrived when it appeared they were done. "Do you want dessert; she asked?" "No thank you, but we will take the check;" Christopher said. Kathy reached in her apron and handed the bill to Christopher. "Why are you giving that to me? She was the one hungry; Christopher said. I didn't even eat. She ate her plate and mine." "So I didn't see you eating that salmon like it was going out of style;" Kathy asked?

"No you didn't and your eyes need to stop lying to you; said Christopher. What? The bill is $63.32. Kathy, I only ate .32 cent worth of stuff for real. Angel ate all this stuff. Can't you get like a radar or sonogram? So you can check our stomach to see where all the food is? This is bullshit!" Kathy and Angel were laughing out loud along with a few diners sitting around them. Christopher said; "Look Kathy, you know times are hard. Don't I get like a Boy Scout discount or something?" "Man, you're wearing a Movado watch. I think you can come up with something;" Kathy said.

"Alright, here take my Visa check card. If you run it and it comes back to a dead guy. I can explain that shit;" Christopher joked. "Lord, this man needs to be on stage somewhere, I swear. Girl, you have something on your hands;" Kathy said. She walked away towards the register. She soon returned. Kathy said; "Thank you both very much for coming in. It was my pleasure to serve you." "Yeah; Christopher said. Well I wasn't pleased. I have some complaints Kathy. As a matter of fact, I'm going to call your 1-800 Wendy's number." "We're not affiliated with Wendy's sir, but feel free to call them anyway;" Kathy said.

"I bet when Wendy come down here and curse you out, you won't be talking all that trash;" Christopher said. "If Wendy comes down here, I promise you, I will apologize;" Kathy said. "Good. What is 15% of .32 cents?" "Sir, your bill was $63.00 and some change;" Kathy said. "What? I'm surprised that card cleared. Angel go start the car before the police come;" Christopher said. "Here is my last $40.00 cash I have Kathy." I was going to use this to buy Angel a birthday and Christmas gift. Then keep $10.00 for myself, but you can have it.

Since you clearly stole money out the cash register to cover our check. You're going to need this when they fire your ass." Kathy burst out laughing. "They probably would fire me just because; she said. I know I can get a job from one of y'all right?" "Sure, I can subcontract you out at my aluminum can pick up job; Christopher joked. You gotta be able to bring in at least ten bags of cans a day. I don't need no slackers messing up the game. If you do well with that, I will move you up. Promote you to selling loose cigarettes on Pennsylvania and Laurens in Baltimore.

Can you expand our business Kathy? I'm trying to take over the next block." I sure can sir, I'll be the best loose cigarette peddler you have; Kathy said. "I'm black, you'll tell me anything;" Christopher replied. Kathy laughed. "What color do you think I am; she asked? I'm surprised with that kind of success collecting cans, you haven't crossed over;" Kathy joked. "Shoot, if I could have found me two more cans, I could have gotten an Asian girl; Christopher said. Then again, I think I got the prettiest girl they had in the stock room." "Boy, come on here and stop with all your crazy stories;" Angel demanded. "Yeah, you get on out of here before she goes upside your head Mr. Crazy;" Kathy said.

"Oh, you see how violent and crazy she is too huh, Kathy? I told you, I need to go to the battered men's clinic; he said. She is really not as nice as she pretends to be. Last week, she shot me in the face for nothing. I know it doesn't look like I was shot in the face. That's because she poured hot grits on me to seal the hole. I had to have like 15 surgeries just yesterday to fix me up. She is crazy. I'm telling you;" Christopher pleaded! "Then why are you with me now, Mr. Victim;" Angel asked? "Duh, because you're violent, and I'm scared to say no;" Christopher replied.

# My, aren't we in a cantankerous mood

Back in the car Angel asked; "Why are you such a clown man?" "I told you woman, I just love to see you smile;" Christopher responded. "You were making Kathy smile a lot too. Almost like you were flirting with her;" Angel said. "What, Christopher said in disbelief! I was not flirting with her. I was just having a good time at dinner with my beautiful date. Trying to make you laugh." "Oh well, that's all that better be. I would hate to have to get violent for real and cut somebody;" Angel said.

"Oh boy! Here you go; Christopher said. First of all, Angel, I only have eyes for you. I enjoy being with you and love talking to you. In fact, I love everything about you. You do know that you're the one that is married between us right?" "I don't care if I'm married or not. I don't want you flirting with no other girls around me;" Angel said sternly. Christopher replied; "Well, I guess you've made yourself loud and clear, but understand this. I am my own man. I am with you because I want to be with you only. However today, yesterday and tomorrow, I do whatever I want to do. Nobody, including your fine ass, is going to make me do anything I don't want to do.

Now don't backtalk me woman. Or I will pull your panties down and put you across my knee. Then spank your bare ass." "Is that a promise;" Angel asked coyly? "Come here sexy girl, with your cute self; Christopher said. How are you going to get mad about me about somebody? Give me a damn kiss;" he ordered. They kissed passionately in the car. Christopher felt her breast before he started the engine and drove back to Maryland.

They picked up her car from his house and he followed her home. As Angel unlocked her front door, they entered. Her son Jamal ran down the stairs. "Ma....oh hey Mr. Christopher;" Jamal said. "What's up, Jamal? How are you doing;" Christopher asked? "Fine. Ma, can I go over to Marcus' house until dinner is ready;" Jamal asked Angel. "Is his mom or dad home;" Angel responded? "Yeah, his mother is on vacation this week and his dad gets off work at five;" Jamal said. "Well don't go over there eating a bunch of junk food. I'm going to make dinner by 7p.m. I will call you on your cell phone so make sure you check it regularly;" Angel told him.

"What are we having ma;" Jamal asked? "Unless you're cooking, don't worry about it. You will eat whatever I fix;" Angel responded. "Don't worry Jamal. If you don't like it, I will take you to our spot to get a turkey burger;" Christopher said. "Man, those were good. I didn't think I would like it at first. I want to go to Ruby Tuesday all the time for them now;" Jamal said excitedly. "I stopped going when they stopped making the peach tea with real peaches; Christopher said. Maybe this weekend we can go scoop up a turkey burger, lil homie." "Ah-ight cool;" Jamal said.

Jamal ran out the door and Angel turned to Christopher. "How do you know I don't have plans? Maybe to do something with my son this weekend; she asked?" "My, aren't we in a cantankerous mood lately;" Christopher retorted. "Nobody is being cantankerous. I just asked you a question;" Angel snapped. "Look, woman. I am not going to argue with you; he said. I had a great day hanging out with you and I am not going to let you spoil it. I am going to the family room and watch some television. When traffic dies down, I will take my behind on home;" Christopher said.

Angel is near completing her meal preparation. She set the table with chicken cacciatore, brown rice, string beans and corn bread. She called to Christopher in the den; "Are you going to eat anything Christopher?" "If you pull down your panties, I will eat you;" he yelled back. "Man, you have a damn one track mind;" she said. Christopher walked into the kitchen. "No I don't, I think about other things too; he said. Remember that time I thought about getting some $150.00 sneakers?"

"I couldn't see you ever spending that much on some sneakers;" Angel said. "You're right. I wouldn't. I try not to invest my money on worthless things. So I can build my net worth like you taught me;" Christopher replied. "Right now, I have to be worth at least $45.00;" he said. "You are probably worth a little more than that;" Angel said, "maybe like $52.00." "See, that's why I love you, Angel. We don't get caught up in how much money each other has. Or try to impress each other by buying stupid shit we don't need. We just hang out and enjoy each other's company.

We can have intelligent conversation about politics, religion or science. Even entertainment or just some stupid stuff. If I could get you to like sports, you would be perfect;" Christopher teased. "I get enough sports when David is home. That's all that man does all day is watch sports;" Angel said. "How is he doing anyway;" Christopher asked? "I talked to him this morning and he seemed to be doing well. They were having trouble getting a permit for something they were doing. I know he'll get it straight and I know he misses home;" Angel said. "He misses home and his family, especially his wife;" Christopher said. Angel looked at Christopher with a slight surprise.

"Hey, I know my role Angel. I know who is number one and number two in your life. I'm am not in any way trying to make any trouble; Christopher said. David is cool people. He has saved me a lot of money working on my patrol cars for my company. I feel probably as bad as you do about this. You must have cast a spell on me or something. I think you're a witch!" "Ain't nobody cast no spells on your crazy tail. You knew what you were doing when you seduced me. Now you're trying to act all innocent;" Angel said.

"I am innocent woman. I was a virgin before I met you. I worked for the Red Cross and I helped old ladies cross the street. Then you just came along. You've risked my chance of making it to glory when I die;" Christopher said. "Man text my child and tell him to come on home to eat dinner;" Angel commanded. "Are you going to eat anything?" "I told you what I want to eat woman. When is that on the menu again;" Christopher asked? "Speaking of that, we have to talk about something. What that was you put in my backdoor the other night;" Angel stated. "What about it;" Christopher asked? "What the heck was it?"

"It was a mini bullet that was supposed to cause good vibrations. Like that song, did you not like it;" Christopher asked? "I didn't say I didn't like it. I was just wondering what it was and why you have it;" Angel said. "Do you want the truth;" Christopher asked? "Of course, I always want the truth from you. Anything less and I would be disappointed;" Angel said. "Well, you know when I got divorced and I had to give up quite a bit of my belongings. I was a little peeved about that;" Christopher began. Then I bought my other house in Marietta and got it like I wanted it. One day I bought a bunch of sex toys. Mainly for this one girl I liked who was kind of into these things. We didn't work out in the end.

No pun intended.  Then I thought I was just going to have a house of sex with a few girls. That didn't work out either.  Many of these women walked in my spot and wanted to go from a visit to a permanent stay.  Most of their ideas of us hustling meant, I go out and do all the work.  Then let them know when to show up and cash the checks.  I had this one girl I really liked and she got a job near my second home so she had to move.  So of course, I am thinking.  She can hold down that house. The house I'm in here is near her family.  So we could become a power couple starting off with two houses.'

I was willing to share and build with her;" he continued.  "So, she was going to be able to go from leaving an apartment to having two houses.  Somewhere in conversation, I asked her did she love me.  She wouldn't or couldn't answer me.  I asked her about visiting her at my house, that she asked me to stay in and she told me no. So, basically she wanted to stay in my luxurious home at a discount. There was nothing in the deal for me.  Then, she got mad because I wanted to make it a business deal.  I put a term limit on how long she could use my house.  So that alleged friendship fell apart;" Christopher said.

Some women just think it is their right to use you because as a man.  Like as a man you're supposed to take care of them.  I'm like bitch not if we're not in a relationship. I thought about that for a quick second and said, fuck that shit. I can do bad by my motherfucking self;" Christopher said. "So, what happened with the girl who was the freak you bought the toys for;" Angel asked?  Jamal comes through the door. "Ma, is dinner ready?" "Didn't you just get a text to come eat;" Angel asked sarcastically?

"Oh yeah; Jamal said  Let me go wash my hands."
"Look here Angel;" Christopher said.  It didn't work out so I
didn't use the toys.  I am about to get on the road and get
myself on home.  I need to wash clothes, sweep and mop my
kitchen. Maybe check out the game tonight." "You're such a
man, Mr. Man. You can cook and clean up after yourself.
Some woman will be lucky to have you;" Angel said. "Is that
right; Christopher asked?  Seems like all the great ones are
taken already." Jamal comes out the bathroom and asks; "Mr.
Christopher, are you about to leave?"

"Yeah bro, I have to roll but let's hook up Saturday.
We'll go get that turkey burger;" Christopher said. "Ok, cool,
but can we do it like by one o'clock?  I want to go to the
movies with Marcus and them around four O'clock.  Then
they are having a party for his sister's birthday. I kind of like
her;" Jamal said. "Go on player player, how old is his sister;"
Christopher asked? "She's like 18 or 19, I like older women;"
Jamal said laughing. "Oh and you're 15, I'm not mad at you
player. Look this is how you get her to want nobody but you.
Is she black or white;" Christopher asked?

"She's black but there's another girl; Jamal said. A
white girl at school that kind of likes me too.  She is closer to
my age." "Damn; Christopher said.  You are the man!  Well
look this works on both of them so just remember this line.
Eh YO trick, bring your white ass over here! Or Eh YO trick,
bring your black ass over here."  "Now the catch is to not
mess up and call the black girl white or the white girl black.
They'll get mad about that. Jamal laughed and Angel yelled;
"DON'T BE TELLING MY SON NO BULLCRAP LIKE
THAT!  He knows he better respect all women.  I wish I
would catch you saying that to somebody Mr. Christopher.
Especially me, I'd beat your behind.

"HEY!" (Christopher yelled pretending to be taking charge of the conversation). "DON'T YOU BACK TALK ME WOMAN! See, Jamal you have to let women know who the boss is." (Angel walks briskly towards Christopher and he runs.) "Then at times you have to let them think they are the boss. I just remembered I didn't go jogging today. I was getting a quick run in;" Christopher said laughing. Look Angel, I don't want to have to knock you out.

Woman you don't have to be trying to beat on me. You know I keep my phone dialed on 9 & 1….all I gotta do is dial that last number." Angel replied; "You're gonna need the Police to come and get me off your ass. If you don't stop acting up." "Okay Ice Cubette, I see you coming Straight Outta Philly; Christopher said. Ain't nobody scurred over here. I just ran because I didn't want to show off my Kung Fu moves in front of Jamal." "You can show all the Kung Fu moves you want. When I hit you with this frying pan you're going to be Kung wounded;" Angel said. "Man you two fight like y'all boyfriend and girlfriend;" Jamal interrupted. "Why would you say that;" Angel nervously asked?

"Man, Angel is too crazy to be my girlfriend; Christopher said. I don't know how your daddy deals with her." He attempted to change the subject. "I think your mama be smoking those flowers she grows out there in her garden." "She don't smoke," Jamal replied. "Did she tell you she doesn't smoke Jamal;" Christopher asked? "Yes, we had a talk about it;" Jamal said. "You're black, she'll tell you anything; Christopher laughed. Remember when we all went to the grocery store? She was upstairs saying she was getting ready. How do we know what she was doing up there? You know I was a cop. I know the signs;" Christopher said.

"What are the signs Mr. Christopher;" asked Jamal? "Well if their name is Angel, it's a pretty good chance they are a crack head. They teach you that the first day of the academy;" Christopher joked. Jamal laughed. "Weren't you about to leave Mr. Christopher;" asked Angel? "Well, I guess I was Ms. Angel; Christopher said in a firm tone. I will holla at you a little later Jamal. Make sure you don't eat and get full before we go get our turkey burger." "I won't Mr. Christopher;" replied Jamal. "I guess I will talk to you later too Angel;" Christopher said.

"Are you going home and go to bed? Or will you be up for a while watching basketball;" Angel asked Christopher? "I don't know yet. I may stay up and watch the game or I might work on a proposal. I need to get it to someone by next Monday for a Security contract;" Christopher replied. "Oh well, call me if you decide to stay up;" Angel said. "Yeah, okay;" Christopher said emotionless. He and Angel hugged. Angel's hand slid across the handgun that was holstered under his shirt. She had become accustomed to him wearing it.

She almost felt a sense to make sure he had it on whenever he left her house. He and Jamal clasped hands and gave a man hug. Christopher walked towards the front door. Angel then told Jamal; "Walk Mr. Christopher to the front door." "I'm good lil' man; Christopher replied. I'm the one with the gun anyway. Plus y'all ain't got no gangsters out here in the suburbs." Christopher walked out the door and Jamal walked back into the kitchen. Angel said to Jamal; "So Mr. Christopher has you eating turkey burgers I see." "Yeah, he took me to Ruby Tuesday and I had never had one before. He told me to try it and it was good;" Jamal said.

"So are you going to stop drinking milk like he does too;" Angel asked? "No, I like milk because I want to get bigger. Maybe be a Karate champ one day;" Jamal stated. "Oh so he hasn't totally got you acting like him yet;" Angel sarcastically asked? "What are you talking about Ma? Y'all are the ones always picking with each other. Acting like boyfriend and girlfriend. Then brother and sister sometimes;" Jamal shot back smartly. "Why would you say we act like boyfriend and girlfriend;" Angel asked incredulously?

"Y'all just do; Jamal said. You always seem to have fun around each other. Then you get on each other's nerves like an old married couple. It's a good thing you're married already. I think Mr. Christopher would try to hit that." "Boy watch your damn mouth. Mr. Christopher and I are friends and that's all we'll ever be;" Angel declared! She began to cut up some celery as she continued her defensive speech. "If I wasn't married, nobody would be hitting anything but some books. Like you need to go do after dinner." They had dinner and Jamal cleaned the kitchen before going up to his room.

Angel went to take her shower and get ready for bed. She mumbled out loud, "If I wasn't married, these children say the wildest things." Then she thought to herself; "I sure do wish Mr. Christopher was trying to hit this right now." A sheepish grin came over her face. Followed by a brief thought of terror. She imagined she had left some type of evidence or clue. Something that could have possibly revealed to her son the truth. Had she or Christopher done something in his presence? Anything that would give him an indication that they were something more than friends?

Did Christopher tell him something when they were hanging out together?  Something in a way of bragging that would have betrayed her?  She decided to call Christopher and ask him.  Christopher answered his phone after the third ring. "Hello;" he answered.  "What have you been telling my son;" Angel demanded? "What the hell are you talking about Angel;" Christopher stunningly asked? Why does my son keep making reference to me and you?  Acting like boyfriend and girlfriend? Or like we're married?  Did you tell him something crazy;" Angel interrogated?

# I'll buy a house somewhere else

"Why would I do that? What would I gain by making the woman I love, hate me;" Christopher asked? "What did you say;" Angel inquired? "I said what would I gain by making you hate me;" Christopher repeated? "No you said something else;" Angel prodded. "Oh, I said what would I gain by making the woman I love hate me;" Christopher confessed? "What, when, why would you be in love with me? When you know I'm a married woman;" Angel inquired? Why are you trying to complicate things, even more than they already are;" asked Angel?

"I am not trying to complicate anything;" Christopher said. I understand your situation and I'm not trying to mess it up. I didn't plan to fall in love with you. Love makes things happen." It's just that for years and more years I saw you as nothing but a dear friend. I felt you saw me the same way. Being intimate with you was the last thing on my mind. Which is why I had no problem bringing other girls I use to date around you; Christopher said. Like I told you, I feel really bad for what we're doing with regards to David.

I know I would be really upset if the shoe were on the other foot. I didn't plan this, I didn't plot this. I didn't ask to feel this way about you. Love just made it happen. Do I wish it never did? Honestly, a part of me wishes it never did and a part of me wants you so bad right now;" he said.
"Christopher, we're going to have to end this;" Angel said. She tried to bring reasoning into the conversation. "I mean I have feelings for you too. My mind is all twisted because of how I feel I should be only with my husband.

All my life I told myself I wanted to find a man that is good to me. I was going to honor that man and love him. Most of all, I was going to be faithful to him. I know if David only knew what I've done he would be ready to fight right now." Angel began to cry and her words became unintelligible. Christopher softly said to her; "Don't cry sweetie. I know, I know but don't cry. We'll work this out somehow, so don't cry;" Christopher repeated. "How can we possibly work this out;" Angel asked?

"I'll leave town. I'll buy a house in San Francisco near my sister Valarie. We can pretend this never happened;" Christopher responded. "That's just it;" Angel said. I don't want you to leave town and I'm not sure what I'm feeling from day to day. Hell, sometimes I don't know from minute to minute." "Well maybe we can go back to just being friends; Christopher said. I mean you were kind of rude to me earlier this evening." "That's because you were getting on my nerves with your foolishness;" Angel said. "I was just trying to act like your friend and not your lover in front of Jamal. Then you had to get all serious with everything;" Christopher said.

"Well you know I don't like it when you start acting like a "Yo" on the damn corner somewhere. That is not my type of man;" Angel said. "I was going to call and apologize; Christopher said. Then you called me up with the third degree. Questioning me about what I was telling your son. Woman I would never betray your trust in me with nobody for any reason." "This whole thing is making me crazy; Angel confessed. I mean once we moved here, we both got married but somehow you and I had this bond. I mean I know you loved your wife and I love my husband. Yet you and I seemed more like kindred spirits.

Now we're here with you divorced and me still being married. Our friendship has grown into this beautiful thing. We built our friendship from the ground up. Without sex in the beginning clouding our judgement. Now I'm wrestling with my feelings. I love my husband and I know he loves me. But he and I don't have the bond you and I have; Angel said. I mean you always know what to say to make me feel better. Now I find out you know exactly what to do to make me feel better too.

I mean we've always had a genuine friendship. That's what I've always wanted in my man. David and I have our good days, but he doesn't see me as his best friend. Or he wouldn't treat me like he does." "How exactly does he treat you;" Christopher asked? "I don't want to get into that right now; Angel responded. Besides for all I know, you may just be having fun with me or may try to blackmail me." Christopher responded; "Even if you stopped speaking to me for whatever reason. Or if we had some type of falling out. Whatever things you have told me. Whatever things we have done. If they were private, they will go to my grave with me.

I would think after all the years of being your friend you would know that about me by now. You have never heard one thing you told me in confidence, come back to you in any way. I listen to you. If you want my advice, I give it and that is the end of that conversation. Unless you bring it up again." "Yes, you have always been there for me;" Angel responded. "You're damn right; Christopher said. I have always loved you. You were the first friend I had that really didn't want anything from me. Nothing but for me to be happy. I mean ever since I was old enough to like girls. It always seemed that if they liked me it came with a catch.

Either they wanted to copy off my paper in school, or they knew they could sucker me into buying them stuff. Even in adulthood. I've dated women who claim to want to be with me and my team member. I invite them over to the house and they want a relationship. Before we even know each other's full name. That's only about trying to lock up a space in my house. Not about me if you don't know me. More often than not it's the women trying to rush me into bed. They don't realized that if real men ask you out. You're not competing with anybody. You don't have to get your panties off before the next girl.

"So you don't think you can find a nice young lady that will love you just for you;" Angel asked? "I have, Christopher replied. She is married already. Her name is Angel." "No, besides me silly;" Angel said. "It's hard Angel. I mean you women always talking about how hard it is to find a good man. It's harder to find a good woman. All these women out here talking to each other. Lying saying they are good women. After they have let some no-good, unemployed bum use their asses up.

Now they have trust issues I'm supposed to deal with. The women who have an alleged good job, make 5 or 6 figures. Won't give you the time of day when you speak to them. I take that back, if I'm in a suit or just got out my ride then they will speak. I know plenty of good dudes who have bad women that don't treat them right. I know men who are trying to save and build a business. While their woman wastes money on weaves so that they stay looking like they got a rat on their head. Fake eyelashes, fake hair and fake nails and can't figure out why they keep finding fake men? Real men are attracted to the real you. There is nothing sexier on planet earth than a black woman with her natural hair.

"You've had to run into some good women with natural hair Christopher. They can't all be bad;" Angel said. "Well I found the perfect one for me. Only she is married already and that creates a dilemma. I just get tired of women's bullshit games." "That's the same thing we say about you men;" Angel replied. "Yeah, women say it but much of what women say is just some drama they create for themselves. How are you going to date an unemployed weed smoker, then be surprised he has no ambitions?

Men don't tend to complain about what women do. Especially not publically, but there are some low down women out here. I was talking to this one girl on online. I mean this woman seemed to be ideal. She was intelligent, beautiful and had been through her share of drama. Yet appeared to keep smiling through it. She was open minded about learning new things. That is really is a turn on for me. I mean we talked online for two years. So this wasn't some 'I saw your picture and now I want you to be my girlfriend' type thing.

All seemed to go well in every conversation we had online and at some point. I became attracted to her and she said she was attracted to me. So I was like I am trying to start a clothing company because she could make nice clothes. Based on this unique brand of material I had discovered when I was traveling out the country. I asked her how she felt about it. She said she loved the idea and wanted to be a part of it. So I'm literally falling for this girl and ready to make her a partner in my new company. I drew up the papers and everything with her name on it. So after two years of all going well, we finally decide to speak on phone. I call and get no answer on the phone. I hit her up on Facebook like when is a good time to call and we finally talk for a good two hours.

Her voice was a little ditzy, but I figured I could overcome that and even learn to love it. After we talk on the phone that night. I can't get her simple ass to respond to anything. Nothing I send her on Facebook, and can't get her to answer the phone again. Now she's posting all these crazy messages on Facebook to someone. Like if you want me you need to come and get me before you lose me? After all we've shared. So I inbox her like, 'what's the deal? If you're checking for someone else, let me know and I will step aside.

Now this broad pretends to act like she doesn't know what I'm talking about. Now she's doing a fake she's mad at me. Then I'm like well, 'let's talk it out and see if we can fix this' but I still get ignored. Then she writes on Facebook: still mad at you. You need to go to Tiffany's or some crazy shit like that. I'm like bitch you're not worth a chicken McNugget, singular. I think when we talked on the phone I was just being me. Not talking all proper like I write and she thought I may not be up to her college standards.

I'm like why the hell you're crying on Facebook? Saying you want a man that can match you in intelligence and ambition. Then when you find him, you let something so stupid ruin it. I bet she ran to her girlfriends talking about there are no good men available. She told me how her ex-husband tried to kill her. Now I'm thinking he was trying to save the world from crazy." "She wanted something from Tiffany's, and y'all haven't even met yet;" Angel asked? "Yes, ain't that some crazy shit. I mean we had talked for a few years over deep conversation. We're proposing for me to fly her up to my other house in Marietta, but we hadn't gotten to that point yet.

We were waiting on her kids to get out of school because I have room for them too. If she wanted to bring them but after we talked she started tripping. So, I was like to hell with it and moved on with my plans to start a different company." "Wow! I can't believe she would let you pass on something so silly; Angel said. She truly doesn't realize what she had. You're a very smart man who is building his fortune one brick at a time. She was too stupid to see the woman who is with you will never live an ordinary life.

Angel continued; why can't there be more guys out there like you? I mean I have girlfriends and they have some horror stories to tell. These so called men out here. Guys lying about their jobs, their cars, their criminal records, their sexuality. Even will lie and tell you it is Tuesday on a Friday. They make these babies and then don't want to pay the child support. They borrow these women's cars and pick up some other hoe in them. They get parking tickets and don't tell the girlfriend.

She doesn't find out she has unpaid tickets until they are towing her car away. Then you have these crazy guys out here who want to control the woman. Want to know her every move. Not to mention, the ones who think they can beat on a woman. All over Facebook you have women talking about some no good man or a deadbeat dad. I'm sorry I don't see as many men complaining about bad women;" Angel said. "Hold on Angel, back that thang up; Christopher interrupted. Like I said earlier, men just don't publically cry about all the wrong that is done to them by these women. Hold on, let me call you on my home phone; Christopher said. My battery is about to die. He dials her number from his home phone and Angel clicks over. Like I was saying; he continued.

I'm pretty sure that's what that Michael Baisden book "*Men Cry in the Dark*" was about. We don't have brother circles where we sit around sipping wine, beer or Malt Liquor. Telling of our woes to each other about women. For all the women who talk about their no good man or deadbeat dad. Didn't they know he was no good before they got involved? Didn't they know he didn't want to be a family man before they decided to have his baby? Not saying every case is like this because I know it's not. But some of these women have babies because they wanted to keep a man that never wanted them.

Just like you said, some men want to control women. Some women feel that once they have a baby by a man, they can control him. With a crooked court system to back them up." "Wait a minute; Angel injected. That is not a woman trying to control a man. If he laid down with her and a baby came then he has to man up. Accept whatever possibilities that may come with that. If that is a baby, then he needs to deal with that. If he didn't want a baby, he should have worn a condom." "Well, Christopher said; if you're going to use that argument, let's flip it like this.

Those same two people who laid down together, if a baby comes he has to man up and deal with it. If he didn't want a baby he should have worn a condom right?" "Right;" Angel responded. "Well, if he laid with her knowing he was HIV positive and didn't tell her. Shouldn't she just woman up and deal with it, right? I mean if she didn't want HIV, SHE should have made sure he wore a condom. Or SHE could have used protection. Same two people, same act, two different outcomes. Now, I am not saying it is right to give a woman HIV by any circumstances. I would kill a moarfugger that hid that from me.

Neither is it right to decide solely on your own that you want to have a baby. Then you're going to force a man to deal with you because you have feelings for him. When you know he doesn't love you like you do him. Just because a dude lays with a woman for a few hours should not mean he has to be connected to her for life, no more than a woman laying with that dude for a few hours should not have her taking HIV meds for the rest of her life. It's wrong both ways. Now if the man and woman talk and both want the baby, then that is fine."

"So you're saying a man should be able to tell a woman when she can have a baby;" Angel asked? "No, I'm not saying that at all. You know I'm a big advocate for Political candidates that support women's rights;" Christopher said. "Why do you think I am a Wendy Davis fan and I don't live anywhere near Texas? What I am saying is there has to be some middle ground somewhere. I don't know what the complete answer is. Today you have hoes camping out at the locker rooms of NBA and NFL players. Just hoping to get pregnant so they can get a $30,000 a month child support payment;" he said.

"They don't know or care anything about these players in many cases. You can't tell me some 20 year old kid who has played sports all his life. Should be wise enough to know he may be getting trapped into financial ruin. All he sees is, I got millions and this half- naked bitch wants to fuck me. Then the system is so corrupt that it makes no adjustments when these dudes get hurt or older. No longer making large sums of money but child support remains at $30,000 a month. It's like that because most of the athletes caught in the system are black males. It looks to ruin them financially before the courts will consider reduction in child support.

This same scheme goes down every day on a smaller scale with working class men. He has an okay job and some skank comes trying to bleed him for child support. Some women know the man doesn't want her. It's not ideal for the baby as she and the man don't get along outside of sex. She will add stress to her own life. Still she will ruin three lives to try to get some stupid scenario in her head. One that is never going to work out. The system helps her out financially but the system can't get you rest and relief from stress. Chicks getting child support, government aid and mama watching their kids. Then they claim they're independent women?

"I agree the system is unfair to men now; Angel said. For a long time women got the short end. Men would leave women with kids while they would go find somebody else. Leaving the woman to struggle in poverty. So a system had to be put in place to correct that huge wrong." "Yes, I am aware of that; Christopher said. That was a great wrong too. I just don't think you over compensate the past wrong by creating a legal system that overly wrongs the other party. America didn't say hey whites hanged blacks for a few hundred years, so now it is okay for blacks to hang white people. All that was needed was hate crime laws. Look! I don't want to talk about this anymore, Angel.

I would rather talk about you;" he said. "What about me;" Angel asked? "What are you wearing;" Christopher asked? "I am wearing the same thing I was wearing when I got out the shower two months ago;" Angel toyed. "What color panties do you have on sexy lady;" Christopher further questioned? "Pink lace but if you were here, I might put on my edible ones;" Angel teased. "If I were there, I might eat you all up beautiful woman;" Christopher asserted. "Oh you think I'm beautiful do you;" Angel coyly asked?

"Yes, I do gorgeous woman; Christopher answered. From your beautiful skin to those beautiful eyes. My God, you have the sexiest lips this world has ever seen!" "Hmmm. Sometimes I don't think I'm all that beautiful;" Angel said. I mean I know I'm not ugly but I am not always confident in my looks." "Woman what are you talking about; Christopher replied. You're built like a goddess. That healthy glow on your skin is such a turn on. Just the way you carry yourself. Every man knows when you walk in a room that a real woman has entered.

I mean you have your ways about you when you want to get moody. Still for a 97.8% great woman with about 2.2% I could do without. I would gladly take you; he joked. Angel, if the world only knew what I knew. They would no longer speak of Cleopatra, Isis or Pam Grier as the most awe-inspiring beauty in history. They would speak of Angel Renee' Robinson. The most jaw dropping, inspirational, powerful aphrodisiac this side of Eden. Mainly because you don't try too hard to be sexy, you just are. I guess all those years we were friends I noticed it, but I didn't notice it."

So we're not friends anymore is that what you're telling me;" Angel asked playfully? "No baby; Christopher said. We will always be friends. No matter what happens in life. I know you get mad with me sometimes. You get on my nerves too sometimes. At no time did it ever cross my mind to abandon you. Or even take a break from you. If I was out of state and you called me and told me you needed me. I would be on my way as fast as I could. That's why I have to keep working. So I can buy a helicopter in case you do call me when I am out of state. Right now you have to wait until my skateboard can get me to you."

"Boy why do you say the most wonderful things;" Angel asked? "What do you mean;" Christopher replied? "I mean I know I will have to let you go. I would love to start one of those fake arguments like your old girlfriend. Then you say something like you'll always be there for me, and I can't see how I will break this off;" Angel sighed. "Well, whenever you want me to not see you like this anymore, then you just say it; he said. One thing you should have been able to tell since we've been friends. Is that I would do almost anything you ask of me;" Christopher said. "I know you would;" Angel said. I cherish that privilege and try to not to abuse it."

"You haven't by any means sweetie and that's one of the reasons I love you;" Christopher said. "Oh really what are some of the other reasons;" Angel asked arrogantly? "Oh now you're pushing it lady; Christopher said laughingly. Hmmm, why do I love you? How about I put it in a poem for you and see what I can do?" "Oh you're going to write another poem for me? I can't wait to read it;" Angel said excitedly! "Damn! I gotta write it; Christopher protested. I was just going to go with roses are red/you have a pretty head/ violets are blue/what's up boo."

"You better not bring me no corny stuff like that. I want something personal and beautiful like I know you can write;" Angel directed. "I will see what I can come up with your highness; Christopher said. What time is it?" "It is almost midnight;" Angel answered. "Man so much for sweeping and mopping my kitchen tonight. Angel why did you keep me on this phone so long; he asked? You know I don't like talking on the phone longer than five minutes. Unless for you." "Oh I'm sorry sir; Angel replied. You could have just hung up, if you didn't want to talk to me this long."

Angel then hears an instant silent. She knows Christopher just hit the end button on his phone. "No this Negro did not just hang up in my face;" she uttered. Her phone rings and she can see it is Christopher calling her back. She lets it ring and go to voicemail. He calls her again and this time she answers. "Oh you think you're funny, don't you punk; Angel asked?

I'm going to get you back. Trust me on that when you least expect it." "What I do? What I do?" Christopher asked astonishingly. Laughing like he has no idea what she is talking about. "You hung up the phone in my face you punk....I'm going to get you back;" Angel promised.

# I'm a long way from buying it now

"No I didn't hang up. I ran out of minutes on my phone and they cut me off;" Christopher lied. "You don't have no damn prepaid phone punk. That's alright, I will get you back;" Angel promised. "Okay, I don't have a prepaid phone. Would you believe the aliens tried to take me to their planet and my signal went out? When I got to the planet Plebolazar." "I got your Plebolazar alright;" Angel said. "That's what I wanted to hear;" Christopher replied. "Get off my phone; Angel said. I have to get up and work on retirement plans for a few clients tomorrow. Do you want to do lunch tomorrow?"

"Well I was going out in the morning to look at beauty salon I may want to buy. Then I will be free; Christopher said. If I get it, I may need your help. In finding some, what do you call the ladies that work in a beauty salon;" he asked? "Stylist," Angel said. "Yeah, them hoochies; Christopher joked. I need women that only do natural hair in my shop. I'm a long way from buying it now though. Have to go see how much money it will take to fix it up. See what the neighborhood looks like. After I am done, how about I cook you lunch at my place?" "Oh that sounds wonderful. What are you cooking;" Angel asked?

"Let's see, you have a choice between my famous meatloaf. With real mashed potatoes, spinach and cornbread. Or you can have Cornish hens with whatever sides you want. Or smothered Turkey chops with brown rice or you can have Poptarts;" Christopher said. "Do the poptarts come with juice or water;" Angel asked? "They don't come with a damn thing, just Poptarts;" Christopher said.

"Well in that case, do you have salmon over there?" Angel asked. It's Pacific Salmon, and I can glaze it in honey or BBQ sauce;" Christopher said. "You know what, I haven't had some good meatloaf in a while. So let me try that but can I get broccoli instead of spinach;" Angel asked? "Anything you wish Angel, and I may even bake you a cake;" Christopher said. "You don't have to go through all that trouble. Just bake me some brownies;" Angel said laughing. "Oh it's gonna be some trouble alright;" Christopher replied. "Goodnight man;" Angel yawned.

When I roll up in that piece, I better smell fresh baked brownies. Or else your eye is going to have a nice brownie ring around it." "Damn! Why are you always threatening me with violence woman;" Christopher asked? Now I'm going to drop your food in the trash and then put it on your plate after the roaches crawl on it." "You don't have roaches punk;" Angel said. "I use to live in West Baltimore. So I know where to get some and put on your food nooka;" Christopher said. "And I know where the cemetery is punk; Angel replied. Don't make me have your family slow singing and flower bringing."

"Goodnight woman; Christopher said. You're too violent for me, but I still love you." "I still love you too; Angel said. That's why I hope I don't have to hurt you. If there are no brownies up in that camp tomorrow; Angel continued. Like Sweet Daddy use to tell JJ, boy you're gonna be in trouble." "I heard you woman. I will see if I can find some little Debbie brownies;" Christopher said. "I'm not playing with you, Goodnight handsome man;" Angel said.

"Goodnight beautiful woman;" he replied. Christopher looked at the time on his phone and went to take a shower. Once out the shower, he went into his home office. He decided to write the poem he promised Angel before he forgot. He didn't want to have to rush one. Christopher sat at his computer and turned on the monitor. He saw he had a lot of emails. Despite being very tired and wanting to get this poem written, he decided to clean out his junk email. A dozen emails about cheap Viagara. About a dozen more telling him that there were horny girls within two miles of him. Just waiting to have sex. One email saying he had won a contest he never entered.

Ooh! Another letter from a Russian girl who fell in love with me just by seeing my picture. Now she wants to come see me. All I have to do is wire her some money, and she will fly to America to have sex with me? "I'll get right on that the day after never;" he thought. Ah, one email from his cousin Geneva, his real estate agent. With some pictures of the salon they are supposed to see in the morning. He clicked on the email and pictures. He noticed the floors were in great shape. 'Man what the hell do you know about running a hair salon?' he thought to himself. "Nothing;" he said out loud. I will hire some woman that does. If she doesn't know what she is doing then I might have some problems.

'Man let me work on this poem so I can go to bed,' he thought. He sat and thought about how beautiful Angel is inside and out. How she excites him. He didn't want his poem for her to be overly sappy. He did want it to convey to her just how she makes him feel. How to proclaim his helplessness to fight her control over him, and yet without sounding like he was whipped.

What to name a poem always seemed to be the hardest part for him to write. However once he got the first line flowing he could easily write the rest. 'What title best described Angel' he thought? He thought about how conversation with her was always stimulating. How being in her presence made him feel alive. How she challenged him mentally. How she pushed him to stay informed, never knowing what subject she may want to discuss. Before he knew it he had these words typed.

# Lovely Woman

Lovely black woman your mind, body and soul feel so good to me

To be inside of one or every part of them, is the greatest of ecstasy

At the thought of your smile or touch, mental and physical
excitement does grow

The pleasures of your beautiful loving spirit, only I and heaven
know


For your love black diamond, there's nothing in this universe that I
won't do

I will call every single star in the sky and tell them all about you

When there is another earthquake, you may find out I am to blame

For I'll rearrange many mountains, to spell out your pretty name


I'm in love with you black woman and there's no way I can deny
this

I'd run across the ocean and jump to the moon, just to feel your soft
kiss

Cleopatra, Isis, Oprah and all the true beauties through eternal time

I would turn away their wealth, beauty and power, if I could only
make you mine


Written By: Christopher P. Watson

Exclusively For: Angel Renee' Robinson

He inserted a rose colored piece of paper into his printer. He thought it was a good poem written in such haste. Tomorrow while out, he would pick up a blank card. Place the poem inside to give to Angel. He already knew going in that this poem would be lost. The card and poem would find imminent fate. Just as all the ones he had previously written for her. Angel could not possibly keep them and risk discovery by her husband. However, he knew she would enjoy reading it when he gave it to her. If it made her smile, it was well worth it to him. He went to bed and got some rest, so he could function later this morning.

Angel was awakened by the sounds of Jamal getting up to shower. After numerous years of Jamal managing his school routine. Her motherly instinct still kicked in. Listening to make sure she could hear him shower. Then brush his teeth and get out the door on time to catch the bus. In her mind, this was the better option. Better than to have to get up and take him to school if he missed his bus. Jamal ate breakfast at school. Thank God she didn't have to get up and fix him anything she thought.

She slowly made her way out of bed and brushed her teeth. She walked down to the kitchen just in time. She said goodbye and kissed Jamal as he ran out the front door. "Let me fix some tea, and get started on these plans for the Johnsons; she thought. Then I'll work on the Crosbys." She fills her teapot with fresh filtered water. She walks from the refrigerator door and places the pot on the stove. Her cell phone starts ringing, she dashes back upstairs where she left it to get it. It is her husband David and she answered. "Hi honey, how are you; she asks? You just missed your son. He just walked out the door."

David tells her how things are going and how much he misses her and Jamal. He asks; "How is Jamal doing in school?" Angel replies; "All is well with Jamal school wise." David asks; "How are you sleeping?" "I'm doing okay but I wish you were here so I could sleep better;" she says. "What color panties do you have on baby;" David asked? Angel almost blurted out; "Why does everybody want to know that?" She quickly caught herself with her heart beating faster. "Why do you want to know that honey;" she asked?

"Because I want to know;" David responded. I've been thinking about you in nothing but your panties." "They're beige, but I can put on whatever you like. Even the edible royal blue ones;" she said. "Why would I want you to put on the blue ones when I am hundreds of miles away Angel;" he asked? "I was just trying to give you a nice thought to think about. Until you get home where I'll be waiting for you;" Angel said.

"I'm sorry baby for snapping. I'm just a little upset because they may halt our work and we may lose money. Have you been recording all my games? So I can catch up on the season when I get home;" David asked? "Yes, I recorded all your games just like you asked me;" Angel said. You get back December 16th right?" "Yeah right before the holidays, and I will be home for at least 45 days. So I will be able to see the Playoffs and the rest of the season on my own T.V;" David said. "Well, glad you're coming home. Glad you're excited about seeing your games;" Angel said. There was a hint of disappointment in her voice.

# What if I wanted to go for a walk?

"Well I want to see you too baby. I can't wait to get some home cooking; David said. They are trying to kill us with this fast food they're serving over here. I can't wait to have Christmas dinner with my family." "I will fix you whatever you want when you get home; Angel assured. When you get upstairs to our bedroom. I will give you anything you want there too." "Look baby, I have to go. The cement truck is pulling up and I have to sign for it;" David cut her off. "Okay baby, take care of yourself. I will be looking forward to your next call; Angel said. I love you David." He replied; "I love you too baby, will call you later."

Angel hung up the phone with a rush of mixed emotions. She obviously felt guilty for things she was doing. Her husband was away working so hard for his family. She also felt terrified of what she almost blurted out. Something that may have disclosed that dirty secret. She didn't really feel left out, just not a top priority with her husband. He seemed more excited about being able to watch his games. Excited more about home cooking, than he was about seeing her. She recalled what Christopher just told her last night. That she would always be priority with him. Over the course of their friendship, he had shown that to be true.

If he had plans and she wanted him to go to the store for a newspaper. He would change his plans. If she needed her son picked up from school. If she needed a client picked up from the airport. Christopher would find a way to help Angel out. Why wasn't she top priority with the man who promised to love her? David was a great father at times but with she and him something was missing.

"I know what I'm going to do;" she thought. "Hello;" Christopher sleepily answered his phone. "What are you doing;" Angel asked? "I am sleeping. Like any normal human would be at 6:30 in the morning;" Christopher said grouchily. "What are you doing calling me this early, is everything alright;" he asked? "What plans do you have for the day;" Angel asked? "Hold on, let me rinse my mouth;" Christopher said and put the phone down. He returned seconds later. "Woman, what do you mean? What plans do I have for the day? The same ones I told you about last night; he said.

I am going to look at this salon building and see if it's a good deal or not." "What if I wanted to go for a walk or to the library; Angel asked? What if I wanted to research on a proposal for my clients?" "Well, if you're going for a walk, then I guess I would have to cancel my appointment; Christopher said. I'd walk with you. If you're going to the library, you can go there by yourself. I will catch up with you later." "What if I wanted you to come to the library with me;" Angel inquired? "Woman, you have a home office and I have a home office. So wouldn't it be easier to research on those plans at your house or for you to come here;" Christopher asked?

"Well, I don't want to be here at my house. I'm not ready to come to your house yet. So can we go to the library;" Angel asked? Her voice was slightly demanding. Christopher knew instinctively that she just wanted to talk. "Hey, now that I think of it, my internet is down. So I guess we're going to the library; Christopher said. Let me text Geneva and let her know I need to reschedule. Probably pass up on what might be a big money- making deal. These opportunities don't just hang out on the corner waiting for a brother. Only for you, would I do this Angel.

Now, you're going to have to do my hair; he continued. Since I won't have a salon anymore. Plus you need to pay me $10.00. I was looking to make at least that much on this deal." Angel didn't feel remorse about making him miss out. She was sure it was a good money- making deal. Yet she knew two things about Christopher: 1) He would never do anything he didn't want to do and….2) He would find a way to make another deal equal to or better than this one. She also knew she was smart enough to make him a good deal of money. There was no doubt about it that Christopher knew how to hustle. He wasn't the guy always in your face with the latest selling something scheme.

Christopher was measured, self-assured. He believed in surrounding himself with the right people that would get him the right information. Ones to bring him the right opportunity. No wonder he had a real estate agent in different states. He also had several mortgage brokers that he kept in contact with on a regular basis. Christopher was a man that never appeared to be hustling. He wasn't the flashy type guy trying to pretend he had made it.

Christopher dressed in a casual conservative way. Usually jeans, casual dress shirt and sweaters in the fall. He would only switch to Polo type shirts in warmer weather. When it came to watches, he only wore one brand and one brand only….Movado. Christopher liked that Movado watches were elegant. They didn't have all that flashy crap that he saw many guys wear. He didn't like the big overstated face watches and extra shiny crap. Movado watches were his reward he would buy for himself every time he would accomplish a goal. He had almost every color he wanted with the exception of one. He just needed an opportunity to add it to his collection.

One thing about Christopher, he was not about trying to impress anybody. He was sure of what he was building in the way of a viable portfolio. Angel was also reserved, but very calculating. She was more disciplined than Christopher and her mind was always in overdrive. If not understanding the next big opportunity on the market. She was helping someone else understand, or reach for their secure retirement.

As a woman who started out with little, she came up well. Angel was introduced in college to a man she called Mr. Powers. He was a RVP in a company called Primerica Financial Services. He talked Angel into joining. The financial education Angel received, she credited with changing her life. She got Christopher to join. While he believed in most of the principles they taught. Christopher just wasn't into being a pitch man. Before long, Angel had her investment licenses. She focused on that portion of the business with a passion. She took additional courses and taught herself so much. Constantly reading and talking to others in the business, she mastered it.

She had become a complete guru on the matter of investments. Some folks even believed she could tell you what and when the next hot market would be. Ultimately she would become a CPA and open her own Accounting firm. Her knowledge of Accounting and Investments made her a financial genius. Most folks felt very fortunate to have Angel come into their lives. Many could not praise her enough for the literal way she changed their future. Most folks believed they had to have a lot of money to get started investing, until they talked to Angel. They were amazed at how Angel could devise plans for what was small money. Then set them on a path to having more than they could have dreamed.

As long as they could discipline themselves and follow Angel's written plan. To many, she was a Godsend. Christopher thought Angel's only flaw was she didn't realize she had built a blueprint. She thought she had to be hands on with each client when her system worked itself. Christopher would often see people that Angel had helped. How grateful they were and he knew he was witnessing a very rare and special woman. Angel also dressed the part, strictly professional and didn't go around showing all of her assets.

She was a woman of great beauty and self-respect. She was not a woman you would ever see twerking. Or degrading herself for a man's pleasure in public. She did know how to throw a party however. Angel and Christopher loved having a get together at their homes. They loved to cook and lay out a nice, fancy spread of gourmet dishes and treats. Their parties centered on having their professional friends meet and mingle. In the hopes that some business arrangement might be made.

Their events were more about those that didn't have but wanted to get. Newcomers were placed in an informal environment with those that had, and wanted to give back. These parties you could find mentors in both education and opportunity. Christopher and Angel knew there were no free rides to wealth building. If you wanted to learn from those that did it, then their parties were must attends. If you got invited to either of their houses for an event, you were lucky. The mentors communicated with each other. One might be asked to do something like find some information. Then call the mentor with it. If you made excuses, that was your last invite. Angel and Christopher carefully screened and watch their associates. Observing where their heads were at and if you appeared to be trying, you may get an invitation.

Were Christopher and Angel the arrogant stuck up type? Not at all. They were Rap music loving, politically informed, Science curious geeks. Both were very conscious of and promoted issues affecting black people. Christopher was a Rap music historian. Both of them were well educated, but from urban environments. They could get ghetto with you and curse you out like a rapper from Compton. However they both preferred to just not deal with people who preferred stupidity. They detested (as Uncle Ruckus from The Boondocks would say) "dumb nigga shit."

Christopher pulled up at the library to find Angel sitting in her car and he quickly found a parking space. He walked over to Angel's car. She appeared to be singing with her windows rolled up. When Christopher was right outside her driver's side window, she rolled it down. He could hear her singing; (Brown Skin) by India Arie. Christopher listened to Angel sing a few bars and leaned in close to her ear. Awww Sooki Sooki now, sang it baby; he teased.

# What, do you want to fight now?

"Angel;" he called. She kept singing. "Angel," he repeated. "What punk; she snapped. This is my favorite part." Angel turned up the music and sang a bit louder. Christopher saw she was trying to be funny with him so he repeated; "Angel!" "Yes man, what do you want;" she asked? "Who sings that song;" Christopher asked? "India Arie," Angel replied. "Why don't you keep it that way;" Christopher laughed. "Forget you punk; Angel said. I was in my groove." She rolls her window up and gets out the car. They walk into the library. Christopher hands her the card and poem he wrote for her. "Why are we here again;" he asks?

"Thank you sweetie; she says. I wanted to check out a book entitled, The World is Flat: by Thomas Friedman. In case it's on a high shelf, I might need you to reach it for me;" Angel said. "Oh, that makes sense Angel; Christopher said. You had me drive all the way down here to grab a book. You could have gotten almost any guy in this library to get for you." "I didn't want any guy to get my book, I wanted you to get it. Now is there a problem;" Angel quizzed back? "No, my Queen, there is no problem. What size cement shoes do you wear and where is the nearest lake or river around here;" Christopher asked? "Whatever nooka;" Angel snapped.

"Did you just call me a nooka;" Christopher asked? "Shhhh…we're in a library; she whispered. Yeah, I did. What do you want to fight now;" Angel jokingly asked? "Look at you, trying to be all ghetto in the library of all places; Christopher said. That's a good thing for you though woman. There has to be a book in here on how to stop the bleeding. You might need that in a few minutes."

"I ain't going to need nothing, but a crowbar to get my foot up out your behind;" Angel replied. Christopher smacked her on her ass and said; "You better watch who you're talking to woman, before I"… Angel cut him off. "Before you hand me that book right there;" she said. Pointing to the book she wanted. Christopher handed her the book and remarked. "This is a damn shame. You brought me all the way down here to hand you a book. What am I going to do with this crazy woman right here Lord?" "Speaking of that, what other gadgets do you have in that house of yours;" Angel asked?

"What are you talking about crazy woman;" Christopher asked? "You know like the gadget you used on me;" Angel said. "You want to talk about this now, in here;" Christopher asked? "Yeah, just keep your voice down and talk;" Angel instructed. "I have a few things here and there;" Christopher said. "Yeah where;" Angel asked? "In my treasure safe;" he said. "Your what;" Angel asked? It's a safe I have in my closet that has a few items in it, such as a whip and paddle, Velcro handcuffs and sexy dice. Maybe some edible and warming massage oils, the blindfold and not much else;" Christopher said.

"Why do you have all of those things;" Angel asked? "I told you. When I got divorced and bought the second house. It was supposed to be just a freak, nasty place where I was going to have lots of women over. At first, all of it was for the one woman I had been pursuing. She was into those things. Those plans never worked out. "Oh, is that the lady you were telling me about;" Angel asked? You really liked her, didn't you;" Angel asked? "Yeah, I kinda had feelings for her and thought she might be the one; he said. You women are all cray cray though. Especially your ass Angel." So, getting back, I saw I wasn't going to be tying her up.

Then the whole lots of women idea got scary. Too many germs being passed around. So I bought stock in Vaseline and Kleenex and I was good; he laughed. I made sure their stock went up. "You're retarded;" Angel said. "A lot of those toys I gave away; he continued. The ones I still have are still unopened. Then the house just became my getaway spot when I needed peace. Now I just fly down to catch up on movies, relaxing and sleep. Sometimes I do business in the office there; Christopher said. I'd be doing business now except, some crazy woman had me cancel that. So I can hand her ass a damn book." "Are you cursing at me man;" Angel asked? "No, I am not cursing at you woman; Christopher answered.

You know I would never disrespect you like that. Even if your ass made me miss out on a damn business deal. Anyway the next time you're over you can go look and see what's in the safe. Not my regular safe you broke into. Another one in the back of my closet. Most of those things have been in my safe for years, untouched;" he said. We can figure out what you like together.

The other night when I was looking at your beautiful body. Just knowing how you respond when I touch you in certain ways. I thought you might really like the mini bullet. I'm guessing from your reaction, you did enjoy it Angel;" he said. "Oh yes Lawd, I did; she replied. That was the most incredible feeling, I must say. I wouldn't be mad if you did that again;" she said. Christopher said; "That reminds me, if I should die for any reason. I need you to get that safe. Throw that shit in the Colorado or Amazon River. Before my family comes and starts going through my things like vultures. Hell, put that shit on a Malaysian flight to somewhere.

You make sure your key is the first one to open my door. If I should go prematurely." "Am I in your will;" Angel asked? "No you're not; Christopher said. My daughter will be over my will passing out leftovers. I need you to make sure everyone knows what to do with $20.00 dollars and not spend it all in one place. Teach my daughter to save a couple dollars or go buy some cocaine. If she sells to the nut wings in Congress she'll be rich. I know those idiots are on drugs. "I will personally fly out to Seattle and give her the message; Angel said. If she is not done with college by then.

Man, her daddy is going to leave her a little small empire. I bet she'll be happy about that." "I ain't leaving her jack because I ain't going nowhere no time soon; Christopher said. Y'all better pack a lunch waiting on me to kick the bucket. I plan on living forever, so far, so good." "Man, let me read my poem and go check out this book. So we can get out of here;" Angel said. "Yeah, you do that, so you can get back in your car and sing. I mean, attempt to sing your song;" Christopher said. "Attempt nothing, oh we're making fun of me now? Is that what we're doing;" Angel joked? "Hey, do you know why India Arie sang that song called Brown Skin;" Christopher asked? "No. why;" Angel responded?

"So that you wouldn't have to;" Christopher said laughing. "Oh let me get this straight because you know I need clarity. You just want me to keep my mouth closed from now on correct;" Angel asked? "Please God no, you can sing or do whatever you like woman;" Christopher whined. "Can we go down by the Washington Monument;" Angel asked? "Why do you want to go down there woman? Let me guess, you want me to buy you a soda. It can only be from the guy in one of those carts on wheels; Christopher said sarcastically. Or you need a baseball cap, with DC on it?"

What difference does it make; Angel asked? You know whatever I ask you for, you're going to buy it for me. They walked outside. Wait, oh this is a beautiful poem you wrote. Thank you so much sweetie; she said. She hugged and kissed him on the cheek and got in his truck. I'll thank you for this poem later; she said. They soon arrived in front of the Monument. As usual, the streets were packed full of cars. So Christopher drove around to a side street. He parked in the residential area several blocks away. He walked around and opened the door for Angel. They then walked over to the park. "Don't think this is getting you out of cooking for me, homeboy. I am still expecting that;" Angel said.

"Homeboy? Were you up watching rap videos or something last night;" Christopher asked? You're trying to get black, cause we're in the hood or something?" "I am black Son Son, and don't you forget it;" Angel warned. "Son Son, oh snap, shorty went NYC on me. What do you know about New York woman;" Christopher asked? "I know you better take me up there soon. So I can get my natural care products in Harlem;" Angel said. "Christopher asked; "So, tell me again, why are we out here in the middle of D.C. Angel?" "We're out here because it is a beautiful day. The sun is shining, it's only 76 degrees, low humidity and I wanted to be outdoors.

Now come on and walk with me;" Angel said. "Where are we walking to old crazy woman; Christopher asked? I hope you're not out here trying to meet with your Russian spy contact. I'm telling the Feds if you do." "Snitches get stitches;" Angel yelled back. "I got your snitch for you;" Christopher said. He then slapped her ass and ran. Angel chased him. Christopher found an elderly woman sitting on a bench laughing at them. He ran behind her bench.

"You can't get me. You can't get me;" Christopher teased. Then stuck out his tongue. "Don't make me jump over that bench, but I will if I have to;" Angel warned. She moved to go behind the bench. Christopher moved to the front. "Ma'am, did you hear this crazy lady, who I don't know, threaten me? Can you please call the police;" Christopher asked? Tell them there is a gun out here and they need to shoot first and ask questions later." "Oh, you dirty dog;" Angel said. She lunged at Christopher and he let her catch him and she punched him on his arm. "You're trying to get me shot. Talk trash now punk;" Angel said.

She placed her hands around his throat pretending to massage it. She slightly squeezed his neck applying light pressure. Christopher pretended like he was choking. He begged the elderly woman to pick up a brick and hit her. The elderly woman replied; "I can't do that. If she is choking you, she must have a good reason." Christopher responded; "All you women stick together. I knew I shouldn't have run over here for help. You probably told her to choke me." "That's right, the elderly lady replied. If you try to run we will both beat you with my cane." "Man, I am scared of both of you; Christopher said.

Christopher walked over to the lady. "Can I get you something to drink, ma'am, before we go?" "Well, if it's no trouble, can you get me a lemonade; the woman asked? "No trouble at all ma'am, Angel chimed in. He'll buy it for you or we'll beat him down and take his wallet." "See, how violent she is, ma'am; he asked? I'm telling you, she just got out of prison yesterday for killing 7 people. She is certifiably crazy;" Christopher said. "She seems pretty normal to me. Yet you seem to be crazy about her, so how does that work;" the lady asked?

"She hit me in the head with a hammer, so I don't know any better; Christopher replied. I will be right back with your drink, ma'am." He and Angel walked over to the stand and he asked Angel what she wants. "I just want a bag of cashews and a small lemonade. I haven't forgotten that you're cooking for me later on today." They returned to the lady and Christopher handed her the drink, along with $20.00. "That's in case, you want to get anything else after we leave ma'am;" Christopher said. "Thank you very much young man;" the woman said.

# The Secret Service

"I really appreciate you postponing your deal to come spend some time with me; Angel said. It really means a lot to me Christopher." "Well, it could have meant I could have bought you three bags of cashews. Instead of one had it gone through, but we will never know that now;" Christopher said. "You're not mad about that are you;" Angel asked? "No, I can never be mad at you Angel. At least, I can't stay mad at you. I don't know why, but I told you I think you're a witch or something. You had to have put a spell on me;" Christopher teased.

Angel poured Christopher some cashews in his hand. They walked and talked. Angel took her empty bottle and bag and handed it to Christopher. "Why are you giving your trash to me? I am not your personal garbage man;" he said. "Can you just walk over there to the trash can, and throw that away? Stop complaining about everything like an old Beeeyotch!" Angel then slapped Christopher on the back of his head and ran off. Christopher dumped the trash in can and chased her.

Abruptly Angel stopped running. "TIME OUT, she yelled! I have to tie my shoe." She pretended to tie her shoe. "There is no time out in war; Christopher said. You could have given me brain damage." "You would need to have a brain in order to get brain damage;" Angel said. She jumped to her feet and smacked Christopher in the head again and ran away. Christopher chased her again and Angel yelled; "TIME OUT! I think I hurt my ankle." Christopher stopped running and went to her. He said; "Let me see it." He took off his shades so that he could see it clearly.

Angel pointed to her right ankle. Christopher knelt down to look at it. She smacked him in the back of the head again, then ran. "You're such a sucker;" she yelled! "I'm going to break your ankle for real when I catch you woman;" Christopher yelled back. Angel stopped again. "TIME OUT! Why are all those FBI Agents walking across the park behind you;" she asked? "I am not falling for any more of your tricks woman. I am just looking for a telephone pole lying around. So I can whack you in your head with it;" Christopher said. "No, I'm serious; Angel plead.

There are a bunch of FBI- looking guys in suits behind you; Angel said. I think you better get out of their way." Christopher jumped and grabbed Angel and wrapped his arms around her. Now I'm going to squeeze all that trash you've been talking out of you. Angel laughed and screamed for help. "Mr. FBI man, can you please tell this man to let me go?" The man says very cool; "I think my boss behind me has somewhere important to go. He might be upset if I stopped to hold this guy so you could beat him up."

Christopher and Angel look behind the man to see who he is talking about. They see The President of the United States Barack Obama walking across the park. Everyone around them started taking pictures and a spectacle ensued. Christopher took Angel's hand and kind of eased back as the President walked towards them. "Why are you pulling me away, when we can take a picture with President Obama;" she asked? Christopher replied; "Remember, I have a gun on me and they don't know I am retired police. If the Secret Service sees the outline of a gun, what do you think they will do? Especially with me standing near the President. Do you think they are going to invite me to the White House for tea? They won't ask a lot of questions.

Let's roll up out of here before we find out the hard way. Barack may have already called in a Predator Drone strike; he said. You know he don't be playing with those things." "Shoot, you stay here. I am going to say hello to the President; Angel said. How many times will I get this opportunity?" Angel ran over and waited on the President to arrive. Christopher watched from a distance. The Secret Service agents visually scanned her and everyone else around. Christopher looked around the park and was not shocked to see snipers on the rooftops. He also saw several cars with dark- tinted windows strategically parked.

He then saw the joy on Angel's face. She literally stood next to the President of the United States. Christopher always liked to see her smile. He wished he could make her smile all the time. Seeing her happy made him happy. He wished he could ask her to be with him for the rest of their lives. Then reality quickly set in. That was not possible because she belonged to another. Then, Christopher felt a bit of guilt. He too, had known the pain of a woman cheating on him. What was worse was he knew Angel's husband and that was a violation of man code.

Yet, here he was enjoying the day. Enjoying life with the woman he adored but was somebody else's wife. What could he do he thought to himself. Everything about this woman is ideal. No other woman can make him so nervous to be around. She is just so well put together that Christopher often wondered was he even on her level. After all, she was college educated and he only had a high school diploma. A diploma from Capitol Senior High, home of those mighty lions. "Yeah, she's lucky to be on my level, Christopher joked to himself.

She better recognize. She is rolling with a Lion. I am the King around this moarfugger;" he smiled to himself. Angel was returning from her visit. "So, what did he say;" Christopher asked. "Oh well, you know. I told him who I was. He was like what do you think I should do about global warming and some other stuff. I told him to give me a call. I would tell him everything he needed to know;" Angel joked. "Whatever punk;" Christopher responded. "Well, I did give him my business card; Angel said. I told him I could hook him up with some great retirement plans.

He said he already had a great retirement plan; she laughed. Who knew? "I asked him to pass my card along and he said he would." "What! You gave your card to President Barack Obama; Christopher asked? You are a woman that is fearless. I am very proud of you;" he said. "Well, actually, I gave it to one of the Secret Service guys. They had to examine it first. "Wow, who would have thought;" Christopher asked? They sat on one of the benches. "Thought what;" Angel replied? "A little black kid from Baton Rouge and a little black girl. From West Philadelphia born and raised, on the playground is where you spent most of your days.... would grow up and be hanging out at the Washington Monument. Then see the President of the United States up close and personal.

Who would have thought with our upbringing of being dirt poor that we would be here? Able to go wherever we want to go, and buy whatever we want to buy? While living like we want to live;" Christopher said. "Yes, you have accomplished quite a bit Mr. Watson. I am very proud of you; Angel added. You're a very intelligent man and you have mapped out your life very well;" Angel said. "Well, I owe a large amount of gratitude to you Angel; Christopher said.

When I first became a cop and saw I could make in overtime money, I was happy. I knew you were doing your thing in finances, but I wasn't thinking about that. Then you started telling me about planning for my future. I was like, I have a retirement plan with the police department. Then you were like why be boxed into what they will give you? You told me I can create my own? Then you were like. Christopher man, you're bigger than moarfuggin Harold Washington, fuck Harold Washington man! Run for President. I was like yeah, fuck that shit;" Christopher said.

"What are you talking about;" Angel laughed? "Oh you don't remember Eddie Murphy's (Delirious), when he was talking about Jesse Jackson being the first black President;" Christopher asked? "Oh yeah, that crazy man;" Angel said. "Yeah and today we just met the first black President. So that skit came to my mind; Christopher said. Anyway, so you got me thinking about being able to control my own destiny. I was able to retire early after you started me investing. Then I moved into buying houses to rent out. I said to myself this buying and renting houses, is a lot more exciting to me than chasing drug dealers.

I had no idea when I made that decision I would be stuck with your ass on a regular basis;" Christopher said. He looked over and saw Angel looking at her phone. Is everything okay; he asked? "Just looking at the price of oil," Angel said. "It's going up, but global stockpiles will bring it way down in the next year." We're going to see gas go close to a dollar again in the next 18 months." "Angel you know I usually trust your judgement. I just don't think gas will ever go back below $2.30 in the country ever again;" Christopher said. "Okay, just keep watching sir;" Angel said. Right now the high prices are good for your mutual funds.

"How so;" he asked? "You have mutual funds and a 401k; Angel said. Like many who hold various funds, you have oil companies somewhere in your portfolio. So speculators and the hedge fund managers are being pressured to make profits. They manipulate and speculate on stocks in the market. Speculation drives up the price of oil and then we end up paying for it at the pump. So in effect our need or greed to make money in our retirement plans. Is driving up the cost of gas. With all the surplus coming on line that will take a dive;" she said. How ironic;" Christopher remarked. "Don't worry, I'll let you know when to move your money; Angel said. I bet God is looking down and is like, you fools have totally screwed this up." They both laughed.

Do you think we're messed up because according to a survey people don't go to church? Not like they use to;" Angel asked? "Hell no; Christopher said. The church is why black people have no money now as it is. Those bloodsuckers take in over 40 billion dollars a year just in the black church. What do we have to show for it? No church where black people can line up and go get jobs. No church we can get funds to start a business. All they have is a bunch of bullshit to offer."

"What do you mean bullshit;" Angel asked? "Think about it. Everything that is said in church is a lie. People just choose to be too dumb to recognize it." "Give me an example;" Angel said. "What are some of the most famous sayings in the church;" Christopher asked rhetorically? "No weapon formed against me shall prosper is something niggas love to repeat. You have to be really stupid to not see how insane that statement is. Slavery was a weapon formed specifically against blacks and it prospered like a motherfucker. In fact, it is the most prosperous system in world history.

Flooding our neighborhoods with drugs and mass incarceration is a weapon formed against us. It's profiting to the tune of billions a year. How does the Government know how much money drugs make, if nobody is making a profit? What else do they say in the church? Prayer changes things…hmmm. Don't you think the first slaves prayed for Slavery to stop? Back then a white man could kill blacks and wouldn't be charged with a crime. Four hundred plus years later, prayer didn't change that when Trayvon Martin & Mike Brown got murdered. Now, do the math.

If you can get 2 million people to work for you for 350 years for free? How much prospering would you have using that weapon you formed against them?" "So, you don't believe in God;" Angel asked? "I never said that; Christopher replied. I believe in God very much, and I know I would not be where I am without him. I just don't believe in the European version of religion. That was forced on us in slavery. It is insane for any people to think someone would come to their home in violence. Kidnap them, kill their parents in cold blood in front of them. Then rape their wives, daughters, sons and them.

Chain them all up like animals. Then give you back YOUR book to connect you to YOUR God, because I respect your religion. When the first slaves arrived in America, they didn't speak English. So how in the hell would they know? That this Bible, which is in English, was the word of God? If I handed you something in Chinese and told you it was the Holy Bible. How would you know if it were or not? It could be a Chinese book of Devil worship for all you know. Once you started practicing what I told you it said, you would pass it down to Jamal. He would pass that belief to his kids with nobody understanding what you're doing."

"Can we just agree to disagree on this;" Angel asked? "Yes, we can. Pimps know women like to believe what sounds good. That is why the church is full of mostly women. I can't tell you with how many times I have seen it in a church. The Preacher screaming like a bitch and they talking about pastor sho' can preach. I'm like, he didn't say a damn thing. Just a bunch of screaming and yelling, which is theatrics. All he did was make you feel good about giving away your money to him;" Christopher said. "The money goes to the church to do the work of the Lord;" Angel said.

"Why does God need money to do anything if He is all powerful? See this is where women don't use common sense. Forty billion dollars a year and an all Powerful God and yet communities like the lower 9th Ward in New Orleans still exist. Compton, South Bronx, West Baltimore exists. Southeast D.C, 5th Ward of Houston, Atlanta, Laurel, Mississippi all exist. All the pastors that collect all that money don't have a fucking care. Not to fix any of these places we live. The black church will seriously say; they're black we can tell them anything. They make billions off of our misery.

"What could the church possibly do about all the crime and problems in the cities;" Angel asked? "That is so easy;" Christopher said. "In almost every inner city, you have a slew of boarded up houses that the city owns. They would love nothing more than to sell, sometimes for a few dollars. The church board could buy these houses. Hire men who have the skills, sitting right inside the church or neighborhood. The ones that know how to do roofing. Plumbing, carpentry and electrical. They can train the young men that don't have any skills. The sorry ass pastor could appoint someone to work with the state to get these kids licensed or certified. Now these young men have skills and jobs, repairing these houses.

You may think I'm going hard on Pastors, but not nearly as hard as they've been on us. The church then rents the house out to the ladies of the church that have jobs. So in effect their rent pays the men's salaries, the women and children have some place decent to live. The men will take pride in something they built and protect it. This way these men, who may or may not have had trouble with the law, will have a career. If they grew up in the church or community then the pastor knows them. He should be willing to help them, but he doesn't. He just sells you a bunch a bullshit about how God is going to bless you with a job.

Why would God give you a damn job that means you are working for someone that doesn't care about you? That same God could give you your own business so you never have to beg again?" He can also connect you to other talent in the Church to do the things in your business that you aren't good at. Then you can focus on frying chicken or whatever, while Sister Jones runs the restaurant. Or give somebody in the church a business that will hire you. Then you don't have to worry about being harassed because you decided to wear your natural hair. Or made to feel hostile because you wore a "Black Lives Matter" shirt to work.

# I want to eat good

"Yeah that's pretty deep; Angel said. You certainly are a strongly opinionated man. I like that about you, even if I don't agree with everything you said." "Well, that's your prerogative Angel. I still love you; he said. I know you will carefully process this information. Then come to your own conclusion in your own time. Meanwhile, don't you have to get home and get dinner started for your son;" Christopher asked? "No, he's staying over at his friend's house this weekend. The little guy named Marcus. He was at our house when you were over there before;" Angel said. "Oh, so what are you going to do? Go home or are you coming over to my place;" Christopher asked?

"You owe me dinner Mr Man; Angel said. Don't try to weasel out of it. It's Friday and I want to eat good. You better have some wine over there. You need to find us a good movie to watch. First, I need to use your office. I have two proposals I need to email to some clients. Oh and print some stuff out for a meeting I have on Wednesday;" Angel said. "Why can't you print at your house woman? Why you have to be using all my ink up;" Christopher asked? "Because I can, you test tube baby;" Angel replied.

They got up from the bench and walked across the park to the car. Angel asked Christopher to buy her a T-shirt that has Barack Obama's picture on it. Christopher approached the man at the stand and asked how much is the shirt? The man says it's $20.00, but he can sell two for $30.00. Christopher pulled out a $100.00 dollar bill and Angel took it from his hand. She got her shirts while the man handed her $70.00.

"Man, how are you going to take my money and give it to her;" Christopher asked? "She looks like she's in charge;" the man replied. "He knows I am;" Angel said. She put the money in her purse and kissed Christopher on the cheek. "I don't like you. Did I tell you that lately; Christopher asked? I really don't like you." They walked across the park and through a construction area. They headed back to the neighborhood where they parked. Angel began teasing. "I had a great day and I made $70.00. Now I'm about to get a home cooked meal and a foot massage;" she said.

"Uh, excuse you...where are you going to get a foot massage from, ma'am? We don't have any massage parlors in the projects where I live;" Christopher said. "You're going to do it, sir. That will be your project;" Angel responded. "I really don't like you, woman. Really, I don't;" Christopher said. Angel said; "Now that I think of it, I think I still have the $20.00. I took it out of your safe about a month ago." "Why were you in my safe woman? Nothing in there belongs to you;" Christopher said. "You left it open and I saw you had about $10,000 cash sitting in there. I didn't think you would miss it, so I borrowed $100 from you.

I didn't want to have to find my wallet in my trunk when I stopped at the pharmacy. All I needed was some detergent that was on sale; Angel said. I ended up spending almost $80.00 and put this $20.00 in my purse to give to you. Here, you can have your raggedy $20.00 back, but I'm keeping this $70.00." Christopher looked up ahead and saw three guys standing on the side walk just before his truck. One pointed toward them. He presumed they pointed at Angel holding cash money out in the open. Christopher took Angel's hand and told her to put her money back in her purse. They kept walking toward his truck.

As they got closer to the men, one of them stepped in front of them. He asked Angel for a dollar. Christopher saw that the other two guys moved behind them and took up wing positions. He and Angel were now boxed in. Christopher calmly said; "Let me get my wallet, because I know I have a few dollars in there." Christopher pulled out his Smith & Wesson .45 caliber handgun. He pointed it in the face of the guy in front of him. He then said; "I don't know what you fellas had planned, but I will kill every one of you punk bitches right here. Right now on this motherfucking sidewalk. Then, I will go through your wallets. I'll find out where your mothers are and go kill them bitches.

If your grandma is alive, I will kill that bitch too. If she's dead, I will dig her ass the fuck up and put a bullet in her motherfucking skull. Now what you probably want to do is get the fuck out of my face. When I count to 5, I am going to start killing whoever is here." The three guys started walking fast out of the area. Christopher used his remote to unlock his truck so he could open the door for Angel. "Dag, we almost got robbed;" Angel said. "Nah, they just wanted to act a fool today. They didn't know I had my anti- fool repellant on me;" Christopher said. "I'm glad you had it on you too. Boy, that could have been a mess, if you didn't; Angel said. Do you carry that thing on you every day?"

"No indeed; Christopher said. Sometimes I carry my .40 and sometimes I carry my 9 millimeter. Sometimes, I carry my other .40 glock. It just depends on what I'm wearing and which gun matches which outfit;" he said smiling. "Dag how many guns do you have;" asked Angel? "I have a few; Christopher replied. I have a few pistols, a few shotguns and a few rifles." "You're one of those gun nuts I see;" Angel teased. "Nope, not at all;" he replied.

I like guns, but I also think people should have background checks to carry one. I don't see any situation where I would need 80 rounds in my magazine. Especially since I am not in the Marines anymore;" Christopher said. "Take me to pick up my car at the library please;" Angel said. "Do you have to go somewhere;" Christopher asked? "Yes, I'm coming over to your house for my dinner, and I need to shower;" Angel said. "What are you showering for? Where else are you about to go;" Christopher asked? "You just saved my life or at least my purse with my money in it.

I want to thank you for that and my poem. Oh and for giving up your deal to spend time with me;" Angel said. "Oh wow. You know I love to be thanked by you; Christopher said. Like MC Hammer use to say; Let's get it started! Angel;" he called. "Yes Christopher;" she answered. "You are one gorgeous, sexy woman. I just want you to know that;" he continued. "Are you just saying that to try and seduce me Christopher;" she asked? "No, not at all. I just think your face and your body are so beautiful. Then throw in your beautiful personality. Add those brains in that pretty head. It is easy to fall in love with you;" Christopher said. "I could easily fall in love with you too, and that's what's bothering me; Angel said.

Why didn't we see this before you got married and divorced, and before I got married;" Angel asked? "Well, they say you never meet your soul mate, until after you're married;" Christopher said. "Do you think I am your soul mate;" Angel asked? Christopher replied; "If you're not, then I don't know who could be. We make each other laugh, we stimulate each other mentally. We enjoy talking about any and everything and sometimes nothing at all. We are both driven and ambitious. I think you would do almost anything I asked of you. You know I would do the same; he said.

You get on my last nerve and I am heavenly to deal with." "Wait! Stop it right there buddy; Angel said. Heavenly? I can't even begin to count the times you got on my last nerve. I have to ask myself sometimes, am I a glutton for punishment? Or do I just like being agitated by you?" "Moi agitate vous;" Christopher asked sarcastically? Little ol bitty ol moi? That is absurd." "Name two things I have ever done to agitate you in one second, times up. See you couldn't name anything; he continued. So this must be a damn lie from the pit of hell, or as you call it Angel……..home." They both laughed at the joke. "I will get you for that too punk;" Angel said.

After picking up her car they both drove to Christopher's house. Angel goes to his office. Christopher asks; what are you doing? "I am going to get on the computer. Then figure out some rates of return my clients need to hit in order to get them retired by 55. Then, I am going to take a shower. If you have to be all up in my business sir;" Angel replied. "Why don't you let me run you a nice, warm, relaxing bath pretty lady? He continued; I know you were crunching numbers in your head while driving. You probably have that figured out already.

I am going to need you to take a break from all of that and just relax. I need you to learn to let go of work and just take some me time for yourself;" Christopher said. "That would be very nice, but I have so many clients that I need to talk to. Just in the last four hours, I have 47 text messages and about 73 emails;" Angel said. "See, that's what I'm saying, you never have a moment's peace for yourself. If you're not running with work, you're doing something for Jamal. Or doing something for the church; Christopher said.

When you come over here, you relax and get pampered. Since I couldn't go to my meeting this morning, I am going to need your phone lady. No text messages this evening after you finish your proposals. I just want you to sit here on the sofa. While I go run your bath water;" Christopher ordered. "Text your assistant Sherry, tell her everything you need done. What the hell are you the boss for, if you're doing all the work;" Christopher asked? Angel went into Christopher's office. She turned on the computer monitor to finalize her two proposals. His office was so much more organized than hers, she thought. Probably because he doesn't do any work in here.

She glanced up and looked at his bookshelf. Looking to see if he had any new books since last week. She saw "Before the Mayflower," "The Isis Papers," "What Color Was Jesus," "From the Browder Files," "Think and Grow Rich," "Dreams of My Father" and so many more, including the Holy Bible and the "Holy Qur'an." Angel loved that Christopher was such a voracious reader. He sought information from wherever he could find it. From whomever would give him information. She too loved to read. She always dreamed of a husband that would share her passion for reading.

Here, in the same house with her, was a man that loved just that. One that loved to cook for her as he was doing at this moment. Treated her like the royalty that she is and yet, this wasn't her house. This wasn't her man and this wasn't her dream. She was borrowing him, and he was borrowing her. This wasn't her reality. "Your water is ready Angel;" Christopher called. She walked in to find the tub surrounded by candles, filled with bubbles and rose petals. "I will be right back;" he said. She undressed and entered into the tub, so the bubbles covered her body.

"Can I come back in;" he asked? "No, a lady is in the tub;" she said. "I have a cold glass of Roscato;" he teased. "Oh, in that case, come on in;" she replied. He gave her the glass and a kiss. "I'm off to cook you dinner;" he said. He turned on one of his favorite CD's Kenny G's "Duotones." Angel sat back to enjoy the ambience. Soon, Angel smelled dinner cooking. "What are we having;" she yelled. "I'm making the meat loaf you asked for. With garlic mashed potatoes. Made from scratch. Sautéed broccoli with cheese and some corn bread. For dessert, I'm baking some brownies. I don't want to get my ass kicked. I have some Ben & Jerry's Cherry Garcia or Chunky Monkey Ice Cream." "Sounds good, you're trying to make me fat with all that Aren't you;" Angel asked?

"I think I can help you burn some calories after dinner. Let me go check on my cornbread, so it doesn't burn;" he said. He returned to the bathroom minutes later and Angel was exiting the tub. "Hey, you're supposed to knock before you come in here;" she said. "I have to knock to come in my own bathroom;" Christopher asked? "Yes, when a lady is present, you do;" Angel played. "Oh, I thought it was just you in here;" Christopher joked. She splashed water in his face. "Aw, I'm sorry baby. Did I hurt your ego? Let me kiss it and make it better;" he said.

He kissed her on her forehead, before taking the towel and helped her dry off. I think your ego moved off your forehead and went into your right eye. He kissed her right eye and then the left eye?" He kissed her nose. Slowly, he moved his mouth over hers. They kissed a long, passionate kiss, as he pulled her naked body close to him. His hands caressed her back. He was careful not to rush to touch any private parts, not just yet.

He led her into the master bedroom. There she found more rose petals spread across the bed and he invited her to lie down. "I'll be right back;" he said. He returned with a bottle of body oil. It had been warming on the stove in heated water. "Let me rub this into your back; he said. Then you should be ready to relax." He rubbed the oil across her shoulders, working his way down her lower back. He slightly touched her ass cheeks and then moved back to her shoulders. He took the time to rub her neck. Gently but firmly and then kissed the back of her neck. Slowly kissing down her spine to the base. Once there, he applied more oil on his hands and he began to rub her cheeks.

He gripped them, squeezing them and rubbing them firmly. Soon moving to her inner thighs. He started with her left thigh. Massaging the back and then slowly moving inwards. Allowing his hand to oh so slightly touch her crotch area before working down towards her knees. Now, on to the right thigh, and the pattern continued. He made deep circular motions on her inner thigh. Just far enough down so that his hands were out of reach of her vagina. He felt her body respond as her legs spread just slightly. That's when he moved down to the back of her knees.

He rubbed them firmly and went in on her calf muscles of each leg. After reaching her feet and giving her heels a turn, he asked her to turn over. He was greeted by very beautiful, well- pedicured feet. He kissed them both and told her how pretty her feet were. "Thank you;" she replied. He rubbed her feet; each foot received its own massage. Next he took her right big toe in his mouth. He sucked it so softly. He then repeated this for all the toes on her right foot. Next he started on her left foot.

After an intense foot worshipping and giving each toe a personal blowjob. He kissed his way up to her knees. He gave each knee their own special time. Getting back to her thighs, he massaged and rubbed them. Like a baker making pie crust he caressed and kneaded them. Careful not to touch her inner thighs until he reached the top. He repeated the same pattern of pressing firm circles on her inner thighs. Only slightly touching her crotch area on the occasional stroke. He then lowered his head and kissed her thighs intently. He slowly pushed them apart to kiss inwardly, while he worked his way up.

When he reached the top he kissed her left inner thigh. Then her right inner thigh but never the center of her joy. Instead, he skipped over it and kissed her stomach and worked his way up to her breast. He made love to her breast with his mouth and hands. Then he moved up to her neck. He sucked and kissed her neck. Like an addict trying to find just the right spot to feel her reaction. Once he found it he locked his lips on it like a vampire. Being careful enough not to bruise her, but hard enough so she could feel it.

His tongue licked all over her neck and breast like he was spelling her name. Kissing each side of her neck before it glides down the center of her body. Between her breast, across her stomach and below her waist. He could see her river flowing, glistening in the dim light. He can see her clitoris swollen with excitement. So he raised her legs for greater access. He placed his tongue on that tiny piece of skin just below her vagina and pauses. Suddenly, his tongue pressed firmly and began to glide upward. Some of his tongue slide inside of her and he pressed it inward and upward. Up until her clitoris was sitting on top of it.

He grabbed her clit with his lips and sucked it gently and as it fell out of his mouth. He stuck his tongue inside of her and then grabbed her clitoris again with his lips. His tongue flickered over her clit up and down, left to right. Around and around as he got it hot enough to glow red in the heat of the night. Her body moved to his rhythm as her voice moaned with pleasure. She felt his finger slide inside of her. The finger pumped as he licked her clit. His smooth shaven face rubbed her inner thighs with each suck and lick. She never planned to surrender herself to him like this. Her mind told her to stop it right here, but her body said damn this feels sooooooooooooo goooood.

He inserted another finger and he licked her and kissed her like a bear licking honey. Her hips were grinding his face, and her breathing became intense. She tried to tell him something. He stopped and asked; what did you say, before rubbing her g-spot and licking her again. She spoke with a breathless whisper; "Don't Stop!" He continued his oral assault on her vagina, until she grabbed his head with both hands. Urgently she rubbed her pussy over his face and released a flood of moisture. She flowed like the water flow over Niagara Falls. She called his name in one long gasp…. "CHRIIIIIIISSSSSSTOPHHHEEER!" He stayed down, while her thighs clasped his head and her body shook. He then softly kissed her vagina until she relaxed from the eruption. He gently licked and kissed her inner thighs in the afterglow, until she pulled him up to lay beside her.

# I have to catch my breath

"Let's go eat dinner;" he whispered in her ear. "Give me a minute; she whispered. I have to catch my breath;" Angel said panting. "Okay, well I am going to go set the table. Your dinner and I will be waiting for you in the informal dining room;" Christopher said. He washed his face and hands and went to the kitchen. He placed the plates on the table. Along with silverware, wine glasses and an extra glass for water. Angel entered into the dining room. Wearing only one of his white casual dress shirts, unbuttoned revealing her cranberry colored panties.

"Oh my God; Christopher said. Can I just crawl under the table and eat you while you eat?" "What? Did I do something wrong;" Angel asked auspiciously? "Yes, you did, woman. Looking sexy times 10 to the 24th power. How am I supposed to concentrate on being hungry with you looking like that;" Christopher asked? "Like what; Angel asked with a coy grin? I just put on your shirt I found in the closet. I wasn't trying to look sexy." "Well you did; Christopher said. Let me fix a plate for you gorgeous." "Oh, this smells delicious Christopher; Angel said.

You know what, you can cook a little bit." "I'm black, you'll tell me anything;" Christopher said. I'm about to tell you why you're getting your black ass whipped; Angel said. You touch me and I'll sue the drawers off of you; he replied. Angel laughed and smacked his hand. Christopher sat in his chair, reached for Angel's hand and said grace before eating. He took his thumb and caressed her hand while they prayed. He reluctantly released her hand when she said Amen. "Do you have everything you need beautiful;" he asked her?

"Everything looks just fine;" she replied. Christopher jumped up and ran to the pantry. He brought back some hot sauce and Tiger sauce. "I know how you black people like to spice up your food;" Christopher said. With a mouth partially full of food Angel said; "No, this is delicious all by itself, Whitey." "Damn, did you just call me Whitey as dark as I am, woman? I know you see all this rich, dark chocolate skin of mine;" Christopher said. "Yes, you do have some beautiful skin; Angel agreed. I bet it even tastes like chocolate." "Well, if you're a good girl. I may let you taste it, but you have to be good;" Christopher said.

"I can be really good baby; Angel teased. The best you ever had. I don't want to brag, but I'll be"… Christopher grabbed his heart in the Fred Sanford heart attack routine. "Oh, Elizabeth, he yelled! "She's going to put it on me. I may be coming to join you honey!" Angel replied playfully; "Who is Elizabeth, and why is she your honey?" "Never mind, Christopher said. You clearly were deprived of your childhood, if you didn't get to see Sanford & Son." "Oh, I still watch it; Angel replied. I was just making a joke and making sure you know. Thou will have no other goddess before me."

"Amen. Can I get you some more food woman;" Christopher asked? "No, I am getting full as it is. Besides, I need to save room for my brownies and ice cream." "Yes, do save some room;" Christopher said. You are done with your work in the office too correct?" "Yep, I just sent everything to Sherry like you said. I just have a couple of emails to send, but I can do that from my phone. You have a movie for us to watch right?" "Yes I do; he said. I thought I'd show you a classic movie from back in the day. It's called; "**The Learning Tree**" by Gordon Parks."

When I was in 9th grade my teacher made the class read the book. I have been reading ever since. Later, I found out they had made the book into a movie. I had to have it;" Christopher said. "What's it about;" asked Angel? "It's about a young black boy coming of age. Back in the early 1900's in Kansas. One day, he witnesses something that puts the fate of his family and race on his shoulders. He has to decide what to do amidst calm racial tension. It's a very intriguing story; Christopher said. You've had your bath. Let me go jump in the shower real quick, I'll be up." She goes upstairs to the loft where the widescreen is and began to channel surf. About 20 minutes later, Christopher came upstairs. Angel was watching The Rachel Maddow show.

"Oh, you've got my girl on;" Christopher said. "Yes, I love her show too;" Angel replied. They sat close and Angel laid her head on his right shoulder. They watched Rachel until her show ended. They talked about a story Rachel presented. The intellectual conversation just turned them on. "Would you like some popcorn;" Christopher asked? "No thank you, sweetie, but you wouldn't happen to have any chocolate brownies, would you;" Angel responded? "Yes and I have some chocolate kisses right here;" he said. "I will take one of your chocolate kisses right now;" Angel said. They kissed and he went and brought two brownies back.

"They kissed for a few seconds more and turned their attention to the television. They continued kissing as the introduction played. Only after the intro faded and the story began did they stop kissing. Every few minutes during the movie, Christopher took Angel's left hand lifted it to his face and kissed it. Angel became really engaged in the movie. Christopher also enjoyed it almost as much as he is enjoyed being with this beautiful woman.

It seemed like the movie was much shorter than Christopher remembered. Probably because he wanted this moment with Angel to last. "That was really good; Angel said. It was an excellent movie with a real good storyline. I am going to have to let Jamal come over here and see this. I know he will love it;" she said. "Yes, I think he would too;" Christopher said. Maybe tomorrow after we have lunch. I will ask him if he wants to come over and hang out." "I think he's going to his friend's house tomorrow night remember;" Angel said?

"Oh yeah that's right. He's got those lil' girls that will be over there. He's gotta get his dick sucked tomorrow;" Christopher said laughing. "My son better not be having sex with those little, fast- ass girls;" Angel said sternly. "He's not having sex. He's just getting his dick sucked;" Christopher joked. Angel punched him on his arm and told him to shut up. "I sure wish I knew where I could get mine sucked;" Christopher said. Angel laid her head across Christopher's lap, and her body was now exposed completely to him. "Well, maybe you should try going to that party tomorrow with Jamal.

Maybe one of those fast little girls will have their fast mamas with them;" Angel said. "I don't want to be with one of those girl's mama; Christopher said. The woman I want is laying right here on my sofa. In my shirt with a pair of cranberry colored panties on." "I'm black, you'll tell me anything; Angel said. "Stop stealing my line;" Christopher smiled and said. "Am I the woman you want Christopher; she asked? If you had me what would you do with me?" "Hmmmm, Christopher said, I would work on building up my little empire into a larger one with you. I'd take you on the nicest vacations each time we accomplished a major goal.

I would pamper you with poetry, great cooking and flowers. I could buy wilted flowers from the Mexican standing on the corner. When you are really deserving, I would get you a bean pie from my Muslim brothers out there too." "You're joking, but I love a good bean pie, they are the truth;" Angel said. "I know, Christopher replied. I bought one the other day on Minnesota Ave in Southeast DC....but let me finish. I would buy you your dream house. Where you and I had our own offices. A sun room, a huge kitchen, so you can cook my food. A large area for entertaining, including a wet bar. Even though I know you and I don't drink too much. Still for you I would not quarrel over spending money.

I'll just have to get a part time at Burger King to make ends meet;" Christopher said. "No, you wouldn't have to work a part time, Chris. You're a smart man, and I am a smart woman; Angel said. So I know we could make a fortune together, because we both are very ambitious." "Shoot, you go out there and flip a house or two. I'll take the profits made and pick some of the hottest stocks out there. We'll watch our money rise like the morning sun. Speaking of rising, what is that sticking in my neck;" Angel asked?

"You know it turns me on when you're talking. Showing off that brain power of yours;" Christopher said. "Well, in that case now that I have shown you how smart I am. Let me show you what else I can do;" Angel said. "Let's go into one of the guest bedrooms;" she told him. I want to thank you for my poem. They got up off the sofa and walked over into the guest room area. "Shall we take the millennium or sleigh bed;" Christopher asked? "Let's take the sleigh bed. I don't want you trying to run if this gets to be too much for you;" Angel mocked.

"Lawd Hair Murcee;" Christopher yelled! Please give me strength." "You wait here, I am going to go brush my teeth;" Angel said. "You have OCD issues don't you woman; Christopher asked? Well, I don't want to be the only one with garlic and brownie breath. I am going to brush mine again too." "I knew you would Mr. OCD;" Angel said. They go downstairs to the Master suite and grabbed their toothbrushes by their respective sinks. "Do you think we could make it together with all our OCD issues;" Angel asked? "I don't have any OCD issues; Christopher retorted.

I just like the beds made daily with hospital folds. No dishes left in the sink after eating, unless they are soaking. I like to keep my house clean. Put everything back where you found it and brush my teeth before making love. Other than that I am fine." They both laughed at themselves. "Yeah, we have a few issues;" Angel said. "That's alright, at least we know and admit it and that's half the battle;" Christopher said. "Okay, let me hit this mouth wash real quick, and I will be ready;" Christopher said. "Let me get a little too;" Angel said. Again they laughed. They calmly walked back upstairs to the guest room. Christopher said; "Let me put on some music to reset the mood."

He goes over to the stereo and picked a playlist off of his mp3 player. Once back with her in the room, he held both of her hands. He got up close to her face. "Angel, you are so beautiful. With the most gorgeous warm brown eyes. The most incredibly sexy lips and oooh this silky, smooth brown skin of yours. I could kiss you all over all night long woman. Tomorrow I'd still have plenty more love to give you." "Shhhhhh, Angel said; let's take off your pajamas and my panties. Everything that needs to be said is about to be said."

Christopher kneeled before this beautiful queen and peeled her panties off. He then helped her out of the open shirt. He quickly undressed and he laid her gently on the bed. He planted kisses on her as they descended. He laid next to her and looked into her beautiful eyes. They kissed and held hands before he guided her hand down to his manhood. She touched it gently, caressing all of his privates in her soft hand. "Pretty nice;" she said. "How do you know? You haven't tried it yet;" he replied.

He then stood in the bed and pulled her up to a kneeling position. She stroked his shaft before her face. "I want you to suck it for me Angel;" he commanded. She looked up at him and took him into her mouth. She made love to him with her mouth. He felt she gave the sweetest kisses he has ever had. Something about the essence of this woman and the self -confidence she possessed. Christopher knew many have tried to be in this position but never succeeded.

# Damn the fate that won't let this woman be....

She worked her juicy lips up and down his shaft. Occasionally glancing up at him for added effect. He was in so much pleasure he was ready to ignite. He pulled out of her mouth and lifted his penis out of the way. Without words ever being spoken she knew what he wanted. She licked his testicles for his blissful delight. As she kissed and licked them, he almost blurted out; "WILL YOU MARRY ME?" He caught himself and talked inside his head; "Don't complicate this for her anymore. She is already married, damn the fate that won't let this woman be mine all the time and forever!"

Angel alternated between licking his balls and sucking his dick. She gently motioned for him to lie down. Once she got comfortable into position she teased his dick. Her beautiful, full lips were ravishing to him. Then she became evil and decided to drive him insane. She licked from the bottom of his shaft up to the tip repeatedly. Christopher was in a frenzy with excitement and joy. This woman took total control over his mind, body and soul. He screamed her name but received no answer.

He called her again and still Angel continued to rub her lips across the bottom of his penis. It was as if she was playing the flute on him. "Oh my God, Angel. I love you, I love you, I love you;" is all he could think to say. Finally in response he felt a pause in the action. Angel said; "I love you too." Without further hesitation she went back to kissing and licking him. "Can you stay with me, Angel;" Christopher begged? "I'm right here;" she said. "No, I mean forever;" he asked? "Shhhhh, let's enjoy tonight and all the beauty that it brings;" she replied.

She lifted his penis and licked his balls in tight figure 8 designs. Christopher could not keep still under the immense pleasure. His body contorted from side to side as Angel worked her magic on him. At this moment, he would do, say or give anything in the world she wanted. He took his hands and ran them through her natural hair. Massaging her brain as she sucked him deeper and deeper. Her hair felt so strong. He could tell she enjoyed his caress on her head. Yet he knew it could not possibly be as good as what she was doing to him.

Angel took her fingernails and gently traced across his stomach. Simultaneously she took her lips and wrapped them around just the head of his shaft. She sucked him nice and slow so he could watch her work. The sight he saw is so incredibly sexy. He soon found himself coming to the boiling point. Christopher pumped his dick in and out of her mouth as his moment was near. Angel only increased the intensity and pleasure. "Oh FUCK, Angel, I'm going to cum. OOOOHHH GOD DAAAAAMMMM I am coming!" Angel worked her head back and forth with renewed energy in her quest to please him. Christopher gasped as she took his breath and set him on fire. His entire body seemed to tense up as he released spurts of hot, sticky cream into her waiting mouth. His hands were clinched ripping the sheets off the bed.

Angel kept her lips locked tight around his shaft until the last eruptions ceased. "My, it does tastes like chocolate;" she said. She worked her way up his body, kissing his stomach and then his chest. Her left hand remained in his crotch, caressing his balls and penis getting him ready again. She cuddled next to him, tracing her nails across his hairy chest. They just lay, enjoying the silence. After a few seconds, Christopher spoke. "Oh that was so damn good, Angel.

You are just an amazingly beautiful, intelligent and might I add, skilled woman. Can I buy you a Pyramid? Or whatever you want I will give it to you baby." "I just want to lay here next to you;" she said. "You can lay here, you can stay here, put your name on the papers here. Woman you have my mind messed up right about now. I might give you both of my kidneys, both lungs and my heart right now;" Christopher said. "I just want you to be happy Christopher. That's all I've ever wanted for you;" Angel said. "I hope you know that is all I have wanted for you too Angel; Christopher said.

"Yes I know; Angel said. I am always very happy when I am with you. Or when we're talking on the phone. Even when you just cross my mind, I smile;" Angel said. "Why do you smile when I cross your mind;" Christopher asked? "Because, I know how much you love me. I know you would do anything for me. I have people in my life who love me but don't put me first like you do. You have always been a friend I could talk to. I can tell my crazy dreams to and you get me. When I talk to most black people about issues concerning black people, they think I'm crazy. You get my passion on that Christopher; she said.

You may be a bit more passionate about it than I am, but we understand the same. You encourage me and that means a lot;" Angel said. "Honestly woman, I just find you irresistible; Christopher said. You have the looks where you could have easily found a man to take care of you. Still you were driven to make your own way. Everything about you is so sexy. From the way you talk, to the way you walk. I love the way you think. You are definitely not your average girl. Many women I meet either don't have confidence or they think they are hot shit with a job.

Like I should bow down to them because they have a job and are buying shit they can't afford. With you I don't feel any pretentions coming from you. You're a woman who knows her worth and are very confident in your abilities;" Christopher continued. "I am confident in my abilities and I feel very comfortable around you; Angel said.

That use to be an issue with me too. Guys would always be intimidated by my ambition. You didn't act like you are intimidated at all. You were like I am going to get on that level. Now look at you. You stayed with it and then branched out. You're living the good life now;" Angel said. "I just wish I could make you a part of my life in a different capacity; Christopher replied. I would be living a great life then;" "What did I always tell you when you first started investing; Angel asked? You have to take what the market gives."

"I think I am ready for your market to give me something; Christopher said. The question is are you ready to take what I am about to give you?" "Yes, I am ready, darling. Give me what you got and show me what you're working with;" Angel answered. He gently turned her from her side down onto her back. He climbed on top of her, kissing her eyes, her forehead, her nose and her mouth. All over her pretty face he kissed her. He used his legs to spread hers and pressed his swollen dick against her opening. He then kissed slowly down her body. Kissing her chin, both sides of her neck and down to her breast.

He lifted each breast and kissed the underside of them. Soon sucking her left nipple as hard as he could. Simultaneously running the palm of his left hand over her right nipple. He then alternated by sucking her right nipple while caressing her left one. After spending some quality time there, he worked his way down to her stomach. He licked and kissed her in a furious assault. He kissed the sides of her body above the hips and it sent shivers through her. He took her right hand and separated her fingers. He then sucked each one of them.

He craved this woman so very much. His mind was racing with thoughts on how to please her. Each finger on her right hand was given a lavish sucking. Then he ran his tongue between each one. He looked her in those beautiful eyes. In the silence of a language only they understood, he said to her I love you. Angel was completely relaxed and at ease with this man. He was taking total control in this bed and she was ready for whatever may come her way. The sensations he was sending through her hands were erotic. She has never had anyone make love to just her hands before. Christopher kissed her palms, the back of her hands, her wrist and sucked her fingers some more.

"This man is going all out making love to my hands;" Angel thought to herself. Amazingly beautiful, enticingly elegant, irresistibly charming and magically delicious. These were Christopher's thoughts about Angel at this time. "I've got to let her know I crave all of her. Not just that spectacular and supreme pussy of hers;" he thought. After he was done spending about 20 minutes loving her hands, he moved to her knees. He let her know this will be the focus of his attention with a kiss on each of them.

He went downstairs and returned with some strawberry- flavored oil. He rubbed the oil in his hands and begins to massage the side of her right knee. He was gentle but firm. "Ummm, that feels good;" Angel said. You're a freak, aren't you?" "I'll be whatever you want me to be, my Queen;" Christopher said. He continued his massage therapy. He moved over to her left knee and with some more oil in hand he caressed both sides. Working her ligaments and letting the oil warm with the pressure of his touch.

He bent before her like a servant bowing to a queen and kissed her left knee. Before running his tongue across it. Then he gave a series of soft lingering kisses on both knees. "Can you turn onto your stomach for me my lady;" he requested? Angel complied with no reluctance and Christopher massaged the back of her knees. He drove his thumbs deep into her tissue as he caressed her. Then followed it with a less intense caress across the back of her knees. He then spread her legs apart and straddled her left leg. Now bowing his head he kissed and licked the back of her left knee.

He ran his tongue across over her tendons like a serpent in quick teasing flashes. His lips quickly kissed as a follow up. He gave her tongue lashes, soft kisses and a teasing caress on the sides of her right thigh. He worked his hands in tight firm circles inching closer and closer to her vagina. His kisses are coming at a measured pace. He planted them one after the other in the back of her thigh area. "Why are you so good to me;" Angel asked? Christopher replied; "Because you are that woman that has always been good to me. He took his tongue and traced up and down her spine leaving a light moist trail.

When we met I wasn't exactly dressed like a baller. You didn't judge me based upon what I had on. You listened to find out where my head was at. You've always been a genuine friend. Never made me feel like I owe you anything even though I owe you everything. You didn't turn your nose up at me, because I didn't have rims on my ride or wasn't driving a Mercedes. You saw that I had brains and took the time to teach me. You took the time to see if I really wanted to help myself and when I did, you helped me more.

You do my taxes and showed me how to make the system work for me. You never charged me so now I would give you everything." He slightly touched her pussy letting just the tip of his middle finger inside. He then sucked the moisture off his finger. He worked his way again up the back of her thighs. With each kiss he paused to look at the beautiful chocolate mounds that were her ass. "This is one ass I don't mind kissing in any way;" he said. He kissed each mound over and over and over and over again. His hands basked in their softness. He kneaded them like a baker does with dough. His lips kissed her mounds from top to bottom and side to side.

Then his eyes came across the small of her back and he planted a kiss there. Letting her know that is the next target of his attention. He placed his tongue right in the center of her back. His tongue started a long drawn out lick up her spine. Slowly inching up her back in this very deliberate lick. Until he reached the back of her neck which he kissed passionately. Angel moaned at the sensations his mouth gave her and her approval urged him forward. He placed his tongue at the base of her neck and worked his way up to her hair. He kissed her natural hair to let her know he loved it too. Back down her spine methodically, kissing every vertebrae.

"You are a Queen that deserves to be worshipped Angel. It is my honor and pleasure to please you;" Christopher said. "The Queen is very pleased; very pleased indeed;" Angel replied.

# The Queen has no complaints at all

Christopher continued licking down to the small of her back. He kissed that dimple for all he is worth making love to the base of her spine with his mouth. "Oh, that feels so good; Angel said. The Queen has no complaints at all my lover." Christopher again began to ascend up her spine with his tongue tracing every inch of her spine. This time, at a slightly quickened pace. Once reaching her neck he drenched it in kisses. Not just in the back, but on either side of her neck as he spoke in each ear. "Angel, I love you, he said in her right ear. He then kissed her left side of her neck. Angel, you're so beautiful." He then kissed the right again.

"Angel, you're so sexy," as he moved over to her left side. "Angel, you're all a man could want and hope for in a woman." He moved back over and kissed her neck on the right. "Angel, I want you so bad right now." Back and forth from left to right, he kissed her neck stopping at the back of her neck in between. Sometimes he would double back to the same side of her neck. Just so she could not anticipate where the next kiss may land. "All I want to do is shower you with love, Angel. The kind of love you deserve," he whispered in her right ear. Angel softly called his name... "Christopher." "Yes, sweet lady;" he answered. "I love you;" she said. "I love you too precious woman."

Just as Christopher uttered those words to her the intro of the song; "He's not good enough" by Solo began to play. Christopher turned her over onto her back and lowered his body over hers. Looking her deep in her eyes as the group sang almost on cue; (I've been thinking maybe he's not good enough for you).

As the intro continued, he positioned himself with his penis pressed against her labia. When the first bass note hit, Christopher rams his dick deep inside of her. She gasped with the feeling of entry as he began a rhythm in tune with the song. Angel is explicitly aware of what Christopher was doing. His body was sending her a message embedded in this song. She knew she should feel wrong about it, but in this moment, it felt so right. She wrapped her legs around his waist as his hands searched on an expedition to find her soft ass. He again lifted her off the mattress and kept moving to the groove of the song.

He was biting and sucking her left shoulder and neck. He drove his shaft deeper and deeper into the depths of her love. Each time the chorus came around in the song, he sang along in her ear. (He's not good enough for you). He grinded his pubic bone harder and firmer against her clitoris. Arousing every part of her body. Meanwhile, the music in the background just keeps on singing; (I've been thinking maybe he's not good enough for you. He can't make your dreams come true. He's not good enough for you).

With each beat of the snare drum of the song, Christopher banged his pubic bone against her clitoris. His dick went deeper inside of her. Driving that message into her mind, body and soul. His lips are now locked on hers, her legs are locked around his hips. Their minds are now locked with one single thought. "No man is EVER going to love you the way that I do;" he said. He keeps steady pace with the song as he makes love to her. Only briefly breaking their kiss so he can say to Angel; "I love you." Then quickly locks his lips on hers so she can only respond with a mumble.

Still holding her ass off the mattress his body crashed into hers with fury. (He's not good enough for you...) the song continued. That message he pounded and sent to the base of and throughout every nerve ending in her spine. Angel's body was electrified by the ambiance of the moment and she enjoyed it so much. Oh, how Angel wanted to cum right now. How she wanted her body to tell this man making love to her that she knew how much he loved her. She knew he would be there for her and take good care of her.

She stuck her tongue in his mouth and they immediately begin to tongue wrestle. The song went to the bridge and seemed to last forever. Both lovers were not wanting this moment to end. They were caught up in their own private dimension. To the best of their knowledge, no two lovers had ever gone there before. The softness of Angel's body is so delectable to Christopher. He just wanted to kiss her over every inch and centimeter. To show her how much he wanted her. After what seemed like an hour, the song came to an end. "What about you and me" by Conya Doss was the next song. He then puts her legs up over his shoulders and made love to her with just the head of him inside.

Her body was moving, squirming trying to get all of him inside. Christopher would not comply. He pumped slowly and picked up the pace and he did this for about two whole minutes. The entire time her hands are on his hips trying to pull him in deeper, he resisted. Angel noticed that this man has a teasing routine he likes to employ from time to time. He continued to dip the head of his penis just to the depth of two or three inches inside of her. While his fingers on his right hand touched her ass. Then without warning, he slammed all of his dick inside of her.

The feeling was so good, he no longer wanted to make love in that moment. He didn't want to see her for the highly intelligent, sophisticated, classy lady that she is. He wanted to fuck the hell out of her. His throbbing dick was plunging deeper and deeper inside her velvety, smooth pussy. At that moment Christopher knew, there was no better place on earth to be. "Why in the hell would fate not put him and this woman together;" he thought? Her body felt soooooooo gooooood. He was trying to wear the lining and tear the stuffing out of her pussy. Her body was taking the intense pounding he was giving her. She screamed; "Harder!"

He gave it to her harder and deeper, then he stopped. He pulled out all of him, except the head and teased her with just the tip. She desperately wanted him back inside of her. It was a struggle for him to not give in to her pleas, squirms and pussy. He wanted this woman to crave him like an addict wanted drugs. He dismounted her and slides down her body until his face is right before her soaking wet pussy. No teasing kisses this time, no working his way up her thighs. He dived in and sucked her clit and licked her pussy. Like a starving man would eat a meal.

His tongue swirled inside her vagina and all over her clitoris, seemingly at the same time. He fingered her hard and fast pressing upward towards her G spot. Trying to force her to cum in his mouth. He sucked her right inner thigh with intent to leave a passion mark. Still he continued to fuck her with his fingers from his left hand. He talked to her in between licking and fingering her pussy. She asked to let her juices squirt all over his face. "I want you to cum for me Angel; he plead. Cum for me, baby, Give it to me...Gimme that sweet, juicy cum of yours Angel;" he begged.

He took his mouth and kissed her pussy as if it were her mouth. His tongue probed inside like a French kiss. He felt her juices seeping into his mouth. Her body seemed to surrender to his will. "Oooossshhhh, Oooooooh FUCK! Don't stop baby! I'm almost there;" Angel said. "That's it. Cum for me woman; he replied. Make that pussy cum for me all over this dark chocolate face." Angel rubbed her pussy harder into Christopher's face, as she took charge of the situation. Both of her hands wrapped around the back of Christopher's bald head. She held it in place so she could fuck his face. Christopher held his tongue out stiff and steady for her to do what she needed to do.

Angel rubbed her clitoris up and down on his waiting tongue. In a matter of seconds she was searching for air. A typhoon wave of orgasm begins to overcome her. Ahhh, Ahhhhhhhhhhhhhhhhhhhhhh DAAAAAAAAMN, I'm, I'm, I'm, I am, Ooooh EEWWWWWW!" She screamed with a sound that shook the room. Her juices flowed freely drenching Christopher's face with her hot lava. As soon as Christopher knew she had cum, he did not give her a chance to enjoy the afterglow. He climbed her body and spread her legs to get his penis back inside of her. He knew how sensitive her clitoris was after just having an orgasm and he wanted to exploit it.

While he was prodding the head of his shaft inside of her his lips found hers. He wanted her to embrace the smell of her scent she had left on his face. They kissed as their tongues wrestled with one another. His hands slid under her ass cheeks lifting them off the bed. Once she was suspended in air, he gave no mercy on her as he drove with force. He knew as he held her in air with her legs pinned over his arms, she couldn't go anywhere.

"At this time, at this moment, she belonged to me;" he thought. She didn't mind her position at the moment either. As he drilled his dick inside of her, she begged for more. He made sure his pubic bone was grinding on her clit with each and every stroke. He noticed her pretty feet shaking beside his head. He took her toes in his mouth once more while he pounded on her pussy. Like a Swat team breaking down a door he rammed her. "Damn Angel, baby I'm falling in love with you; he moaned. I'm falling in love with your pussy baby. I just want to fuck you all night tonight." "Then fuck me all night Christopher; she replied.

Take this pussy and fuck it! Eat it, do whatever you like to it;" she urged. Her response left no doubt they were both enjoying the moment. He let her legs come down and turned her over on all fours and got behind her. He slid his manhood up and down her slit rubbing over both of her holes. He then grabbed her hip with his left hand and slid into her wet pussy. "Oh, how beautiful her body was;" he thought. She gave as good as she got. With her beautiful cheeks spread, he took his thumb and moisten it off her juices. He then massaged her anus while still ramming inside of her pussy.

She seemed taken back at first, but quickly got into to groove, as they were making love. "What do you want, Angel;" he asked? "I want you to do whatever you want tonight;" Angel replied. "I want to look into your gorgeous eyes when I come." So he took a seated position with his legs stretched out and he takes her hand bringing her to him where she can sit on his dick while they face each other. They kissed intently again and they both wiped each other's forehead. They were both slippery with perspiration but didn't care.

Once she lowered her pussy onto his dick they wrapped their arms around each other. Angel felt him throbbing inside of her. "He felt her walls grip and massage his shaft. She was driving sensations through him that were exhilarating. "Don't stop, Angel. Please Don't Stop;" he begged. "I won't stop;" Angel said. "I won't stop until you get enough of me." "I don't think there is any such thing as enough of you gorgeous;" Christopher responded.

Angel lifted her body up and down in a sensual pace. She brought Christopher to the brink of his orgasm and then she stopped. She kissed him like a lost lover and squeezed his penis with her vaginal muscles. At this point Christopher knew she was in charge. She wouldn't let him cum until she was ready for him to do so. Christopher tried to push his penis deeper inside of her. He was very close to coming before she stopped him. Angel took her lips off of his and gives him a look that says; "be still and wait until I let you cum."

Like a child scolded, Christopher complied and he waited for her permission. After Angel knew his dick had calmed down. She again began to ride it as her hands caressed his shoulders and back. "Your beautiful brown body is 100% pure unadulterated heaven;" Christopher said. "I am so in love with you, Angel." "I love you too my strong, dark and handsome man;" Angel said. Again Christopher was building towards an orgasm. Angel squeezed his shaft with her vaginal muscles, pausing those plans. "How are you going to torture me like this Angel;" Christopher whined? Angel did not respond and began riding him again.

# I love you

"Why are you torturing me woman;" Christopher asks her? "If you think this is torture, then I can stop;" Angel replied. "No, Don't Stop; Christopher begged! Don't stop, baby, please! I will do anything you ask, give you anything you want, just don't stop." Angel does not say a word. She just starts to grind her pussy on his dick once again while she massaged his broad shoulders. Christopher was holding her soooo tight as she had taken total control of him. He didn't want her to ever give up control.

Once again, she brought him to the brink and she clenched his dick with her pussy. After she lets him calm down once again she got off of him. She laid on her stomach with her legs spread apart. Her ass was slightly raised in the air. Christopher was torn between admiring this beautiful sculpture and diving in. After all she delayed him the last several minutes. He slid his dick over her slit and quickly found the entrance to paradise. He frantically went in search of the orgasm Angel had kept him from. He is pounding inside of her at a hysterical pace, as if he is trying to rattle her spine.

Angel knew she would take some pounding for teasing him like she did. Everything was working just like she planned. Watching her ridiculously sexy body willingly take his dick was too sexy. It was too much for any man to bear too long. He watched her soft round mounds of ass jiggle each time he drove his dick into her. The sounds her voice made as her moans urged him to fuck her. Their lust levels were animalistic at this point. Angel toying with him moments earlier made them insatiable.

Now he definitely did not want to make love to her. He wanted to fuck her silly and Angel wanted to be fucked. She reached her arms back and spread her ass cheeks apart. Christopher could see all of her and heard her scream she was cumming. Her voice and that pose overloaded his senses with desire. Three deep strokes in her pussy and he felt his dick shatter in a million pieces as he came. He pulled out of her and rubbed his dick right between her spread cheeks. Spurts of milky white cream poured over her asshole and ran down over her vagina. Angel moved her body slightly to make her cheeks help get out every drop. She wanted nothing more than her lover to be satisfied.

Christopher finally able to see looked between her spread cheeks. He admired the sight of his handy work where he had cum on this beautiful ass. He then turned Angel over on her back. She motioned for him to come to her. He moved around to put his penis in her mouth, which she readily accepted. "Oh my God, oh my God; Christopher said. I love you, Angel. I love you. I love you, I love you, God Damn I love you!" Angel made sure when she took his penis out of her mouth there was nothing on it. Nothing coming out of it and she said; "I love you too; Christopher."

He lay next to her once again and he just stared at her gorgeous face. "What are you looking at;" Angel asked? "I am looking at a very beautiful woman; Christopher replied. You are one of the most beautiful women in the history of the world." "Thank you; Angel said. You're not so bad looking yourself." They smiled at each other, and Christopher kissed her forehead. "Are you falling asleep woman;" Christopher asked? "No. Angel said groggily. I'm still awake." "Well, if you are sleepy, you know you are more than welcome to sleep here; Christopher said. He kissed her softly.

As a matter of fact; he continued. I will be up cooking your breakfast in the morning. Do you want some money baby? How about some chicken wings, do you want some fish and grits? I'll hurry and go get it. Whatever Angel you want me to do baby." "You're so silly; Angel said. Let me get up and take a quick shower; she continued. Then, I am just going to lay in bed in the master room and take a quick nap for about 8 hours."

Angel awakens and can hear the distinct sound of pots and pans clanking in the kitchen. The sweet smell of breakfast is cooking. Clearly, she has been asleep longer than she had anticipated. She dragged herself into the bathroom and begins to make herself presentable. After 15 minutes she is done in the bathroom. She walked out of the master bedroom into the common area of the house. Christopher opened all the blinds and let the sunshine stream in. Angel looked out the window to see a rabbit, birds and a deer. "What are you doing in here man;" Angel playfully demanded? "I am fixing your breakfast, woman. Now sit down and get ready to eat," Christopher said.

"What if I wanted to eat in the formal dining room, instead of in here;" Angel asked? Christopher immediately stopped stirring the grits and removed them off the burner. He then picks up his and Angel plates and carries them to his formal dining room. He then moved all the other items as well. "I didn't say I wanted to eat in there; I just asked what if I wanted to;" Angel said. "Well, you wouldn't have asked, if you didn't want to eat in here. So as you wish my queen;" Christopher replied. He completes setting the table in the formal dining room. He then goes back into the kitchen and continues to cook. What are we having for breakfast;" Angel asked?

"I am making you an omelet with veggies, grilled chicken and cheese. We have some veggie sausages, hash brown casserole and grits. A fruit cup with watermelon slices, cantaloupe, pineapples and grapes. Plus your choice of wheat toast or pancakes. For drinks, I have regular coffee, homemade latte', tea or cappuccino. Oh and your choice of pineapple, cranberry or orange juice. Plus we have maple syrup, molasses and premium strawberry preserves. If you want or need anything else, too bad. I am tired;" Christopher said. "Boy, you love you some maple stuff don't you;" Angel said.

"Are you going to move to Canada, since you love to vacation there;" she asked? "No; Christopher said. Not move up there permanently, but I'd like to buy you a summer home in Niagara Falls." "That sounds wonderful;" Angel said. I wouldn't mind visiting there regularly." Christopher looked to make sure he has set everything on the table that they needed. Next he checked that he has turned off the burners on the stove. They said the grace and Angel started with her omelet. "Wow, this is so good;" she said. I can't believe you can cook like this, and don't have a steady girlfriend."

They both give a quick glance at each other then looked at their plates. They brushed off the awkwardness of her statement. "I guess I just haven't found the right person. That makes me feel like I feel right now; he said. I mean I've found her, but there is just one little technical issue that is hard to overlook." "Yeah, those technical issues can be a bitch;" Angel said. Besides, we spend a lot of time together, but you don't get to see the real me all the time. I mean, I am moody, I can be consumed by my work. I like things done my way, and sometimes I have OCD issues."

Christopher replied; "Really, that may make for a difficult relationship. I can be moody. I can be consumed by my work. I like things done my way sometimes and I have OCDs too. Not only do I have OCD; Christopher said. "I have N.W.A, TLC and apparently I am down with O.P. P." Angel replied; "Well you know I can R.E.S.P.E.C.T. that." They both laughed. Christopher said; "That's all I can spell with a 3rd grade edumakation. I quit." "Oh, so no Scrabble game today;" Angel asked? "Oh, I have the deluxe Scrabble and Chess game upstairs. I will gladly put a whipping on that ass when you're ready.

It's just that I have to go pick up Jamal. I am going to take him to go get our turkey burger. What is on your agenda for today beautiful lady;" Christopher inquired? Angel said; "I think I am going to stay here at your house. Go in your office and get some things done. Then I may find a movie to watch on Pay per view. Find out what nice kind of wines you have here and enjoy." I am going to eat up your snacks and relax when I finish about an hour's worth of work." Christopher said; "I have some Tokaji white wine, which is imported from Buda Pest Hungary. I have some Freixenet from Spain. And I think some Tormentoso Mourve'dre imported from South Africa."

I also have several bottles of domestic wines I picked up at the liquor store. Sorry, if you were looking for some Mad Dog 20/20. I can run up to the store real quick and get you a bottle;" he laughed. "Just for that, I am going to open all of your imported stuff and have a glass. Then you will need to order some more;" Angel said. "Well, while you're online, can you order me some more anyway, Ms. Lady Ma'am. Try to find me a nice Tunisian wine for my collection, please;" Christopher asked?

"You're lucky I like you or I wouldn't be buying you anything; Angel said. I will get you your precious wines, including the Tunisian one. I may surprise you with something else. From somewhere around the world;" Angel said. "Okay, do your thing; he said. I have to clean up this kitchen and get showered and dressed. Jamal may beat me up for being late." "I can clean up the kitchen;" Angel said. "Angel, you don't have to work in this house; Christopher said. Unless it's your business stuff you're working on. My mama taught me how to clean my own house. So go on up to the office and do what you need to do."

"I will take care of everything down here. I'll put this stuff in the dishwasher. Angel excuses herself from the table and kissed Christopher as she walked past him. She heads to his office. Christopher cleared the table. In a matter of moments, he had all the dishes stacked. He wiped down the table and the glass top stove. He did a quick sweep of the floor. "I will mop this when I get back;" he thinks to himself. After the kitchen is clean, he goes to shower. Dressed, he goes to the office to kiss Angel goodbye. Then he leaves for her house to pick up Jamal. Jamal has texted him already to see if he's going to be on time.

"What up little homie;" Christopher asked? Jamal gets in the truck. "What's up Mr. Christopher, how are you doing;" Jamal asked? "I'm alright black man. How was your stay over at your friend's house;" Christopher asked? "It was good;" said Jamal. "Did the hoochies come over last night and break you off some nookie;" Christopher asked? "Nah, Jamal said laughing. Jasmine and Tina did come over there, but Tina's mom brought them. My friend's dad was all up in our mix too." Christopher drove off and said, "What they were cock blocking…those dirty bastards!

Do you want to go do a drive by on them fools;" Christopher asked? "Nah, Jamal said laughing. You can't kill people for just being at their house or guest at a house." "Why not;" Christopher asked? "Because you will go to jail;" Jamal said. "Not, if they don't know who did it;" Christopher said. "Somebody will tell, somebody always tells;" Jamal said. "Kill them too;" Christopher said. "You can't just go around killing people;" Jamal said. "Why not;" Christopher asked? "Because you will go to hell;" Jamal said. "Kill the Devil, and walk up out that joint;" Christopher said.

"You're crazy Mr. Christopher;" says Jamal. Christopher laughed; "I'm crazy? Man I should climb down this magic beanstalk and smack you for that. You know I'm just kidding Jamal. I don't want you to ever be out here doing some dumb nigga shit, as Uncle Ruckus would say." "I know; Jamal said. Too many people out here think they need to fight somebody over dumb stuff. Like my dad, he's always starting stuff with people for no reason when he's home." "What kind of stuff;" Christopher asked? "Well, he started drinking a lot lately. When he is drunk he yells at everybody when we ain't even do nothing;" Jamal said. "Didn't do anything;" Christopher said. So does he yell at you?"

"Yeah, the last time he was home he went off on me for not making my bed. It was the guest bed that he had just got out of;" said Jamal. "Does he ever yell at your mama;" Christopher asked? Jamal says; "Sometimes, they are going at it. He is real nice to her sometimes, and then other times he be like cursing her out. He accused her of going out to the clubs while he is not home. Or seeing some man from our church. Which is crazy because the man is gay." "So has he ever hit your mom that you know of;" Christopher asked?

"I've never seen him like punch her; Jamal said. Although sometimes she stays in her room when he's home. I have seen him push her a few times. She tripped over my skateboard I left in the floor and fell one time. Then he cursed me out for leaving the skateboard." "Was Angel hiding a secret from me;" Christopher asked himself silently?

## Painting in your dining room

"So how do you feel when he's going off on you and your mother;" Christopher asked? "When he's yelling at me, I just stand there and think of something else. You know try to block him out. I feel bad for my mom when he yells at her. He calls her all kinds of names and will then leave the house. He goes to a bar or somewhere and gets really drunk. Then he comes home, like he doesn't remember what he said to us." "I'm not going to make excuses for him; Christopher said. What your father does for a living is probably not easy.

I can imagine some of his work is very physically demanding. Probably mentally demanding too. Then being away from home so much has to be tough. Again, not saying it is right. Not giving a reason for him to treat you and your mom like he does. Maybe some unresolved issues are going on with him too." Jamal asked; "Mr. Christopher, are we going to get some snacks, before we go into the movies?" "I'm not really hungry Jamal ahhhhhh, I had a, a big bowl of cereal. Right before I came to pick you up;" Christopher said. "I will stop and let you go into the pharmacy to pick us something up. I know your mom gave you some money."

"She was supposed to leave me $60.00 on the counter this morning. I guess she forgot before she left out. I tried calling her when I came home about eight this morning. She must have been driving since she didn't answer her phone. I must have just missed her. I didn't text her urgent, because I knew I was going to see you. I figured I could borrow $50.00 until you see my mom and get it from her;" Jamal said. "She must have been meeting with a client again."

"Why do you think she was with a client that early in the morning on a Saturday;" Christopher asked? "Shhh, mom, don't care what day or time it is; Jamal said. She lives, eats and breathes her business. So I try not to bother her unless it's an emergency. If I would have texted her 911 she would have called me back. Like I said, I figured I could borrow a couple of dollars from you, Mr. Christopher." "A couple is two; Christopher said. You know that don't you Jamal. I don't know where you think I would get $50.00 from. Times are hard, ou'chere." "Man, Mr. Christopher, you got like all that nice stuff in your house. Plus you be like going to all those different places; Jamal said.

You couldn't do that, if you didn't have no money. I think my mom told me you had a painting in your house. One you bought from some dude named Poncho Jones or something like that." "Larry "Poncho" Brown is his name;" Christopher said. "Yeah! That's him. My mom said you made a good investment on that painting in your dining room;" Jamal said. In mom talk a good investment means money." "Nah yo, she meant to say like $5.00 for that painting. More than that is too rich for my blood;" Christopher said. "I've been to one of his shows; Jamal said. He doesn't sell anything for $5.00 and you have two original pieces by him." "Look at you knowing a little sumthin' sumthin' about art; Christopher said.

Alright, tell me which piece is more valuable out of original, artist proof or limited edition. If I'm impressed I will give you $50.00. Jamal said; "That's easy, the originals are the most valuable. They are the only one of that particular painting in the world. Next the artist proofs because the artist has personally looked at those replicas. They signed off that those copies are an accurate depiction of his original.

Lastly, the limited editions are the third most valuable paintings. The closer you get to the final number the more value. "Damn son, I'm impressed. Who taught you all of this stuff;" Christopher asked? "My mom took me to a few art galleries when she was buying stuff. A lady was schooling her and I kind of like listened; Jamal said. I also liked a lot of stuff by Charles Bibbs and Gwen Redfern. Both of them are great painters too. "Well, that's impressive, indeed. You just earned a little more than $50.00 homeboy; Christopher said.

I am going to give you fifty dollars and two cents. "Two pennies, Mr. Christopher! Come on, man, you can do better than that. Can't you make it like at least $75.00? In case Tina asks me to buy her something. We're going to the mall later this evening. I don't want to be embarrassed and be like I don't have any money." They pull into a shopping center and Christopher gets his wallet. He hands Jamal a $100.00 bill. "Well, you should have said you were trying to impress a girl. This should get your dick sucked tonight;" Christopher said. "Wow, thanks Mr. Christopher for the money. We can't do that nasty stuff. Her mom and some other parents are going to be there the whole time;" Jamal said.

"Show her mom this hundred, and her mom will suck your dick;" Christopher said laughing. "You're crazy Mr. Christopher;" Jamal said laughing. "Here is a $50.00, go get us some chocolate- covered raisins; Christopher said. See if they have some Malt Liquor and whatever else you want and don't break your $100.00." "Mr. Christopher you don't drink and I can't buy that stuff anyway. I will be right back;" Jamal said smiling.

While Jamal was in the store, Christopher decided to text Angel. *"Hey sexy lady, what are you doing over there?"* Seconds later, a reply comes from Angel: *"I am putting together some booklets for some clients and using up the ink in your printer again."* Christopher responded: *"There are more ink cartridges in the office closet, if you need them and I will put that on your bill."* *"Ah! I have a bill. How much do I owe you as of right now:"* Angel texted back? *"You owe me some kisses, and I will take some nookie if I can get it:"* Christopher replied. *"How is Jamal doing and what are you guys up to:"* Angel asked? *"He is in the store right now buying us some candy for the movies, and he's doing fine:"* Christopher replied.

*I have to tell you about our conversation, when I see you later:"* Christopher sent. Angel responded: *"I know he called me this morning. I must have been passed out in your bed. What did he say?"* Christopher replied: *"He said you owe him $60.00. He thought you left early for a client."* Angel texted: *"Dammit, I was supposed to leave him some money and forgot all about it. Can you loan him a few dollars and I will pay you back when you get home?"* Christopher replied: *"Why would you ask me that, woman? You know if I have it, then you have it.*

*Besides, Jamal has $100.00. He doesn't need a loan."* *"You gave him a hundred dollars; Angel texted? You didn't have to do that."* *"I know I didn't have to do it. I don't do anything I don't want to do so shush. I got this. He's coming out the store now, ttyl. Love you:"* Christopher sent. *"I love you too. You guys have a good time:"* Angel replied. Jamal returned to the truck and Christopher asked; "Are we all set?" "Yeah, we're good, Mr. Christopher. I got you, your chocolate- covered raisins; Jamal said.

I got me some Sugar Babies, two bags of popcorn, two sodas and some Sour Patches." "Man, you're going to have cavities on 36 of your 32 teeth;" Christopher said. "You're eating candy too Mr. Christopher;" said Jamal. "Yeah, you're right I will shut up now; Christopher said. "Let's go see this movie and watch some people get killed!" "You're a crazy nutcase Mr. Christopher;" said Jamal. "You know a little kid your age called me a crazy nutcase just yesterday; Christopher said. Rest his soul in peace;" he laughed.

Jamal's phone rang and it was Angel calling to talk to him. They chatted for a few minutes. Jamal said; "I love you too mom." He then sat his phone on his seat. "You wouldn't kill me because you're scared of my mom;" Jamal said. "Man, your mom is a punk. She ain't even in no gang. I can't respect that; Christopher said. The other day some fool was looking at her crazy. She ain't even smoke his ass; Christopher continued. She could have at least made him break his self, run his jewels or something. What, because she be reading books, she thinks she's too good to peel a sucker's cap? Not me, I be going out looney like O' Dawg from Menace II Society."

They drive down the street a few blocks on their way to the movies. Christopher sees a few old ladies standing on the bus stop." Christopher yelled out the window; "BREAK YO SELF!" They're lucky, we have to get into this movie. I was going to bust a U and clear that corner out with my nine." "Mr. Christopher, you don't have any sense;" Jamal said. "See how you're lying bro. He opens his ashtray. I got change in here;" Christopher said. "No, not cents as in money but, never mind;" Jamal said. "What would Uncle Ruckus say about you doing dumb nigga stuff;" Jamal asked?

"He wouldn't say jack to me because I would peel his cap too; Christopher said. Just kidding Jamal, let's make a deal. Neither one of us will do any stupid nigga shit. Nothing that will get us locked up or in trouble, right;" Christopher said. "That's a deal Mr. Christopher. Have you ever been locked up;" Jamal asked. "Nope and I'm proud to say I've never been to jail and never used drugs;" Christopher said. "Not even marijuana;" asked Jamal? "Nope, not even that;" Christopher said. "I get high off of my mind, thinking of funny shit to say.

I go to bed and I get up when I feel like it. I don't work for nobody but me. Any business I have to do I tell them what time I will meet them. Your mom, who is my Accountant and investment advisor. I tell her what time we can meet to talk about that. If you don't learn anything else from me you should learn this. As a black man, life is not going to be fair. In spite of that, you can succeed. You don't have to act white to do it. But you damn sure won't make it acting like a nigga. Always be an intelligent black man and you can conquer the world."

"You think one day, when I get older, you can show me what you do Mr. Christopher;" Jamal asked. "Of course, but why wait until you're older; Christopher replied. What if I die tomorrow then you wouldn't know these things. So we'll start today and I'll keep teaching you. In the event something happens you will at least have the building blocks to start. It's really not that hard. You just have to be a man that does what he says he going to do. By doing that you will build the respect of people around you. They will do most of the work to make you rich. If you tell someone you will meet them at 7:00pm. You need to have your ass there by 6:45pm if not sooner.

If you tell somebody you will take care of something and get it done. Then that shit needs to get done by the time you said. People don't want to hear excuses, they want what you told them you would or could do. Once you establish yourself as a reliable and responsible person. You will see that even white people will line up to work with you. In life and business, your reputation is everything. When people know they can count on you, to be where you say you will be. Do what you said you would do. They will have little reservations about working for or with you. I have real estate agents trying to get me to buy deals all the time. I have mortgage brokers and banks trying to give me $20,000 to $200,000 all the time.

All these motherfuckers know I don't get a paycheck. When I was working I worked steady. I paid my loans that I borrowed. I increased my net worth and got to the point where I didn't need to work anymore. White folks are cool with that. I have a lot of things I can bargain with if I want to ask them for money. I didn't buy dumb nigga shit like rims on my ride. Only a fool invests a lot of money in something like a car that loses value every day. I have precious metal dealers trying to sell me more gold coins and gold bars. I have artist trying to sell me artworks. Things that go up in value.

Whenever I do want to buy something or borrow money, they do all the work. They draw up all the paperwork, and I just sign my name. That's a pretty cool life isn't it, Jamal?" "Yes it is, Mr. Christopher. I want to do that kind of stuff when I get a job;" Jamal said. "Well, you will young blood. You will; Christopher said. Just remember, you're in competition with nobody but yourself. Just because Oprah or your classmate goes out and buys two houses. It doesn't mean you have to. If that's not in your budget.

You only buy what you can afford. This game is not about impressing anybody. It is doing what you can on your level to move forward. It requires sacrifice. Sometimes my friends would be going to concerts or trips out of town. I couldn't go. I needed money for closing cost on property I'm trying to buy. That's okay, everybody that went to the concert will be begging you for money one day. Then you will have to show your compassionate side. Remember all the teachings Pastor taught from your church. You tell'em; "I don't know what you heard about me. A bitch can't get a dollar out of me."

Most importantly, don't ever fuck with a whore that ain't got nothing to lose. If she doesn't have a business or her own house, then you shouldn't talk to her. I don't care if she is as fine as Teyonah Parris and makes $50,000 a year on her job. A lot of these hoes will trade that in for you to take care of her with alimony and child support. A good woman with a brain doesn't use a child for financial gain. They plan when they want to have kids. Usually in partnership with you and not to extort you."

# Show up and do what I'm being paid to do

"Mr. Christopher; Jamal said. If I'm only in my mid 20's in 10 years, then most women I know won't have a business or their own house." "Exactly; Christopher said. Get your money before you get your honey, my teacher use to say. If you do that in reverse, you will always be broke. This shit isn't hard, but a lot of motherfuckers will come at you. Trying to make your life hard. They don't have shit going on in theirs so they will try to fuck up yours. Watch how many people are in your circle.

Keep your circle small and you can easily figure out who did what. Then get rid of the problem. I mean kick them out the group not get rid of them like the mafia or something. When you're a man, you don't have to resort to violence. Unless violence comes to you. If they punch you, you break bones. If they use force, you use deadly force. Putting that ink to paper can destroy somebody much worse than a bullet in many cases. Learn to fight with your mind. People may not like you, but they will respect the fuck out of you. That's all you can ask for in this world is that people respect you.

They will respect you, because you do what you say, when you say. So it all comes back full circle, homie. Now let's go in this movie and see some people get killed; son" "Thanks, Mr. Christopher;" Jamal said. "What I do Yo;" Christopher asked? "Thanks for talking to me about how to succeed in life;" Jamal said. "Well, if that shit don't work out; Christopher said. I've got two ski masks in the back seat. We can go hit this bank down the street." "Nah, I'm good. I think I will try to do what you do. So I don't have to go to no job;" Jamal said.

"Hold on brother, I did work a job. Most days, I showed up to work on time ready to work. When I accepted a job that is the promise I made. You pay me, and I will show up at the time I am supposed to show up. I do what I am being paid to do. A job is your stepping stone to get here. Anything you have to do in life. Let it be a stepping stone to get you to the next level; Christopher said. Now, let's go in this theater, before we miss something. You know they kill all the black people in the first two minutes of the movie."

They got out the truck and walked into the movie theater. Jamal carried a jacket stuffed with candies and popcorn. Christopher walked behind Jamal who was trying his best to be discreet. Christopher whispered in a conspicuous voice; "Hey, if you get busted, I don't know you dude. Don't have me going to jail with you because you decided to break the law;" Christopher said. "We're not going to jail Mr. Christopher. They would just put us out;" Jamal said. They went in and found seats to enjoy the movie.

Meanwhile at Christopher's house, Angel was stapling her booklets together. She looked around the office at the collection of art and items Christopher has collected. Items from many places he has visited. There were pictures of him at the Lionsgate Bridge in Vancouver, City Hall in Toronto and Safeco field in Seattle. The Epicenter in Charlotte and Comerica Park in Detroit. The Superdome in New Orleans and Wrigley's Field in Chicago. American Airlines Arena in Miami and AT&T Park in San Francisco. Of course, the Inner Harbor and Camden Yards in Baltimore. Angel was not a huge sports fan but thought it might be nice to go to some games. Just to yell and cheer for either team Christopher wanted to win.

She looked through his vast music collection and how many genres of music he had. "This man loves him some Anita Baker;" she thought. She then went back to grab a CD. A compilation of slow jams Christopher made many years ago. She turned on the 2nd floor stereo and let the music play. She then went down to the bar. She looked through his wine rack to see what she might want to try. "Ah, this looks good," she said to herself as she grabbed a bottle of Freixenet. She grabbed the ice bucket off the bar and decided to spruce up the place. She went into the master bedroom and removed the sheets. She placed them in the laundry room.

Then, she entered the guest room and removed those sheets as well. She checked the laundry basket in the master bedroom. She went to all 3 baths, plus the half bath, and collected hand and floor towels. She had the music turned up as she sang along to The Manhattans; "Wish that you were mine." She separated the clothes and started with dark colors. She dusted the great room. "What am I doing cleaning this man's house; she thought? He has a maid that comes over every week." For the most part, Christopher kept his house clean and neat. After she finished dusting and cleaning the glass tables, she moved back into the master bedroom.

She found ink pens on his night stand and decided it should be in the drawer. Upon opening the drawer, she found the flavored massage oils and various junk, including old cell phones. "Why does he have all this junk in here; she asked out loud? What other kind of stuff is in this junk- filled drawer?" She started moving things around and noticed some business cards. One in particular belongs to a Shenequa M. Grey. She is an Attorney apparently. Must be an old friend of his from Louisiana; she thought.

"She found many keys and wondered what locks they all belonged to. Just then she recognized the song being played. It was "Seven Days; by Mary J. Blige. The lyrics seemed to sum up perfectly her feelings. She didn't want this CD to make her contemplate. After the song she went and shut it off. She turned on the radio to hear what April Watts was talking about. "Next Lifetime; by Erykah Badu had just begun playing. Angel listened to the words and scenario of that song. It then dawned on her that many people have been in her exact situation.

From "Secret Lovers;" by Atlantic Star to More than Friends by Jonathan Butler. People have sang about the dilemma of being in one relationship, and then caught up in another. This didn't make her feel any better but at least she knew someone understood. April Watts went back in the day and played; "I can make you feel good;" by Shalamar. That was Angel's jam and she ran to the mirror to sing along. She pretended she was singing it to Christopher. She kept touching her crotch as she sang; I can make you feel good. She pulled down her panties slightly, pretending to tease. Then she checked to see if her pubic hair has possibly gotten too long.

She reached down with the intent to check her hair length, but her finger grazes her clitoris. "Ummm, that felt good;" she thought. Turning the radio off, she touched herself again. This time moving her finger in a slow circular motion. She went into the walk- in closet and grabbed a towel. Then laid it on the bed since the sheets have been removed. She hadn't gotten around to putting new sheets on the bed. Sitting down she started to insert a finger inside of her. She imagined that Christopher was there. Kissing her vagina like only he could as she closed her eyes.

Using the moisture from inside of her, she began to rub her clitoris intently. Her mind raced with sexual images of Christopher licking her pussy. Imagining she was down on all fours and she told him exactly how and where to lick her. Her finger movements intensify, as she imagined herself sitting on his face. Forcing her wet pussy lips and clitoris all over his face. She jammed her middle finger inside. "Oooh yes, boy, ram that tongue in there. Lick it! Lick that sweet pussy," she commanded. She spoke out as if Christopher were there. "Ummm, you nasty boy, you want to lick me front and back too, don't you?

Oooh damn, now suck my clit…suck it, like I suck your dick. You better swallow my juices when I come. You better swallow them boy. Tell mommy how good her pussy tastes." Angel took her finger out of her vagina and inserted it into her mouth. "Oooh, yesssssssss. Lick that pussy good boy. Lick all of my juices up. Knowing exactly where and how to get herself off Angel quickly had an orgasm. "Oh, yesssssss, I'm going to cum all over that chocolate face of yours." She visualized Christopher working his tongue feverishly on her pussy and released with an intensity that made her body shake.

After she was able to come back down to earth she slowly sat up. "Well this towel needs to go to the laundry;" she said. She wanted it cleaned before Christopher returned home. She stood and took the towel to the laundry room and tossed it on the floor with the rest of the dirty laundry. She then showered her body and pampered herself in the bathroom. "Now, what was I supposed to be doing;" she chuckled to herself? Just then the bell rang on the front load washer indicating it was done. She walked over and put those clothes in the dryer. Next she began putting the light bright colors in the washer.

She then put some clean panties on and started dusting in the bedroom. "Let me finish this work so I can get on to relaxing and drink me some wine;" She thought. She decided not to open up any more of the drawers on Christopher's nightstand. In a bit of time, she had dusted furniture, vacuumed carpet, then swept and mopped the floors. The fragrance from the carpet powder had the house smelling good. Still she decided to light some scented candles. "Wow, this is a beautiful home;" she said out loud.

# Lover & Friend

Angel had a much bigger house as hers was made to hold a family. She noted Christopher has really nice taste in furniture and art. This house just looks like a bachelor pad and could use a woman's touch. Some curtains over those blinds. A few other nips and tucks and this place could be even more special. I wonder what he would say if I told him I wanted to put some curtains up. Or change a color of one of the rooms. I can hear him now; "Woman; I don't need no damn curtains!" I know how to get him to break down though. When I'm finished he will let me put up anything I want.

She walked over to the bar and grabbed the ice bucket with the bottle of wine in it. She grabbed a wine glass and the wine bottle opener. She poured herself a glass. "Umm, this is not bad; she said. What kind of snacks does he have in here to go with this wine I wonder?" She looked in the pantry and saw crackers, cookies and chips. Along with an assortment of all types of food preparation items, sauces, flour, sugar, syrup, rice and various other things. On the floor, there were cases of soda, bottled water, extra virgin olive oil and rice milk.

"Does he have any dip for those chips;" she asked herself? She looked in the refrigerator and found some sour cream and onion dip. "Perfect; she said. Damn but what will I eat when I get hungry later? Those two monsters are out at the movies and then are going out to eat. I don't feel like cooking. I guess I will order something from one of the places that deliver. What I really want to do right now is take a darn nap. Let me put some sheets on his bed and finish this glass of wine. One more glass and I may be too tipsy to do anything."

She snacked on some chips and dips and then sipped some wine. She turned on WHUR and heard Minnie Ripperton singing "Lover and Friend." What a perfect description she thought of her love with Christopher. There was no doubt that they were friends, or lovers either for that matter. She finished the glass of wine and washed her hands again. She didn't want to get any grease from the chips on anything. She then went into Christopher's walk in closet. The shelves had fresh sheets she could put on the bed. "Now, do I want the chocolate sheets, cream colored, royal purple or magenta?

I think I will go with the cream colored ones;" she said. After making the bed, she turned on the home alarm system. She usually works long hours and definitely had missed sleep. She turned off the music and got in bed. Then turned on HGTV. It is so rare that she got to relax like this at home. Her home office phone was always ringing. Or some kids were always ringing the doorbell to see Jamal. She was always cleaning because someone from her church may drop by. Usually to pick up some food her Pastor asked her to cook for something. "He don't ever offer no money to buy the food; she thought. That nigga has been pimping me for years."

Over at Christopher's house, she was almost at total peace. Most clients don't have her cell phone number. She could check her office messages from her cell, so that was perfect for her. "Oh wow, look at that bathroom;" she marveled as she watched T.V. They had a Jacuzzi with a wall in between his and her side. Two people can have different temperature water. "That's nice; but I like this Jacuzzi where we both sit together. Christopher just has to toughen up and learn to deal with warm water." she smiled.

"Oh boy, that wine is kicking in. Let me close my eyes for just a little while. Maybe I can touch myself just one more time. That will definitely help me sleep. Just then, the bell rang on the dryer in the laundry room, as it had stopped. "Oh shoot, time to put that load in the dryer. I will put the dry load in the basket;" she said. I will fold them later, because I am going to enjoy my day of relaxation." She got up out of bed and put the new load in the dryer, after emptying it of dry clothes and then went to brush her teeth. "Now, let me get some much needed rest and I guess Christopher will wake me."

She looked at the television for a few moments more. Her eyes began to get heavy. She was quickly drifting off to sleep and there seemed to be nothing she could do about it. She shut off the television and her eyelids came together. The sleep monster had got her and she was out of there. Jamal and Christopher walked out of the movies, and Jamal asked; "How did you like the movie, Mr. Christopher?" "It was alright. Just wasn't enough killing for me;" Christopher said. "There were like a 200 people that got killed in one scene; Jamal said. When the guy shot the office building with the rocket launcher and killed everybody inside."

"Well, they should have killed 201 people. How can he justify letting that old lady live? She was across the street;" Christopher said. "You know she is going to snitch, so he should have taken her old ass out." "You have issues Mr. Christopher. Did anybody ever tell you that;" Jamal asked? "My therapist says I don't have issues; Christopher said. He said it is perfectly normal to talk to aliens from Neptune or Jupiter. My therapist should know. He came here from a more evolved planet Xzasabar on a magic washcloth."

Jamal just shakes his head. "I'm going to get you some help someday Mr. Christopher." "You can help me now punk by buying dinner;" Christopher said. "No, you told me not to cash my $100.00. I was always told to listen to my elders;" Jamal said laughing. "Are you trying to call me old, boy? I bet this old man can whip your little ass. Now, laugh about that;" Christopher said. "Calm down Mr. Christopher. I don't want you to get your blood pressure up. You might have a stroke or something;" Jamal teased.

"I bet I'll stroke this belt across your little ass and get your ass pressure up. You lil' whippersnapper;" Christopher laughed. Jamal retorted; "Is that how they talked back in slave days, when you were a kid Mr. Christopher? Lil whippersnappers and stuff like that?" "Oh, you got jokes huh; Christopher said. Well, I tell you what, young grasshopper. Whippersnap DEEZ nuts!" They both laughed hard, as they got into the truck to drive to Ruby Tuesday. "That was dirty what you just said back there;" said Jamal. "Dirty deez nuts;" Christopher replied. "Why you play so much;" asked Jamal?

"Play with deez;" Christopher replied. "I'm not talking to you anymore;" said Jamal. "Talk to deez!" Christopher yelled. They both laughed until tears came out of their eyes. Jamal not wanting to here another Deez joke went silent. After several minutes driving towards the restaurant, Jamal spoke. "Mr. Christopher, can I turn on the radio?" "TURN ON DEEZ;" Christopher yelled back! They both laughed. "You saw Rush Hour; you ain't never supposed to touch a black man's radio; Christopher said. What do you want to hear, grasshopper?" "Hop on Deez;" Jamal replied.

They continued to laugh at the silliness of the moment. Christopher turned on his mp3 player. "Who is that;" Jamal asked? "Is that KRS-One?" "Yeah son, that is the Blast Master, the Teacher. The greatest MC to ever pick up a microphone in my humble opinion;" Christopher said. "A lot of dudes say Rakim is the greatest. Some people that don't have a clue of what Rap skills are will name some of these wack- ass studio artists of today. Nobody had more styles, more skills, than Mr. Parker. His thought provoking content and viciousness on the mic is legendary.

This dude could literally murder an MC's career off the top of his head." "So what do you think of today's rappers, Mr. Christopher;" asked Jamal? "Well, as one of our great black leaders of the Civil Rights Movement, Uncle Ruckus would say. It's a bunch of dumb nigga shit; Christopher said. I mean there are a few rappers out there with some lyrical content but not many. Lupe Fiasco is deep. Kendrick Lamar is definitely a man with brains and has something heavy to say. Jay-Z is a freaking icon because he is by far a great student of the game." "What do you mean student of the game Mr. Christopher;" Jamal asked.

"I mean, Jay-Z is very well educated not just on the streets. He knows books, politics, business, the history of pop culture, especially rap. You will always hear Jay refer to some rapper, or scenario from a movie or other historical context. That makes his music connect with everybody. Which is why he is still top of the food chain. Jay-Z is sharp, if you're going to mimic a rapper, mimic his business skills." "Did you ever want to be a rapper Mr. Christopher;" asked Jamal? "Nope;" said Christopher. "Why not;" Jamal asked? "Because I can't rap;" Christopher said. "I can quote the hell out of some lyrics, especially Ice Cube lyrics."

"Ice Cube, why do you like Ice Cube Mr. Christopher;" Jamal asked? "Ice Cube is the greatest story teller in Hip Hop history. I have almost everything in the Ice Cube library. No other artist could paint such a vivid picture of what they were saying. When you listened to Cube you feel like you were right there in South Central; Christopher said. Who is your favorite rapper Jamal?" "I like K. Lamar, Mos Def or Yasiin Bey, Common, Lupe Fiasco and Jay-Z;" said Jamal. "Ah, Mos Def really is Brooklyn's Finest which really makes him one of the greatest to ever do it.

Far more advanced in Rap Skills than any Rapper from Brooklyn including Jay-Z and Biggie. Anyone who says differently is judging on subject content of the Raps. Like somehow Rapping about selling drugs makes you a better artist. Now that's stupidity. You like rappers with skills, I likes that;" Christopher said. "Anyone with a brain will have more to talk about than getting high, bad bitches and dumb nigga shit."

Industry rule # 4080

"Yeah but Mr. Christopher, they're making a lot of money talking about that stuff;" Jamal said. They arrived at Ruby Tuesday, parked the truck and walked in. "They may be making money, but at what cost when it's all said and done Jamal;" asked Christopher? Many people have gone into the record business and made millions. Then walked out of it broke." "How does that happen;" Jamal asked? "Industry rule # 4080;" Christopher replied. "What; asked Jamal? *"Industry rule # four thousand and eighty, record company people are shady.*

*So kids, watch your back/ cause I think they smoke crack/ I don't doubt it/ look at how they act;"* Christopher rapped. "Who said that Mr. Christopher;" Jamal asked? "That's A Tribe Called Quest, Check the Rhyme. Now let's check out some food;" Christopher said. "Table for two;" the hostess asked? "Shhhh, I don't know this fool lady; Christopher said. This kid has been following me around all day. Look, I'm not no snitch or nothing but I think he has a nuclear bomb in his pocket. You might want to call security. "Why you be playing so much Mr. Christopher;" asked Jamal?

"Little kid, my name is not Christopher. I told you that. "It is Thorton Winthrop III Esquire & Ebony Magazine, Duke of Black Enterprise;" Christopher said. "You two, follow me this way;" the hostess laughed. Once seated at the table, Christopher spoke. "You're lucky they let you come through the front door. Once upon a time, you wouldn't have been able to eat in here with everybody else." "Yeah, I read about that and the Civil Rights Movement back in the day; Jamal said.

I am sure glad it's not like that anymore." "Really;" Christopher said. You think things have changed and are different today than say back during slavery time?" "Yeah, things are a lot different Mr. Christopher. They couldn't try that slave stuff now; Jamal said. Brothers would be giving out beat downs on anybody who tried that today." "Oh my goodness. This is why you negroes need to stop listening to that dumb shit the radio. You need to pick up a book. All that dumb shit is only preparing you to go back into slavery." "Good afternoon gentlemen. My name is Melodie, and I'll be your server today.

Can I start you off with something to drink?" Jamal said; "Actually, we are both ready to order." "Okay, great. What would you like first young man;" Melodie asked? "We will both have a peach tea and turkey burgers. On my burger, I don't want any pickles and extra mustard." "For you sir? How would you like yours prepared?" "I want a light amount of mayo, extra pickles and a slice of cheddar cheese on that joint. Oh, and instead of fries, can I get rice pilaf;" Christopher asked? "You sure can;" Melodie said. "Do you two want the salad bar?" "Nah, we're good;" Jamal said.

Melodie said; "Well, I will get this order in and have your drinks out right away." She then walked away, and Jamal and Christopher continued their conversation. "Mr. Christopher, how are you saying we could go back into slavery; Jamal asked? When a Rapper talks about getting high and shooting niggas. That is going to get the average black person arrested. What do you think that is? Prison is slavery and Rappers are a corporate tool used to help put more black people in prison. Back in the day Ice-T, Cube and others told Gangsta stories. They also told you the outcome of a life of crime. So it provoked thought.

They did that because Rap was mostly controlled by blacks. Now the other folks are the pimps controlling Rap. They hire hoes they use to sell you bullshit. In the songs the bullshit has no real consequences but fun. In real life the consequences are very real. Let me ask you something Jamal. What exactly would stop white people, if they wanted to start slavery up today? Blacks are unorganized. You have Rappers, talking about how many guns they have. But like most niggas with guns, they probably can't shoot.

Most blacks have no idea of the layout of the city they live in. Not beyond their own neighborhood. So even if we have guns, what good are they if you're rounded up in your hood? Then even radio host are talking like getting high is okay. Many blacks listen to these people because they're making money. What happens when you're high on weed the day they bring slavery back? How much resisting being captured could you do if you're high? All white people have to do is arrest you when you're high. They can tell your mama you tried to overthrow the government then. Seeing pictures or video of you high, the world will believe it. Now everybody understands why "they" are killing you.

What happened in Detroit Jamal?" "I don't know;" Jamal said. "Exactly, most of us don't know it. Yet we know who is fighting on Real Housewives. You'll hear people say they wish whites would try to put them back in slavery today. They would beat their ass. In Detroit City, they cut off the water. Thousands of black folks who can't drink, cook or clean without water. If whites decide to stop that truck that refills your local grocery store. What would you do for food? I mean most blacks can't grow vegetables and damn sure can't raise cattle. So how much ass beating can we do with no food or water?

Too many boys your age are looking to Lil' Wayne for knowledge on how to be a nigga. Too many girls your age spend more time learning to twerk than how to read. We are imposing on ourselves the same level of education the slaves had. So what exactly will stop slavery from happening today? Detroit is a test run. Blacks need to wake up and start working to own a business. If not they are going to find that Motown is coming to Yo-town." "You mean a business like my aunt Janice, who is a hair stylist and works for herself;" Jamal asked?

"You call that a business Jamal;" asked Christopher? Let me tell you something about business, little man. A business makes money whether you are there or not. If your ass is not in the shop doing hair, then you don't make money. So that is not a business. You have a job working for yourself is all that is. See, when Oprah is sleep, she's making money. When Bill Gates is on vacation, he's making money. While I'm here talking to you and about to eat my turkey burger. I'm making money. Somebody is at work so they can pay my rent. That's a business;" Christopher said.

"Why do you think more black people don't try to own their own business Mr. Christopher;" asked Jamal? "Oh, that's easy," Christopher said. The Black Church. They've taken over 400 billion dollars from us in the last 30 years. Preachers with no common sense. Preachers too stupid to help us build businesses are our enemies. I think it was Dr. Julia Hare who said at the last State of the Black Union, that blacks are functionally illiterate when it comes to money. I say preachers are the leaders in that category. "What about all the preachers everybody be quoting? Who say a lot of good stuff about having your own business;" Jamal asked?

"I want you to remember this as long as you live Jamal. Never listen to what a man says; Christopher said. He can say anything. Watch what he does and you will find out the truth about that man. Let me ask you something else Jamal. Don't you think with over 400 billion dollars collected? A God that can do anything? Shouldn't we be not as dependent on whites as we were 30 years ago;" Christopher asked? We're closer to slavery now than in 1960. "So, are you saying there is no God; Jamal asked?" "Absolutely not, I am just telling you, God never has and never will be in the church. The Devil is in the pulpit, he calls himself Pastor.

Look at where they led the sheep. We are 98% dependent on whites to take care of us. Jobs, houses, schools, everything we have to get from them; Christopher said. Now look at the mood of the country and tell me how that can be good? "So, you think that God doesn't do anything good for people;" Jamal asked? "Nope, I'm not saying that. I am just saying before we threw away 400 billion dollars plus. Black people in Detroit had water." "Here you go guys. Two turkey burgers. I believe, this one is for you sir, and this one is for you, young man;" Melodie said. Christopher and Jamal said, "Thank you."

"You're welcome. Can I get you anything else? I brought you some extra napkins right here;" Melodie said. "No, that's all we needed;" Christopher said. "Dag, that is messed up that they turned off their water;" Jamal said. "Yeah, it is; Christopher said. All your dumb preachers in Detroit can do is tell people to pray. They have squandered away all the money. On his clothes, his wife's clothes, his side bitches clothes and that new car he has to have every year. I'm almost certain a few billion of that 400 billion was collected around Detroit. Now we're praying for water?"

"Yeah, but praying is good isn't it Mr. Christopher; Jamal asked? I mean, if you ask God for something, he will do it for you. Maybe not when you want it but in time;" "Man, they have you programmed really well;" Christopher said. "Ask yourself something? Don't you think when the slave ship Jesus carried the first slaves from Africa, they prayed to be free? Yet 250 years later, Jesus and other ships were still going to Africa bringing folks to enslave them. See the preacher man won't tell you is Jesus saved the crops here in America, not you. God is not going to do anything for you, if you don't get up off your ass and do something for yourself. Whatever you do has to have a thought out plan.

Also you and your oppressor cannot possibly pray to the same God. Then both of you expect that one God to answer both of your prayers. If you're praying to be free and your Massa is praying to have slaves how does that work? Your team plays a game against your rival. You both want to win the game. Impossible God will let both win. Even if they tie but the rival has more wins from other games you're behind. So if Massa is reading a certain playbook and he has been winning. It's probably not the smartest thing for you to use the game plan he gave you. If a man is abusing a woman in a relationship, doing whatever he likes. Why would he give her a phone and the number to the battered women's clinic?

Why would he tell her he doesn't care who she talks to. That would be counterproductive to his grip of control. So if he lets her talk to anybody it would be his crazy brother. Or somebody that's going to tell that woman how lucky she is. How rough the world is out there. She should thank God she has a man like his brother who can fight and protect her. Except she's not being protected, she's being beaten. That's the role many black Pastors play in America.

They quote that Faith without works are dead. At the time of the Jena six crisis T.D. Takes lived next door to George Bush. He was also a Bush "spiritual advisor." How hard would it have been to pick up the phone? George I don't know if what my people are saying is true. Could you send the Justice Department to Jena? That shows you right there how much God is in them. Black people literally dying, but that's not the mega-pastor's concern. He's too busy telling you a slave ship is going to save you. If you don't believe it, it's because your faith ain't strong enough. Look close, you'll see it's all smoke and mirrors.

The reason blacks are conditioned to love a slave ship is simple. Bringing slavery back has always been an option in this country. The key to that is keeping you mentally enslaved, you'll fight less if you think it's God's will. Now eat your food;" Christopher said. Jamal filled his mouth with food. "So you don't think the reason people's lives don't get better, is they don't give back to God; he asked? "You mean like tithe;" Christopher asked? Let me tell you something, young blood. The Bible says, the Earth is the Lord's and the Fullness thereof. So, if God owns the earth and everything in it, why does he need money?" "So, that the church can do God's work;" Jamal said. "Tell me what works has the church actually done? I know they feed the homeless; Christopher said.

So does the Red Cross. Funny how the church can't help blacks get into business because that's not their role. Those motherfuckers ain't the Red Cross either. Even worse is Preachers waste the talent in the church." "What do you mean by wasting the talent in the church? There are a lot of good singers that came out of church;" Jamal said. "I'm not talking singing bullshit; Christopher said. I'm talking how you may have in a church, women that can sew their asses off and make nice clothes.

Why can't a pastor from New Orleans call up and pastor in New York? Then say I'm sending 50 shirts made by Sister Jenkins to sell to your congregation. The pastor from New York sends down 50 pair of shoes, hats or whatever. Black people start becoming financially independent? Why can't a church in Atlanta ship peach cobblers around the globe to other church houses? Or a church in Baton Rouge ship out pecan pies to a church in Baltimore?

If these preachers weren't so fucking stupid, they would work together to change the lives of black people. Nobody would have to be praying for a better job because we would be creating them. T.D. Takes can sell a million books. How does that help the lady that lost her job and has kids to feed? Oh, he'll tell her some bullshit that sounds good. What he won't do is use his 140 million dollars. He could make sure nobody in his church is in her position ever again. He just don't give a fuck like 2Pacalypse." Every church going black woman will say on cue; "Not my church, they do what they're supposed to do." Then ask them what that church does and they start telling you about some land or a building they own and a community center that feeds the poor.

Then I ask them how much of that land or building is theirs? They usually get mad then. So to throw salt in the wound I point out something. They put all their money in the church. Yet their name is not on anything but the Pastor's name is. That's called "Dumb Nigger Economics". If the church is doing what they're supposed to do. You wouldn't have to go out here and jump through hoops to get into college. You wouldn't have to apply for a job. Essentially banging your head against the same walls your parents did. You'd go work for your parents or Uncle and know at 10 years old your future was secure.

Jamal's phone rang and he answered. "Hi, mom. Nothing sitting here with Mr. Christopher. Talking about the black church and how they don't help nobody start businesses and stuff. Huh? Oh the movie was good. Mr. Christopher wanted to see more killing. You want to talk to him? Oh, okay I will tell him. Hold on. Mr. Christopher, my mom says she just came from a client's house up your way. So she is going to stop by your place to get some maple tea. Christopher replied; "Tell her I spit in the pitcher, because I am tired of her stealing my stuff." "He said he spit in the pitcher mom, cause you be stealing too much; Jamal told her. She said that's okay. The last time you ate at our house, she washed your plate in our toilet. Then put your food on the dust pan and swept it on your plate;" Jamal repeated.

"Tell her I said, don't let my white neighbors see her go through the front door; Christopher said. They know to call the police, if any thugs come to my house." "You heard that mom; Jamal asked? She said she ain't worried about your neighbors or you Mr. Christopher. Okay, bye mom. I will talk to you later. No, Mr. Christopher is going to take me over their house when we leave here. He gave me some money, so I'm good. Okay, I love you too mom. They hung up. I'm glad she aint' try to talk me to death this time. It must be because I'm talking to you."

# It should be for you

"Oh, so I saved you a long-winded conversation, huh;" Christopher asked? That's got to be worth at least $100.00." "Nooo! Mr. Christopher, I will call her back and talk as long as she wants;" Jamal said. "You're funny kid. You know she only calls you because she loves you. You being her only kid and erriethang;" Christopher said. "Yeah, I know, but sometimes she treats me like a kid too much;" Jamal said. "Well, you are a kid and should enjoy your childhood now; Christopher said. When you get to be an adult, the world is going change like a 40 degree temperature drop.

You will wish for this time when all you have to do is bring home good grades in school. Your mom loves you, that's why she works like she does. All you have to do is go to school. I told her to trade you in for a Mexican kid, but she wouldn't listen to me. Excuse me, Melodie. Can we get the check please;" Christopher asked? "Here you are sir. I'll take that whenever you're ready;" Melodie said. "Hold up, Melodie. Why is his food on my receipt; Christopher asked? I told y'all, he escaped from the looney farm." "You want me to pay for it Mr. Christopher;" asked Jamal? "Nah, I got it this time." He handed Melodie his check card.

"You can pay when we go to an expensive place. Where the food is like $200.00 a plate;" Christopher said. "I don't have that kind of money Mr. Christopher;" Jamal said. "Rob some moarfuggers yo;" Christopher said. "You can't go around robbing people Mr. Christopher. That will land you in jail;" Jamal said. "Why not, preachers do it every day. They have robbed the fuck out of black people." "Aren't you supposed to tithe like it says in the bible;" Jamal asked?

"We don't have time to get into who concocted the book you call the Bible. Let me tell you this. As you live, your body, just like my body and everyone else. We're going to become old, our bodies will get tired. It simply will not let you work. Especially if you have a job that requires you standing or sitting a lot. At that point, you are going to wish to God you hadn't thrown your money away in a church. You will wish you had that money to take care of you in your old age.

Yes you should be putting up 10% of your earnings but it should be for YOU. When you can no longer work. That day is coming for me and it's coming for you. It's coming for everybody else who has thrown away their retirement savings. Lining some preacher's pockets;" Christopher said. "My mom thinks I get a lot of wisdom from talking to you; Jamal said. That right there makes a lot of sense." "I know right; Christopher continued. Why would God have you throw away your money in a church? Especially since they won't do a damn thing for or your family worth anything; Christopher asked? "Old and young people today are dying, because they don't have healthcare. Four hundred billion dollars we threw away in church. That should have gotten us a network of doctors.

"Are you familiar with Obamacare;" Christopher asked? "Yeah that's the Healthcare law right;" Jamal replied. Christopher continued; "well when it went into effect a lot of Republican controlled States refused to accept it. Racist Governors and State legislatures didn't want you to have it. As a result a lot of people still didn't have healthcare." Jamal responded; "Yeah that's messed up those states did them like that." "Maybe so but why didn't the Church get these people healthcare; Christopher asked?

They could have done that long before Obama was born. They don't give a damn about black people." How can the Church get people Healthcare Mr. Christopher; Jamal asked? Easy, the Church goes to BlueCross with 10,000 people. Ready to sign up for Healthcare. Then they would get a group discount rate just like any big employer does. What has stopped First Baptist from calling up Good Sheppard? Then 40 other churches just in the same city or town? Putting names together to get group discount rates on insurance? Nothing but stupidity. Now the dumb hoes who defend these preachers will say; the church ain't supposed to be doing healthcare.

Well church people are dying from lack of adequate Healthcare. If you're too stupid to see how that's your business then that Pastor should be shot. Four hundred billion dollars should put every black person that wants to go, through college. Without Tom Joyner having to raise more money. Four hundred billion dollars should have started a lot of real businesses. That money is long gone in pastor's nice house. Let's roll up out of here homie. So I can get you over to your boy's house and I can go home;" Christopher said.

"Do you have something to do at home Mr. Christopher;" asked Jamal? "Yeah, you could say that, Jamal. I have something I need to get into when I get there;" Christopher said. "What's that you're going to be doing Mr. Christopher? Is it something to do with looking for a new house;" Jamal asked? "Why are you asking me all these questions kid;" Christopher asked? Are you wearing a wire? I know you got people in Baltimore. I know The Wire was there too. Now I'm thinking you're a Snitch. Am I going to have to take you behind this restaurant and cap your little ass;" Christopher joked?

"Quit playing Mr. Christopher. Why would I be wearing a wire? Who would I be snitching to and what information would I have to give them;" Jamal asked? "That's pretty convincing Jamal. Exactly what I would expect a Gov'mint informant to say;" Christopher replied. "Whatever Mr. Christopher, can you open the truck;" Jamal asked? "No, not yet. We have to check it for bombs; Christopher said. I will check the seats, and you get down and roll under the truck to make sure they didn't put one under there."

"I'm not rolling on no ground Mr. Christopher. Besides why would anybody bomb your truck;" Jamal asked? "That's exactly how the man wants you to think, little whippersnapper;" Christopher said. "Yep, you're crazy Mr. Christopher. I just want you to know that;" Jamal said. They arrive at Jamal's friend's house. Jamal removed his seatbelt and said; "Thanks Mr. Christopher for everything. Especially the talk, some of it was real deep. I appreciate you explaining it to me. Christopher responds by calling his name, "Jamal." "Yeah, Mr. Christopher;" replied Jamal. "EXPLAIN DEEZ;" Christopher said. Jamal burst out laughing and closes the door.

Christopher rolled down the passenger side window and said; "Have a good time, lil homie." "I will Mr. Christopher. I will see you later;" Jamal said. "You can SEE DEEZ;" Christopher yelled as Jamal ran to the front door laughing. Christopher, while still in the driveway, grabbed his phone to see that he had text messages from Angel. *"I'm missing you and wishing you were here, so I could rub your shoulders and whisper some sweet nothings in your ear."* He then opened the next one that read: *"This wine has me feeling some type of way, and you might be able to take advantage of me, if you were here."*

Then he opened the last one: *"I am a classy lady so I don't send nude pics of myself, but if you could see what I have for you, then you wouldn't be reading right now."* Christopher backed out of the driveway and burned rubber as he raced up the street. Right now at this moment, he has only one person and one thing on his mind….Angel. He pulled off of 63rd Ave onto East West Highway. He didn't stop for the stop sign just as a police car was coming up the street.

The officer turned on his blue and red lights to initiate the traffic stop. Christopher pulled over to the right side as soon as it was safe to do so. He rolled his windows all the way down so the officer could see inside. He then turned his music completely off. "Good afternoon sir. Do you know why I stopped you;" the officer asked? "Yes sir I do. I ran that stop sign back there;" Christopher replied. "Are you in a hurry to go somewhere;" the officer asked?

# A woman that can be quite expensive

"No sir. I was just trying to get home. I have a beautiful woman waiting on me. If you know what I mean;" Christopher said. "Well hell, I might run a stop sign or two myself if I had that; the officer said. How about I just check out your license and registration. If everything is good, we can get you out of here with a warning." "Yes sir officer. Here you go, my license, registration and here is my retired I.D. card;" Christopher said. "Man, why didn't you say you were retired law enforcement in the first place;" the officer asked? Man, go home to that lovely woman and have a good time."

"Thank you very much officer. You be safe out here;" Christopher said. Christopher drove off then he noticed a flower shop. He decided to stop in and get Angel a bouquet of flowers. He came across a dozen of pink and white roses. He also bought a crystal vase. He had the roses boxed, so he didn't have to worry about the vase while driving. After purchasing the roses, he continued to drive. He arrived home sometime later pulling into his garage. He went into his house empty handed and turned off the alarm. He yelled; "Don't shoot, it's just me a burglar."

"Oh, Mr. Burglar why are you here;" Angel said. She spoke in her damsel in distress voice. There is nothing here to steal. The only thing here is just little old bitty old me." "I will take that Ms. Lady. I think I just hit the lottery;" Christopher replied. He walked up to her and wrapped his arms around her as she did the same to him. They kissed like they've been apart for ages. Christopher ran his hands all up and down her body.

"Somebody's been drinking wine I see;" Christopher said. "Somebody has been eating onions I see;" Angel replied. They both giggled and kissed again. "Oh yeah, let me go and get my toothbrush out of the truck;" Christopher said. "Why is there a toothbrush in the truck;" Angel asked? "Just in case Janet Jackson was in town. She might say something like can you come over to my hotel and lay in bed with me now. I would need my toothbrush for that;" Christopher said. Angel gave him the look, but let him go.

He went out to the garage and came back in a few seconds later. He said; "I can't find my toothbrush, but I found these flowers lying on my seat." "Awwww, that is so sweet;" Angel said. She opened the box. "Ah pink and white, they are so beautiful;" Angel said. "Just like you. I love you woman, and much more than you know;" Christopher said. She walked up to him very seductively and kissed him passionately on the mouth. Christopher was ready to explode at her touch. "Why don't you go put those in some water with this vase I found? I will run and go brush my fangs; he said.

Then, I will be ready to spend some time with the most beautiful woman in this galaxy;" Christopher said. Soon Angel joined Christopher in the master bathroom. They both brushed their teeth at their respective sinks. Christopher looked over at her, rinsed his mouth and said; "Hmmm, jamming something in your mouth, white stuff all over your lips. I think I love you woman. What do I have to do to make you all mine?" Angel rinsed and said; "Boy, you are the silliest man I have ever met. Anyway I don't think you can afford me." "What! Christopher said acting startled. Here it is, I saved all my money from my allowances as a kid.

Well what price to have such a lovely, beautiful, rare and precious woman like yourself Angel? I am willing to sell my porn collection if need be;" he said. They both placed their toothbrushes into their holders. Angel turned to him. She said; "well I am a woman that can be quite expensive as I have lots of wants and needs." "Go on;" Christopher said. "Well for instance, I need love;" Angel replied. "Woman, if you don't know that I love you by now, then we have a serious communication problem;" Christopher said. "Yeah, well I know you love me as your friend. I know you would do anything for me. I wonder sometimes if this love is just because I am convenient;" Angel said.

"What do you mean convenient;" Christopher asked? "I don't just call you over here for a booty call. Then forget you exist, until the next time I want some." He then walked up to her and wrapped her arms around his waist. He wrapped his around hers, so they are nose to nose with one another. "Woman, you mean everything to me. I know I didn't realize it all those years we were good friends. I was lying to myself and by the way we make love we were lying to each other." "I'm not saying you don't care for me; Angel said. I'm saying maybe you think this relationship is easy for you to deal with. I mean the reality is I'm married.

You can act like my husband while he's away. We both know that you don't have to keep me if you get tired of me. You know my issues but you don't have to deal with them per se. You know there is only so much attachment I can get because of my situation. I just wonder, would you act the same if things were different?" Christopher replied; "Different, the same, logical, insane, in a car or a plane, green eggs and ham, I don't give a damn. I love you woman. Nothing you or anyone else does or says will change that.

I don't have the best feeling about being with another man's wife. I don't think it's my place to break up a happy home. If it's happy. If it ain't happy and we were talking about your home. We're talking about you Angel Renee' so I would tell you to leave that dude. Whatever you would lose in the divorce monetary wise, I would replace it. Then add a lot more on to it. Whatever you were getting in love. I will multiply that ten times. Then put some whip cream and cherries on top. I am not promising you the moon. Nor saying every day will be sunshine. I know we are both strong minded people and we like things done our way.

What I can tell you is, I have never felt this way about a woman since I got married. I said I would never love like that again and then came you. So, if I have to bite my tongue, swallow my pride and digest my macho attitude. I am willing to do that for you my Nubian Queen." "Yeah, because you can be a smart mouth, sarcastic somebody at times; Angel said. That won't play too well with me as your woman. I know you like to joke a lot and that's fine when I'm in a playful mood. When I'm not you could be headed to Death Row." "Damn it's like that;" Christopher asked?

"Oh, I wouldn't let you die. You might be wounded. Until you learn how to curb your smart mouth;" Angel said. "You women can be so vicious and cruel; Christopher said. I hope I never get on your bad side, but I am a realist. I know it will happen at some point. Don't be ignoring me because I will make brownies. Then you will have to talk to me to get some." "Now that is low;" Angel said. "No worries, I will cozy up to you and get me some brownies. You better be more of a Baker than Anita when you get in the doghouse.

Christopher looked in her eyes and asked; "Why are we standing here in the bathroom talking?" "I don't know;" Angel said. Now that I think about it, let's go. I don't want to be like I'm falling for a man, who seduced me by the toilet; Angel joked. They walked into the living room and sat on the sofa. Angel asked; "So do you really think this wouldn't be any different if we could be together all the time?" "Not for me it wouldn't be;" Christopher said. "I not only love you, I am in love with you and that for me is an irrefutable fact.

"How do we know if we got married it will end up any different than our first;" Angel asked? "We're both a little more mature now;" Christopher replied. Experience and life have taught me why so many marriages fail. "Really what is the reason; Angel asked? "Society;" Christopher answered. "What does that mean;" Angel inquired? "It means from the time we were kids, society told us who to marry; Christopher continued. They told boys to find ourselves a "good woman". One you meet in church, one that you can bring home to your family.

When we get older we meet that girl that is a total freak. She does everything we love in bed. She makes us happy. However we won't marry her because she's been around the block. Everybody knows she's been around the block. We would feel embarrassed to make her our wife. So we end up marrying that church girl. Who doesn't do many of the things we want. At least not on a regular. It's like pulling teeth or you get a blowjob on your birthday. Fuck that bullshit. So many men end up creeping back to that girl that has been around the block. That's where there happiness is because they're getting what they want. For girls they're told to grow up and be that wholesome girl. One that a man would be proud to marry.

Reality is those women want to do those freaky things. They're just as horny as men. They want to try porn type sex and everything else. They're just afraid if they say that to their husbands, he'll have a bad reaction. They think he'll be like; bitch where did you learn all this freaky shit from? Are you some kind of whore? Are you fucking somebody else? So these women are guarded. When their husbands ask them about anal they can't say yes the first few times. If they appear too eager, he may think they've been around the block. They hope he'll ask again so it looks like he talked them into it. Too late, he's stepping out to where he doesn't have to beg. Where he can be satisfied of his desires.

Now the woman isn't being satisfied because her true desires aren't being met. Then she ends up creeping out to find a guy. One that has no qualms about asking her to do all the things her husband won't. Both husband and wife caught in the illusion of what a "good woman" is. Trust me Angel. I don't have an ego. Whatever you want to try in bed is okay with me, and you've proven not to be shy. I also will have no issues asking you to do what I want you to do. I'm not going to assume that you've been around the block over a request. Even if you did, it was before me. People shouldn't get mad about what happened in the past." "Interesting;" Angel said.

Besides sex doesn't make you a good or bad person. It only enhances who you already are. So nothing would change if we were together all the time. I know what an amazing woman you are. I not only like making love to you. I love making love with you and sometimes I just want to fuck your brains out. You have a lot of brains up there woman, you could lose some and still be smart. It's those brains of yours that turn me on so much with your sexy self. So if you wanted to go home right now and bring your things over.

I could find some room for you in my king size bed for you to sleep." "What would I eat if I stayed over here;" Angel asked? "Well, I could cook you something if you like. Or we could fly out to San Francisco and eat out on Pier 39. Or ride over to Oakland and catch dinner at Jack London Square;" Christopher said. "I would love to take you to Oaktown someday pretty lady." "What's so special about Oaktown;" Angel asked? "Some places just have that feel that you can't really describe. When you're there you feel creative and Oakland is unique. A lot of talent has come out of Oaktown.

Or if you like I know a place that has some great grilled chicken. Smothered in fresh vegetables and cheese on that West side of Canada in Vancouver. After we eat, we can drive down to Seattle and sit outside the very first Starbucks on Western Ave. You can sip on a coffee or cappuccino. We'll go shopping afterwards in the Pike Place Market. However, if you wanted to stay on the East coast we could catch the train up to NYC. We can go see this play they have up there with some guy. I can't remember his name, Denmark or Denzo Washington. Somebody who thinks he can act;" Christopher said. "Denzel Washington;" Angel screamed!

"Oh yeah. That guy; Christopher yelled. My nephew just happens to have some tickets to tomorrow's show. I know tomorrow is Sunday. Usually I like to be in church giving away my money. I want to be like Pastor. Selling my soul for material wishes, fast cars and bitches. Wishing I lived my life a legend, immortalized in pictures. Or would you like to go to New York? "Hell yes, I want to go;" Angel screamed! Let me just call my sister. Maybe she will stay with Jamal tomorrow night at my house. In case you had plans to stay until Monday."

"That won't be a problem let me call my nephew; Christopher said. Make sure we're still good with those tickets. We may have to stop by his spot off of Metropolitan and 118th in Queens. That's where the tickets are then we can go back to Midtown." "Okay; Angel said. Let me call my sister and you do what you have to do to make it happen. Wait I need to go home and get something to wear in case I see Denzel." "You don't need to go home and get anything woman. Your toothbrush is here and your comb and brush is in your bag;" Christopher said. "I'm not talking about that man, I need a nice outfit to wear;" Angel said. "Have you heard of Saks Fifth Ave woman;" Christopher asked? "Yes I have, are you taking me there to get something to wear;" Angel asked?

"No, there is an alley behind the store. This dude named hustle man sells t-shirts;" Christopher laughed. "See, that's what I'm talking about. Your smart mouth there sir; Angel said. I have to call my sister. I am going to your office, so I can explain this to her." Angel walked to the office and Christopher turned on the radio low volume. He then took his phone and called his nephew. He asked if they can pick up the tickets tomorrow. His nephew advised that he still has tickets, but they will not be home tonight. So he will leave the tickets on the coffee table in his apartment. Christopher has a key already.

Christopher then booked a King Suite for two nights at the Courtyard Midtown East overlooking the city. He then booked a rental car. Now all they have left to do is leave. Angel came out of the office and said; "My sister said she'll stay over at my house. So I'm good to go. What time are we leaving?" "Now; Christopher said. Since we do have to get up to New York and we're in Maryland right now."

They grabbed a few essentials and two clothing bags with nothing in them. They would not be empty when they came back. They grabbed some headphones for their phones. Christopher grabbed his .45 handgun and an extra clip. They went out to the garage and left for the Aberdeen Train station. Christopher parked the vehicle and they went inside the station.

"Excuse me ma'am. What time is your next train going up to Penn Station in New York;" Christopher asked? "Our next one leaves at 3:25pm, sir. Would you like tickets;" the lady asked? "Yes, I'll take two round trips leaving today and coming back Monday afternoon." They sat down in the waiting area. Many people were coming and going through the station. "Hungry;" Christopher asked? "A little but I want to wait until we get up to New York;" Angel said.

## All Aboard, Departing For New York

"How do you know I might not get into a dice game on the train; Christopher asked? I may not have any money in NYC. Then you'll say, I should have eaten in Maryland." "Man, you don't know the first thing about playing dice; Angel replied. Even if you played, you would quit when you lost more than $20.00." "Yeah, you're right. I would never waste my money on no crap game. I'll spend it on porno or something good, like God intended us to do; Christopher joked. Do you want a bag of popcorn and some tea until we get up there?" "Are you going to eat some too;" Angel asked?

"Yeah, but only if you promise to not spit the shells on my shirt. You know you're ghetto at times;" Christopher joked. Angel punched his arm gently. He bought the bag of popcorn and two medium teas. They sat with Angel leaning her head on his shoulder as she took a few kernels of popcorn. "Do you think we can go uptown? I want to look for a movie I can't find anywhere. I also want to check out some deals on some perfume;" Angel said. "We can do whatever you need up there my beautiful woman. Then some of whatever you want;" Christopher said. "What did you have in mind Mr. Man;" Angel asked?

Christopher unlocked his cell phone and went to YouTube. He searched for and found Luther Vandross' "If Only for One Night." He then sent it to Angel's phone via text. "What did you just send me;" Angel asked? I know this is you texting me. It better not be something simple." She opened the text message and read the name of the song. "Awww, this is one of my favorite Luther songs;" she said. "Go ahead and play it then woman;" Christopher said.

She put in her dual headphones. Once the video started they listened to the words. They were two people in their own little world. Christopher kissed her on her forehead. He took her phone to hold it for her while they both listened. They were interrupted halfway through the song by the intercom: "Boarding in 15 minutes will be Amtrak 1867 to New York City, making stops along the way in…." "Oh! That's us; Angel said. "Let me run to the restroom real quick and I am done with this popcorn.

Can you watch my purse too please;" she asked? "Yes woman, I got you. I will be right here until you get back;" Christopher said. Angel came back out about 7 minutes later. Christopher said; "Let me run in the restroom real quick too and I'll be right back." Shortly after Angel could hear the hand dryer going. She knew it was Christopher who came out after a few moments. A line of about 17 people had formed to board the train. Angel took the tickets out of her purse and they walked in line. They found a seat on the train and Christopher placed their bags overhead. He took the window seat and Angel took the one in the center.

Soon, the train was headed north and they were holding hands. "Thank you very much;" Angel said. "I didn't do anything;" Christopher replied. "For taking me to New York to see "A Raisin in the Sun." For buying my train ticket, booking the hotel. Oh and taking me shopping in the alley behind Saks 5th;" Angel joked. "Nothing but the best alleys for you, my dear precious woman; Christopher replied. I will take you shopping at the finest alleys all over the world." "You're so good to me;" Angel said. "That's all a man is ever supposed to be to a treasure like you; he said. I better not find out any man is ever pushing you around or else." "What???"….Angel replied.

"Nothing, I was just saying if anybody messed with you. They would have to deal with me;" Christopher said. "Anybody like who are you talking about;" Angel asked? "Like that big apple head man up there sitting by the door. He was looking at you like he got it on his mind;" Christopher said. "Leave that man alone; Angel said. He wasn't thinking about me, you and probably nobody on this train. "Well, if he was I would have to let him know. I'm from East Baton Rouge and West Baltimore. I will put an East/West whipping on that ass. Call that shit a half and half."

"You're so silly, man. I don't know what I'm going to do with you;" Angel said. "I have a few ideas; Christopher said. We can try tonight in the hotel room. If you'll let me." "Oh yeah, we can talk about those when we get to the room;" replied Angel. "You're such a lady at all times, Angel. I like that;" Christopher said. He then squeezed her breast discreetly. "Hey I didn't say I was a gentleman at all times;" he said. Arriving at Penn Station, they walked to the subway platform. They purchased two subway tickets. They looked to see which train would take them to Lexington Ave Station near their hotel. Once they figured that out, they boarded the next subway car. It was nearly crowded.

There were a group of rowdy teenagers talking loudly. Laughing as a few of them were randomly walking up to people. Asking them have they ever seen an elephant fly? When the random people looked up or ignored them, the rest of the group burst into laughter. One middle aged man tried to ignore one of the kids in his face. The juvenile slapped his face and the man did not respond. Christopher pushed Angel to the front of the car with her back pressed against the window. He stood in front of her to protect her. He had Angel hold both empty clothing bags.

He then pressed his back gently against her breast and they both held on as the subway car moved. Two of the juveniles made their way up to the front of the car. They walked towards Christopher and Angel. Christopher stood in a firm stance. He looked the biggest juvenile right in his eye showing no fear. The juvenile then turned around to his group and said; "Yo, let's get off at the next stop Yo." When the subway doors opened, the rowdy group got off together. Now there were seats that Christopher and Angel could take.

"Do you want to sit down;" Christopher asked? "No, we only have three more stops and we'll be at Lexington Ave;" Angel replied. "Did you think that kid was going to say something to you?" "Nah, he didn't want them kind of problems; Christopher said. He knew I wasn't scared for a reason. So he took some advice from Spike Lee. He thought it was better to do the right thing and leave." "He didn't know you had a .45 on you. So how would he think you'd give him problems;" Angel asked? "These kids aren't as dumb as they try to pretend. He saw my hand under my shirt; Christopher said.

Yes, I could have been bluffing. But he knew if he was wrong about me bluffing that was his ass. I don't play poker, so I don't bluff. He did the right thing. This is our stop, so come on woman and get off the train. Before we end up on Riker's Island or somewhere." They scurried off the train and looked for signs that directed them to 59th Ave. They walked a few blocks to 53rd Ave and around the corner to the hotel. They checked in with the front desk and took the elevator to the 30th floor. They had a luxurious room overlooking the city of New York. Their room was also facing the lipstick building. "This is very nice; Angel said. You have a little taste I see."

"I wouldn't classify you as a 'little taste" woman. You're too hard on yourself;" Christopher joked. Angel dropped her clothing bag and ran toward Christopher. He was standing by the bed and she tackled him onto it. "I wasn't talking about me, you punk;" she said. She pinned his arms under her legs without his resistance. She gently pinched his face and lightly across his chest repeatedly. "Stop playing woman;" he said in a pseudo mad voice. "Or what;" Angel asked? "Stop playing before I turn into the Hulk on you up in here;" Christopher said. "You can't do nothing Mr. Man. Except beg for mercy. So shut up all that crying, before I give you something to cry about;" Angel replied.

"Who do you think you're talking to black woman;" Christopher asked? He then muscled his way to topple her off of him onto the bed. He then straddled her, with his knees pushed up by her armpits. He began to tickle her frantically. Angel laughed hysterically and pleaded with him. "I'm sorry, I'm sorry Christopher. I didn't mean to make you angry Mr. Hulk! Now get off of me before I have to kick your green ass!" "You're going to do what;" Christopher asked? He tickled her sides. "I didn't hear you. What did you say?" "Nothing, I didn't say nothing, punk;" Angel retorted. She was still laughing wildly.

"Oh, I'm a punk huh, woman?" He tickled her some more. She laughed insanely and finally decided to submit. "Okay, I give up, let me go; she said breathlessly. You win Mr. Man." With that, Christopher leaned down and kissed her lips then looked into her eyes. "That's right and don't you ever forget who the King is;" he said. Angel uttered playfully; "That's Michael Jackson isn't it?" He started to tickle her again and Angel stopped his hands. "Yes, my king, I humbly acknowledge your dominion over me."

She wrapped her arms around his neck and pulled him down for another kiss. She then said; "Only because I didn't want to have to kick your tail up in here." Christopher raised up to start tickling her again, but her grip was firm. With her arms around the back of his neck she pulled him in for another kiss. It was abundantly clear to both of them who submitted to whom. The feel of her lips pressed against his and he had no fight left in him. "No fair, you're cheating Angel;" he said. "How am I cheating;" Angel asked?

"You're using the power of your sexy lips as Kryptonite. Your naturally beautiful face and hair. You've weaken me and crush my resistance;" Christopher replied. "Did I do all of that;" she asked coyly? "We better get up and grab some clothes real quick, before the stores close;" Christopher said. "Yeah, let me freshen up real quick in the bathroom; Angel said. I'll be ready in one minute." They freshened up to head outside towards Times Square. They stopped on 5th Ave at Saks and Angel quickly headed to the door. "They are closing soon at 8:30pm, but will be open on tomorrow at 11:00am; Angel said. Okay, we will have time, since our show doesn't start until 3:30pm. So we will have to be here when the doors open."

Christopher whined pretentiously; "Get up early? It never ends with you woman. I'm on vacation. Angel replied; "Okay I need clarity, so let me get this straight. You don't want to get up early for me nigga? "You just called me a nigga again woman; Christopher said. Put your ass in the city and you go straight ghetto. I'm scared of you if we took a ride over to the South Bronx. Or if we went out to Compton. You would probably be throwing up gang signs and Crip walking." "Yeah, I might have to ride on a couple of fools who owe me some grip out on that Westside; Angel teased.

Or I just might jack me a mark.  If I catch them slipping at the light with them gold Daytons on that six foe." "Get the hell out of here with your crazy self. Where did you learn all that trash you're talking;" Christopher laughed? "I was listening to your Ice Cube "Death Certificate" and "Lethal Injection" CDs earlier today when you were out with Jamal;" she said.  They walked to Times Square and Christopher took her hand as they walked down 7th Ave.   "Are you ready to get something to eat yet woman;" Christopher asked?

"Yes, I could go for something good right about now. What did you have in mind;" she asked?  "Angel, I brought you on this trip; he said.  So I am taking you to eat wherever you want to eat tonight.  Tomorrow we will go to Sylvia's or Amy Ruth's in Harlem.  Tonight is your pick;" Christopher said. "Okay, let's go in there;" Angel said. She pointed to a restaurant across the street. "Sounds good to me nigga;" Christopher said.  Angel slapped him across his arm. "Come on man; she said. Let's go before I have to hurt you." "Like you were hurting me in the hotel? When you were crying how sorry you were;" Christopher asked?

"Man, please I was about to do my move and bust you up in there. I didn't want to show off my fighting skills;" Angel said.  They crossed the street when the light changed with the crowd.  Christopher said; "Oh! You have fighting skills now.  You must have bought them when we got to Madison Square Garden or somewhere." "Whatever punk, you know I could have hurt you if I wanted to; Angel said.  I kind of like you a little bit so I took it easy on you." "I believe you;" Christopher said.  He opened the door for them to walk into the restaurant.

"It's about a 30 minute wait;" the hostess said. She handed Angel a restaurant pager. "Is that okay with you;" Christopher asked Angel. "That's fine. I have some files I need to review and a few emails to send out;" Angel said. "Alright, well you do what you have to do and I'm going to watch some basketball on my phone; Christopher said. You're in New York and you're working. Ain't nobody got time for that;" Christopher teased. "My business isn't set up like yours, Christopher. So I have to stay on top of some things; Angel snarled. Here hold this pager on your lap, so we'll know when our table is ready;" she said."

# The Hotel, The Show, The After party

"Okay, I'm putting on my headphones, so I can hear the game; he said. Don't try to walk off and leave me here while you're eating." "I wouldn't do that; Angel replied. I need you to pay for my meal." "Okay, next time I tickle you I will have no mercy;" Christopher said. They had a nice candlelit dinner in a very romantic place in Times Square. They came outside holding hands and walking down the street without a care in the world. "So what do we do now;" Angel asked?

"Well, let's go get our car, which is over on 48th and we can ride over to Queens. We need those tickets for tomorrow. Then we can drive down the Westside Hwy to 125th and see what's happening in Harlem;" Christopher said. "As long as you know where we're going I'm fine; Angel said. I want to pick up some things in Harlem anyway. Like the skin cream you brought me the last time you were up here. Oh and some peppermint soap." "Well, that's why we have the car, but we'll get a better deal on Peppermint soap in Brooklyn; Christopher said. Flatbush and Fulton is the spot.

After leaving Queens and driving a few minutes, they made it to Harlem. They saw the famous Cotton Club. Angel asked; "Can we stop and take a picture in front of the Cotton Club? Christopher said; "Let me see if I can park. Probably nothing available until 128th St. Then we'll have to walk back down here or catch the bus." They parked on 128th near Madison. Christopher walked around to open the door for Angel. They walked back towards 125th St. They walk across Malcolm X at 125th St. They immediately see a guy packing up his perfume and cologne stand and stop.

"Man, you ain't got no Brut 33 or no Stetson out here brother; Christopher joked? This ain't no real stand, homie." "Nah, I don't carry either of those but if you really want them. I can get them for you;" the man said. "That's alright, my brother;" Christopher said. I will go with this Tom Ford and this Creed Virgin Island Water;" Christopher said. The man joked; "Okay, but you know they cost more than Brut 33, don't you?" He had a heavy Nigerian accent. "Don't worry about it brother. I will borrow money from her. She just got a job at the Red Lobster down the street. Angel hit Christopher and pointed out some perfume. "Can I smell that; she asked?

He sprayed some on her hand and she smelled it. She placed her hand under Christopher's nose. "What is that;" Christopher asked? "It's called Ferragamo;" Angel replied. "Yeah, that smells good;" Christopher said. "Oh, you have to try a bottle of this "Angel" perfume named after you;" Christopher prodded. Angel smelled it and agreed she had to have it. After they were done buying fragrances they walked towards the Apollo Theater. They see a guy selling DVDs. He had some of the classic performances that happened inside this theater. The Jackson 5, Stevie Wonder and The Supremes. Smokey Robinson, Gladys Knight and The Pips and many more compiled onto a DVD.

"How much for this DVD sir;" Angel asked? "For you pretty lady, I will let you have it for $10.00;" the man said. "Let me ask you something; Angel said. I'm looking for a movie that starred Matthew Broderick. He was a tourist in Russia, who fell in love with this lady. Then got caught up in scandal of the governments and the church trying to hide the fact that Jesus is black." "Back in the U.S.S.R;" the man yelled! "Yes, that's it. Do you have that;" she asked?

"No, that's out of print but will you folks be in town tomorrow? I can get it for you on VHS by then and put it on DVD for you." "Yeah, we'll be here homie;" Christopher said. "Okay, good, come see me tomorrow any time after 9:00a.m." "Tomorrow our schedule is kind of tight sir; Angel inserted. Will you be out here Monday morning?" "Yeah, I will be out here Monday at 9:00a.m. So any time after that is fine;" the man said.

"If I'm not here when you come. I just went across the street to use the restroom or get something to eat. The guy that will be here can reach me by cellphone. I'll be right back;" he said. "Cool; Angel said. One more thing can you take a picture of us in front of the Apollo?" "Sure pretty lady that will be no problem;" the man said. After they took the photo they walked towards the Hudson River. They crossed the street near the Cotton Club. "Excuse me sir;" Angel said to some guy walking up the street. "Do you mind taking our picture with the Cotton Club in the background for us?"

"No, I don't mind;" the man said. They stood with their arms around each other taking the photo. The man let them look to see if they liked it. He handed Angel her phone upon approval. "It's a beautiful night out here, don't you think;" Angel asked? "Yes it is beautiful. The temperature is unseasonably nice for this time of year at 76 degrees and low humidity. I LOVE NEW YORK;" Christopher screamed! "I don't know this man;" Angel yelled. Christopher wrapped his arm around her and said; "This is my woman and she loves me and NEW YORK! They walked back up along the street towards Malcolm X Blvd. Angel bought some natural care products out some stores. They then stopped to get ice cream cones from one of the local shops.

After a few hours of walking around, they decided to head back to their hotel room. Christopher drove down Broadway back into Midtown. They found a garage close to their hotel. They gathered their things out of the trunk and walked back to the hotel. "I think I need to take a shower now;" Christopher said. Angel turned on the television and began flipping through the channels. As she lay across the bed for several minutes, she heard Christopher rinsing with mouthwash. Christopher came out the bathroom and was wearing his Sean Jean pajama set. He said; "I'm all done."

"Why are you wearing all of those clothes; she asked?" "It's colder than a motherfucker up in here, that's why;" Christopher replied. He turned the temperature up and ran and jumped under the covers. Angel kissed him and went to the bathroom. Christopher turned the channel to ESPN to catch up on all the NBA highlights. "Damn, woman I could have flown to San Antonio and watched the game. Then came back before you would be finished in there;" Christopher yelled. "Anything worth having is worth waiting for;" Angel yelled back. "Then I will say duly noted and I will shut the hell up;" Christopher said in response.

Angel came out after spending quite some time it seemed to Christopher. She was wearing her silk pajamas and the slightest hint of lip gloss. No makeup but her hair had a fresh sheen and she smelled delicious. She strutted over to the bed. Angel said; "You don't rush beauty like this, my dear. I have to make sure I don't unleash it on you all at once. Too raw and uncut and you might overdose." "Well, call me a junkie, a crack head, a dope fiend or whatever you want; Christopher replied. Damn you look good woman." He got up from under the covers to a kneeling position. He kissed her until she was lying in bed.

He then unbuttoned her pajama top and was delighted to see her exposed breasts. He removed her top and worked on pulling her pants off of her. Only to find she was wearing no panties. Angel motioned to him to come to her and he does. She unbuttoned his shirt and she removed his pants. He slides off the bed to the floor. Immediately he turns the T.V. off and starts kissing Angel's pretty feet. Licking the bottom of them that were so soft and supple. He puts her feet together taking her big toes in his mouth to suck them together.

"Ummm," he moaned as he worked his way down each toe on her left foot. Then did the same on her right foot. He then kissed his way up her right leg to the depths of her valley low. His nose and lips brushed against it slightly. Next kissing his way down her left inner thigh. He then worked his way back up her body to her secret garden. He probed his tongue across it oh so softly, as if he had never done this before. Angel's body waited with anticipation as Christopher lay there staring at her vagina. He marveled at how beautiful it is with its perfect lips. He can see her wetness oozing out. He blew on her labia with intentional warm breaths of air.

He flicked his tongue out like a snake. Teasing her clitoris with just a slight touch. Then breathed on it again with a heavy, warm breath. Angel moaned at that touch thinking he would begin to feast. He made her wait seconds more. When he decided it was time, he spread her legs wider. His fingers exposed her clitoris, which he quickly grabbed with his soft lips. He gave it one long passionate suckling before running his tongue under it. His tongue drove downward between her moist vaginal lips. Just as he had driven her down the Westside Hwy earlier. When his tongue found her opening, he slowly pushed it inside of her.

From wall to wall further and deeper inside. Until his tongue can go no more. He spread her legs even wider and he licked her vaginal opening 360 degrees. Resting his tongue on that tiny space below her vagina. Angel was moaning in sweet agony. His tongue began a relentless probe of all the beauty that lay before him. Her head tossed from side to side. Christopher kissed, licked, sucked, tongue fucked and made love to her vagina. Her pussy was radiating heat of about 1000 degrees at this point. He pushed her knees up towards her chest. He could now have access to everything. He gave Angel a masterful tongue lashing.

He took his tongue and placed it on the right side of her clitoris and swept it to the left. He then placed his tongue on the left side and drove it to the right. His tongue went under her clitoris and he drove it upward before going up top and pressing it downward. He ran the tightest circles he could all around her swollen clitoris. Clockwise and then counter clockwise while his fingers pushed their way inside of her. He curled his fingers upward looking for that magic spot. "Oooh FUCK;" Angel screamed! "Oh you eat my pussy so good. Ohh baby, you eat it soooooooooooo fucking goooood.  I want to cum, oooh yes right there I want to cummmmm."

Christopher knew when she was ready as she grabbed the back of his head. He stiffened his tongue and lets her grind her pussy on his face. He slid his fingers inside of her. Trying to match her rhythm, but her hips seemed to be moving at 100 mph. "Oh God, yes right there, keep it right there….Oooh yes lick my fucking clit, lick it, lick it, LICK IT!" Christopher repositioned his head. His tongue was right in front of her swollen gland. He then sucked it firmly, while Angel tried to ram her clitoris down his throat.

"Ahhhhhhhhhhhhhhhhhh OOOOOOOOOOOOOH!" Angel screamed as her body exploded. Spraying out gushers of warm sweet juices in Christopher's face and mouth. Her inner thighs were soaked. He gently licked up all that poured from her onto her beautiful brown skin. He gave her darker toned areas special attention while cleaning up the spill. He placed his hands into Angel's hand and held them while she slowly returned back to earth. Breathing heavily, she said; "Oh my God, you're a, you're an animal when it comes to that. I can't lie and say you don't know what you're doing down there."

"Well, if I didn't I would gladly take lessons from you. Until I learned how to please you my lady;" Christopher said. "Boy it's hot in here. Did you turn the heat on or something;" Angel asked? "No, I just turned the A/C temperature up;" Christopher said. Angel got up to go adjust the temperature again. While she was bending over the controls, Christopher walked up behind her and spread her cheeks. He pushed his dick inside of her with no resistance. "Oh damn, your pussy feels so fucking good Angel. Oh baby I want this pussy. I want to eat this pussy. I want to marry this pussy."

Angel moaned in approval and Christopher ripped the curtains open. They were making love while staring out over New York City. Angel placed her hands against the glass window to brace herself. Christopher held her hips steady and rammed his dick into her with the force of a jackhammer. The cold air rising up from the A/C unit was cooling to Angel who was so hot right now. Christopher grabbed her breast with his hands. Fondling her hard nipples and ramming into her. They looked at the skyline, all the cars and people down below. "Woman, you're so perfect for me Angel; he moaned.

I should have told you the day I met you I wanted to marry you. I want to fuck you so good, your pussy calls my name in the middle of the night." "My dick's name is Kunta. Call his name Angel!" Angel screamed; "Oh yes, fuck me Kunta, fuck me Kunta! Just like that baby. Christopher rammed his dick in her harder and faster. Angel's juice was drenching him until his dick was glistening in the night lights. Then Christopher pulled his dick out of her and kneeled behind her. He tasted her sweetness yet again. He spread her legs and cheeks and buried his face in her pussy from behind.

Angel closed then opened her eyes to see the panoramic view from high above the city. Christopher licked her like she was the sweetest candy in the entire city. Angel arched her back to let him have greater access. Christopher licked her up and down devouring her pussy in open view for all the world to see. He stuck his finger inside of her then licked her in a hasty pace. Her river flowed like the Nile and he licked her oh so sweetly. He then nibbled on her cheeks before having his tongue find its way back over her dripping pussy. He took her clitoris in his mouth again between his lips. Making deep loud moaning noises he sent small vibrations through her vagina.

"Angel baby, I want you so bad; Christopher said. I need you, woman. I have to have you right now." With the curtains still wide open he grabbed her hand leading her to the bed. He then pushed her down onto the bed and quickly climbed on top of her spreading her legs with his knees. "I'm going to work this pussy tonight, and you're going to let me aren't you;" he asked?

"Yes, YES, work it baby. Take this pussy. Take it, Christopher;" Angel replied. "Take this pussy and do what you want with it." Christopher drove his dick all the way inside of her. He scooped up her legs over his arms. He fucked her intently for a few moments. His slides his arms under her shoulder blades letting her legs lay flat. He then shifted to straddle her left leg wrapping his ankle under hers. Once again, Angel had a human dildo that she could use to make herself cum. She worked her hips pressing her clitoris against his pubic bone. Quickly she came. She came again. She came again and yet again.

Angel was hysterical as her body kept erupting. Then quickly Christopher picked up her legs over his arms. He quickly started to pound into her. Her arms were wrapped tightly around him. They were both semi aware as they heard a helicopter flying near their hotel. They are possibly being watched, but neither of them cared at that moment. He slid Angel's legs further up over his shoulders. He was now power driving his dick into her. Her pretty feet were dangling on either side of his head. He turned his sweaty face and kissed her left foot and then turned to kiss the other. All the while maintaining a steady heavy pounding into her body.

"Oh yes, I want to fuck you just like this Angel; he said. Damn, you feel so fucking good to me woman. I swear I would do anything to make you mine. Anything in the whole fucking world. He licked the bottom of her feet as they were next to his face. Angel moaned in delight. "Whose pussy is this Angel; he asked? Tell me who can have this pussy anytime they want this pussy baby; Christopher asked? "You baby, you can have it, it's all yours Christopher;" Angel replied breathing heavy. "Oh fuck me, take this pussy. Make it yours. She's calling your name baby."

"She's called your fucking name and she's called this good dick's name. "Oooh that Kunta dick is so hard and so good. Don't stop fucking me like this Christopher. Don't stop baby! Promise me you won't stop making love to me like this." "I promise I won't stop Angel, as long as you let me. I will love you like no other man ever can or ever will; Christopher replied. You're the most beautiful woman from here to heaven. I will never stop kissing this lovely brown skin. Those gorgeous lips and eyes you have."

Angel then motioned for him to let her up and Christopher complied. As she lay him down, she prepared to sit on his dick. She lowered herself gently onto his rod and slowly started a rhythm. She pressed her hands firmly into his chest. Her fingers rubbed his chest as she stroked him. Up and down with the sweet movement of her hips. She adjusted position to make his dick hit her spot. Then she started to fuck him like he had just done to her. She drove her fingernails into his chest as her hips swirled and took control of his body. She leaned in to kiss him while causing her body to push his dick all the way inside of her. "Oh fuck yeah Angel, that feels so damn good baby; he cried."

I love you woman. I love you. I love you. I love you. I love you." "Whose dick is this;" Angel asked? "Nobody but yours Angel; Christopher replied. It's your dick baby. All day or all night anytime you want it. It's yours Angel." "Say my name again baby;" Angel commanded! "ANGEL; he screamed. It's your dick Angel! I don't want nobody but you baby. I need you in my life;" he pleaded. "Do you want me to let you cum baby;" Angel asked? "Oh yes ma'am, I want to cum, please let me cum Angel, he begged! I want to cum inside your pussy or wherever you will let me cum baby.

Just don't stop doing this magic you're whipping on me right now baby;" Christopher said. Angel leaned down and kissed him some more. Working her pussy with the softest grind bringing his dick to a boiling point of ecstasy. "Oh damn, Angel. I'm about to cum. I'm about to cum baby. Oooooh you're making me cum pretty baby;" he cried. Angel then drove her hips down on his dick for three quick strokes. Just as he was exploding, she slid down and took him in her mouth. If he was not her prisoner before, he completely belonged to her at this point. Christopher grabbed the back of her head to try and stay inside her mouth. Angel moved his hand and worked her mouth up and down. Without a word she told him, she's got this.

Christopher's body shuttered with delight as she drained all of him into her mouth. He lost all sense of time, space, place and his identity. The only thing he could think of at that moment was Angel. After the last spurts of his juice came to a halt, Angel kissed his inner thighs. Then his stomach and worked her way back up to his chest. "Did you like that;" she asked him?" "Liked it? I feel like I can moonwalk from here to Eritrea right now;" Christopher said. Angel laughed and they kissed before she laid her head on his chest. She gently ran her fingers through his chest hairs.

"Do you think we better get some sleep, since we have a pretty busy day;" Angel asked? "As long as I am with you woman. I don't care whether we are sleeping, walking or talking. I just want to be with you;" Christopher said. "I love being with you too Christopher. I could really get use to the fun we have together;" Angel said. "So, why don't you;" Christopher asked? "You know it's not that easy because of how things are;" Angel said.

"How are things;" Christopher asked? "You know. I'm married remember;" Angel said. "Woman, you're married to him on paper. Your mind, body and your soul are married to me. The way we make love, your spirit and DNA are also happily married to me. So do you want to do what society says is the right thing? Work out whatever issues with him, or do you want to be happy;" Christopher asked? "It's not that simple Christopher and you know it; Angel said. I took a vow before God. That was supposed to mean something before I ended up crossing the line with you.

What would my parents say if they found out? What would everybody be saying about me, about us? How could I face the people at my church?" Christopher replied; "Who gives a damn about them lonely bitches at church, or what the hell everybody has to say. Those cackling hens don't make you happy like we're happy together. I know damn well Pastor won't give anybody a fucking dime to pay any of your bills, unless you're fucking him. So some of the dudes in church may be getting their bills paid, but you ladies ain't got a shot. Women, so many of you are unhappy because you go to church and believe the dumbest shit these shady pastors have to say.

They tell you women to find you a church going man. Nigga look around you in the church. There are 20 women for every dude. This stupid ass preacher can't even count or divide. How the hell can you find a dude in there when the freaking numbers don't add up??? That's like telling me to find a California girl, we're in New York right now. Yes, I know there are some women from California here now, but the odds are real weak that I will find one my age, single and compatible for me right now."

"Yes, well I found my husband in the church. He is my age and some of the things I want;" Angel said. "Did you hear what you just said woman; he asked? You said some of the things you want. He doesn't make you happy, and you know it. Yes, he fits this ideal cliché bullshit of a man that provides and goes to work. All that yada, yada, yada. But he shouldn't be yelling at you. Calling you out of your name or pushing you around;" Christopher said. "Wait, what, where did you hear something like that; Angel asked?

Damn Jamal, always running his mouth and doesn't know what is going on." "So what is going on Mrs. Robinson;" Christopher asked? How much does he need to understand when he sees his dad pushing you? What I'm curious about, is what he may not have seen go on between you two? Has he ever hit you more than just a push;" Christopher asked? "I don't want to talk about this right now; Angel said. Can't we just enjoy the moment? Without you being all up in my business;" she asked? "You are my business woman. My corporation, my entity, my LLC and my partnership. If somebody is trying to mess with my business. I will put that motherfucker out of business;" Christopher said.

"Nobody is trying to mess with anything; Angel countered. Can we just go to sleep? So we can try to get up tomorrow and enjoy the day? "Yes, we can go to sleep, but only if you do two things for me;" Christopher said. "What's that;" asked Angel? "I need you to promise me, we'll talk about this later. And I need you to give me a kiss right now;" Christopher demanded. "Ummm, goodnight my dark and handsome man;" Angel said before kissing him. "Goodnight sweetie, I love you and you better not forget that;" Christopher said. "I love you too darling, and you better not forget that either;" she replied.

She snuggled up to him with her back to his chest. He wrapped his arms around her kissing the back of her neck. "You know men can only do this spooning thing for about 20 minutes before our arm falls off right;" Christopher said. "That's fine; Angel said. You have a spare arm, you should be okay." He tapped her buttocks with his pelvis and gently bit her on the back of her neck. "This is all I can do to hit you; he teased. Since you have my arm trapped under you woman. You're lucky I can't reach one of those light poles outside." "You need to make up your mind which pole you want to hit me with and soon; Angel said.

If I like the pole, I will let you hit me with it. If not, then I will have to get my A.K, and learn you not to hit a woman;" Angel said. "Damn, you're violent and you use bad English. You must be in a gang from Philadelphia;" Christopher said. "I'm about to be in sleepadelphia Mr. Man, goodnight;" Angel said. "Goodnight, John boy;" Christopher replied. "Goodnight grandpa;" Angel mumbled back. Goodnight Kunta;" she continued while reaching behind her to touch his penis. Christopher reached over with his free right hand and began to rub her vagina. He inserted a finger inside. "Go to sleep man;" Angel ordered. "She'll be here for you tomorrow night."

Christopher removed his finger and put it in his mouth. Tasting the moisture he uttered an "ummmm" as he sucked his finger. They soon both drifted off the sleep facing the window. Watching the night as the many people and cars moved beneath them. At some point in the night, Christopher got up to close the curtains. He didn't want the sun to awaken them first thing. At 8:30am Angel's alarm on her phone started ringing.

They both slowly started becoming conscious. Angel went to brush her teeth. Christopher lay in bed trying to steal a few more minutes of sleep. Angel came back to bed to kiss him. He turned his face away. "No woman, I haven't brushed my teeth yet;" he said. He got up to head to the sink. Angel checked her office messages on her phone. "I've told this man a million damn times;" Angel said exasperated. "What happened;" Christopher asked? "This damn man calls me every other week. Asking should he sell his stock before they go down. I've explained to him that you can't just jump in and out of the market on a whim;" Angel said.

"Why are you even getting his calls; Christopher asked? Have your people deal with him. What is the point of being the boss of your company, if you can't delegate? "Yeah, I will text Kathy and have her call him for me." "Wow you're a great assistant yourself there, Mr. Watson. I may need to hire you to be my office manager;" Angel said. "Shhh, not me; Christopher said. I don't work for nobody anymore. Especially I wouldn't work for you. I would work with you. Having you as my boss though? One of us would have to die, either by murder or suicide;" Christopher said.

"Why couldn't you work for me? I couldn't be any more difficult than working for you;" Angel said. "That's the point woman. We're both perfectionist. We want things done how we want them done. We both think our way is best so that would be immensely conflicting. In our personal lives we always compromise. In business we're both too serious. I would have to jump off the Empire State building. Or throw you off that motherfucker;" Christopher laughed. I think we could work with one another. You run your department and I run mine. If we're both working on same goals that would be a tough team to beat."

"Let's get up and get to this store so we can beat the rush; Angel said. Then get back here in time to get to the auditorium and see the play. "Yes oh mighty Isis. I hear you;" Christopher replied. In Saks fifth Ave, Angel found her way over to the evening gowns. Where she found something black, something red and something navy blue. "Hold my purse, she told Christopher. I have to try these on." "Woman, I don't walk around with a purse;" Christopher snarled. You should have brought your girlfriend for this. My doctor said I need to be watching "The Daily Show" on my phone. Not holding purses." "Man shut up and hold my darn purse please; Angel said.

I will be right back." Angel came out first with the red dress on and doesn't say anything. "My, my, my;" Christopher said. Now I know why Johnny Gill sang that song. You sure look good woman." "Thank you; Angel said. It's nice, but I'm not crazy about the straps over my shoulders." She goes back into the dressing room. Moments later, she comes out in the navy blue dress. "I likes that too; Christopher said. Not as much as the red one, but I like it. I can't reach a button in the back; Angel said. I would need you to get it for me please. If I find a blazer to go over it, I would be fine. Hold on let me go try on the black one that I think I will really like."

She returned and Christopher sat her purse in a chair and grabbed his heart like Fred Sanford. "Oh Elizabeth, I think I've already died and came to join you honey. There is an Angel standing here at the dressing room. Waiting to show me my wings." "You're so silly and simple man; Angel said. I take it you like this one. It does fit me kind of nice but I don't know." "What don't you know about it;" Christopher asked?

"Well, the purse I brought doesn't go with this dress;
Angel replied. I did bring some black pumps, but they are not
right for this dress." "So what is the darn problem, I am
asking one more again;" Christopher asked? "Well, I'm not
trying to get you to spend all of your money on me;" Angel
said. "This is not my money sweetie; Christopher said. This
is coming out of your allowance that I am giving you. So you
can blow it all in here or spend it at a coffee house for all I
care;" Christopher said. "Oh! I have an allowance? How
much is it;" Angel asked? "I'll let you know when you're
getting close;" Christopher said.

Hey remember that popcorn you had yesterday back in
Maryland?" "Yes, what about it;" Angel asked? "Well you
almost went over your limit with that;" Christopher joked.
"No, I am only kidding woman. Your allowance is about what
you make in a month, Angel." "I get twelve thousand
dollars;" Angel whispered excitedly. "Damn, you make
$12,000 a month woman. You need to give me an
allowance;" Christopher whispered. "If you needed any
money from me you know I would give it to you;" Angel said.
"I know, go ahead. You can spend your $12,000 on whatever
you like;" Christopher said.

She ran to him and kissed him three times on the lips.
"Awww thank you sweetie;" she said. I am so excited I need
to find me a pair of shoes and a new purse." "You won't have
any problems finding shoes in here; Christopher said. You go
right on ahead woman and knock yourself out. I will be right
here, watching Trevor Noah acting a fool." Angel came back
to where Christopher has been sitting for about 55 minutes. "I
think I am ready;" she said. "I am going to get the all three
dresses; she said. I couldn't decide on which pair of shoes so I
got five pairs.

I also found three perfect purses that can go with either outfit. All of it is waiting up there at the cash register for you." They walked up to the register and the clerk said good afternoon sir. How will you be paying for this cash or credit card? That will be debit card ma'am;" Christopher says. "Well would you like to apply for a Saks card and save 10% off your total today;" the clerk asked? "No ma'am, I don't believe in credit cards and haven't had one in years.

If I don't have the money in the bank, then I shouldn't be buying anything;" Christopher responded. "Well that's a good motto to live by; the clerk said. Your total comes to $5257.16 and you can swipe your card whenever you're ready." "See, I saved you almost $1800.00; Angel said. You should be thanking me." Christopher swiped his card and the lady placed all the items in bags for them. "Yeah, I will thank you alright; he said. You saved me $1800? Woman I'm black, you'll tell me anything. I hope you aren't planning to eat for the rest of this trip. We have to walk back to Maryland;" Christopher said.

"No we don't; Angel said. You know I can cover whatever other expenses that come up. On this or any other trip, so we're good." "I know you can baby. That's why we make such a good team;" Christopher said. "I think you should do a LeBron James. Opt out of your contract and come on home." "I didn't have any options in my contract silly man;" Angel said. "Yes you do, I have a lawyer that can make you an unrestricted free agent;" Christopher said.

# Let me try this black one

"Yes, but would I be the star player on the new team or just a role player;" Angel asked? "I can't believe you would even ask me that woman;" Christopher said. "Not only would you be my star player. I will build the franchise around you." They start to walk back towards the hotel to drop off the clothes they just bought. "So what type of incentives would I have to sign with this new team;" Angel asked? "Well that depends on your ball handling skills;" Christopher quipped. "Didn't you think I handled them pretty well last night during the game;" Angel asked?

Christopher rips a flyer off of a light pole as they pass by. He turns to the back handing it to Angel. "Yes you did, sign here and you're the number 1 draft pick on the team;" he said. "I better be the only damn draft pick on the team;" Angel demanded. Or we will go from playing basketball to kick balls;" Angel said. "Damn, you're a violent woman; Christopher said. I think I know what I want for my birthday now." "What do you want dear for your birthday;" Angel asked? "I think I want a restraining order;" Christopher said.

Angel burst out laughing. "Man I tell you, you're too much with your crazy self." "You're talking about kicking me in my balls and I'm crazy;" Christopher asked? "Let's hurry up and run over to the Brooks Brother's store. I will show you how to shop. You walk in the store, find what you want and roll the hell out;" Christopher said. "Men, that's because you guys grab the first thing that you find on the rack and don't care;" Angel said. "No, that's not true. You look at me woman. I have impeccable taste in clothes. It just doesn't take me 12 years as a slave in the store to find them."

They reached the hotel and someone was just stepping off the elevator. Once in the room, Angel hung up her dresses and sat her shoe boxes on the table. Christopher walked up behind her. He grabbed her hips and pulled her over to the bed. He slung her down on the bed and climbed on top of her. Kissing her lips and smiling at her big, beautiful brown eyes. "Damn, I love you woman;" he said. Angel wrapped her arms around him. She pulled him closer for more kisses and she said; "I love you too."

"Good, now let's go find me a suit;" Christopher said. They get back downstairs and hailed a cab. 346 Madison Ave please; Christopher said. Angel paid the driver in cash and they went into the store. Christopher looked at the suits they had and saw a nice black one, a light gray and navy blue suit. "Let me try this black one my man;" he said to the store clerk. The clerk unlocked a dressing room for him and he tried it on. "Everything fits, except the pants are a little too long. Can I get these hemmed up bro;" Christopher asked? "I'm sorry. The tailor is not in on Sundays and won't be in until tomorrow morning. Would you like to pick them up tomorrow afternoon;" the clerk asked?

Christopher turned to Angel and said; "Angel, give me five hundred dollars please. I don't have any cash on me right now." Angel handed Christopher five one hundred dollar bills from her wallet. Christopher handed them to the clerk. "Hey, my man, can I get these hemmed up like in the next twenty minutes;" Christopher asked? "Our tailor can be here in 10 minutes. I will get him down here right now for you sir. In the meantime, let Jack chalk those pants for you. So that they will be ready when he arrives;" the clerk said. "Thank you homie, I appreciate it;" Christopher said.

"Now, can you recommend a nice shirt and tie for this suit. I'll go look at some sweaters while my suit gets fixed; he said. See I'm done Angel. Get in and get out, just like sex;" he smiled. "I'm watching my man take charge and make things happen for himself;" Angel said. He kissed her quickly on the lips as the guy finished marking his pants. Christopher went back into the dressing room and changed back into his jeans. He handed the pants to Angel to give to the tailor. The Tailor had just arrived to do the alterations. Christopher came out and found some shoes and said; "Perfect."

Now, all I have to do is get a Movado from down the street. I will be as sharp as a Johnny Cochran use to be in a courtroom." "I hear you sharp man, that suit does look nice on you;" Angel said. "Well it was either a suit or I was going to let my jeans hang off my ass. With my drawers showing;" Christopher said. "Shoot, you wouldn't be going nowhere with me looking like that;" Angel responded. "What! After all we've been through together; Christopher said. You would kick me to the curb? Just because I like to show my underwear to a bunch of dudes? I thought our love was stronger than that Angel."

"Oh, I would still love you Christopher; Angel said. I just wouldn't be seen anywhere in public with you, that's all." "So, you only date men with self-respect is what you're telling me woman;" Christopher asked? "You know it, brother man;" Angel replied. "If you don't respect yourself, it will be hard for me to respect you." "Alrighty then;" Christopher said. "Remind me not to do no gay shit like sagging my pants. I don't need no dudes to watch my ass." "I don't think I have to remind you of that at all;" Angel said. "Here you are sir, your alterations are all done; the clerk said.

If you will follow me over to the register, we can get this taken care of this for you right away." They walked over to the register and the clerk asked will that be cash or credit? "That will be cash;" Angel said. She cut Christopher off from responding. "Alright ma'am, that comes to $1987.33, but I can get you 10% off. If you'd like to open up a charge account with us today;" the clerk said. "No, I don't need an account;" Angel said. She counted out 20 one hundred dollar bills and handed them to the clerk. "Damn, are you carrying a bank up in there woman;" Christopher asked? "Man, hush; I got this;" Angel replied.

"Okay, shutting the fuck up in 3, 2, 1;" Christopher said. "Sometimes that's the best thing to do. When your lady wants to take charge;" the store clerk said. "Yeah, I know; Christopher said. Especially when they are violent like her." "Oh, I don't believe this beautiful lady has a violent bone in her body;" said the clerk. "Okay, you're letting her pretty looks fool you my man; Christopher said. You can't do that. Look, I need you to do me a favor. Check the back of milk cartons next week. If you see me on one of them, show the police the surveillance tape from today. So they know who they're looking for;" Christopher said. "I don't know what I am going to do with this man I swear;" Angel said.

"Did you hear that? She's already making plans to do something to me sir. Please dial 911 right now, before it's too late. You may be the last one to see me alive;" Christopher pleaded. "Oh, my Lord, this man and his dramatics;" Angel exclaimed. "Come on here, man. I have no plans to kill you, in New York;" Angel joked. Christopher wore an expression of stunned surprise and mocked fear. "I'm black, you'll tell me anything. Then kill me in New York; he said.

Angel handed him his clothes to carry in one hand. She took the other hand and led him out the store. They ran back to the hotel and both felt a little hungry. They ran downstairs to a Café' and ordered lattes made with almond milk and baked goods. They didn't eat anything heavy, because they were pressed for time. They also wanted to be hungry for after the show. Once they left the café, they returned to the hotel. Christopher took a shower and then came out to shave his head. Angel then showered. He made sure to clean the sink, so that Angel could use it once he was done.

Once they were dressed and both looking like royalty, they headed downstairs. Angel waited in the lobby, while Christopher retrieved the car from the garage. The afternoon was absolutely gorgeous. The temperature once again, was only in the high 70s with low humidity. Christopher pulled up in front of the hotel. A concierge escorted Angel to the car and opened the door for her. "I don't have any cash on me right now homie;" Christopher told the concierge. I will stop at an ATM before I come back. What's your name?" "My name is T.J;" the man said. "Okay T. J, what time do you get off tonight;" Christopher asked?

"I will be here until 11p.m sir;" T.J. replied. "Cool, we should be back before then;" Christopher said. They then drove to the theater and parked in a garage. After the play, they walked out of the theater arm in arm. Angel raved about how good the play was. "Yes, it was very good;" Christopher said. That Denzel guy, if he works on his craft, he may turn out to be big time someday. I can show him a few things about acting. I didn't want to go onstage and embarrass him in front of erriebody." "Yeah, I'm sure you could have taught Denzel nothing;" Angel said.

"Lawd that man can step on my stage and act anytime." "So what are you saying? You think that amateur can act better than I can;" Christopher asked? "There is nothing amateur about Denzel baby. Nothing at all and seeing him live just made my day. No my week, hell the whole year;" Angel said. "Alright, I get it. You think he can act and whatever, whatever;" Christopher said. That play was well produced though." "Of course it was; Denzel was in it;" Angel said. "Damn, do you want me to try and go get his phone number for you? You're drooling all over this dude like he's a star or something;" Christopher said.

"No, I'm sorry baby. I have the only star I need right here holding my hand;" Angel said. They walked toward the garage they parked at. They waited for the valet to bring them their car. The streets are extremely crowded with people and cars. Hundreds of cabs trying to muscle their way on the streets. To pick up people leaving the theater and other venues in the area. Christopher and Angel finally got their car to return to the hotel. Christopher saw an ATM and pulled over to withdraw money. "What are you doing;" Angel asked? "I'm going to get some money. So I can hook my man T.J. up, when we get back."

"Man, I have plenty of cash in the safe in our room. I told you I got you sugar;" Angel said. "Alright, I guess I will just trust when you say you have my back that you have my back. I hope you know that I have yours too, my African Queen;" Christopher said. "Of course I know that; Angel said. Which is why I don't mind having your back. Now let's get back to the hotel. So I can get out of this dress and into some comfortable clothes. Then we can go eat. Those cashews and Malibu/pineapple we had at intermission just made me hungry." "Alright woman, I'm driving right now;" he said.

When they get back to the hotel, T.J. is standing right outside. Christopher called to him. "T.J, my man, my woman has a couple of dollars in her other purse upstairs. We are going to go and change clothes real quick and be right back. Can you watch this car for us and make sure it doesn't get towed? We promise to take care of you when we come down okay." "No problem sir, I will guard it with my life;" T.J. said. They ran upstairs and carefully hung up their suit and dress and change into jeans and shirts. Christopher grabbed his lightweight jacket. Just in case Angel was cold inside the restaurant. Angel grabbed some cash out of the safe.

Christopher looked at the amount she had in there. "Remind me to rob your ass when we get back;" he said. They went downstairs and T.J. was waiting patiently with the keys to their car. He handed the keys to Christopher. Angel handed T.J. 100 dollars. Thank you so very much, ma'am and sir. You are too kind. They drove down 53rd Ave and maneuvered through the city. They ended up on the Westside Hwy headed towards uptown. They drove past 116th and continued to 125th. Angel wanted to take some pictures of some of the historic buildings. She snapped a picture of General Grant Projects as they passed by. Christopher pulled over quickly. Angel stepped out and take another photo of the Cotton Club behind them.

Once they drove up to Lennox Ave, Christopher turned right heading towards Amy Ruth's. They parked near that location. "My, look at all these people in line waiting to get in for some soul food;" Angel said. "Yeah, it's like this at Sylvia's and here; Christopher said. We just have to wait with all these people." "I'm black, you'll tell me anything; Angel said. I bet we can walk right in." "Go ahead and catch a Harlem beat down if you want; Christopher replied.

# The purest friendship

While standing in line Christopher took a few pictures. Angel posed under the awning. She looked so beautiful in her flowered pattern dress. Angel snapped a few photos of the restaurant and streets. Then they asked the guy in front of them if he would snap one of them together. Christopher walked over to Angel and stood behind her. He wrapped his arms around her waist. He put his face next to hers while the man took the photo. "Now, let me take one of you;" Angel said. She thanked the man for helping them out.

Christopher stood so that the background of 116th St. was behind him. As Angel snapped the picture, his lips formed to say; "I LOVE YOU!" Angel burst out laughing as she looked at the photo. Christopher asked; "why are you laughing?" "I caught you with your mouth open; Angel replied. You look crazy." "Well, I am crazy woman, crazy about you;" Christopher said. Just then a hostess came out and allowed a few more people inside. Now they were certain to be in the next group. They were the first two in what was becoming an increasingly long line. "Hey, you can go ahead and delete that picture now Angel;" Christopher said.

"Why would I do that;" asked Angel? "Because you got me looking all funny when you took it. People might think I was yawning or something;" Christopher said. "First of all, nobody is going to see these pictures but me; Angel said. I will know exactly what you were saying when I took it. I have a time and date stamp on it. I will know when you told me you loved me.

"Man this line is getting long;" Christopher said. "I didn't realize so many white folks loved Soul food like this;" Angel said. "Oh this place and Sylvia's packs them in; Christopher replied. Harlem and Northeast DC are both changing. "Yes there are a lot of new places opening along Benning Road in DC; Angel said. "Hey how are you doing Chris;" a voice spoke. Christopher turned to see it was his friend Andrew. "Hey what's up Andrew;" Christopher said. They shook hands and embraced. "This is my girlfriend Angel here Andrew;" Christopher said. "How do you do Angel;" Andrew said. "I'm fine, nice to meet you;" Angel replied.

"Baby, you know how blacks are always saying the white man be holding us back? The white man won't let you get ahead; Christopher asked? This is him. Don't let the "Al Bundy" look fool you. They all laughed. "No you can't pin that on me my friend; Andrew said. I just work at the Virgin Music store. They only gave me power over 8-Tracks. Ooops next group is up, let me get in line. Come by the store sometime Chris. You know when I'm there. Nice meeting you Angel." "Okay, next 10 people can come in now;" the hostess said. Christopher and Angel hurried inside. Angel excused herself to go to wash her hands. Christopher sat at the table and texted his investment group.

Angel returned while he is waiting on a reply. Christopher put his cell phone down. "Who was that you were texting;" Angel asked? "I was just talking to April about a deal;" Christopher said. "Oh is that the building in East Baltimore;" Angel asked? "Yeah, that's the one; said Christopher. They've moved the settlement date on us about three times already. I'm about to say to hell with them. April and the group really wants this in our portfolio."

"It's an old apartment complex. We are going to have to renovate and convert to luxury Townhomes. Then we can sell them. My brother owns a home improvement company so we're using him. Everything done at, or close to cost to save us some money;" Christopher said. "Wow, you guys have a lot going on. How did you get into all of this stuff;" Angel asked? "Well, I have always had an idea that I wanted to be a business man of some kind. I just didn't know exactly what; Christopher said. Then, I met this lady who did bootleg taxes. I was just trying to get back $5000 in my taxes when I went to her. She starts telling me what kind of investments I should pursue. Now and down the line. She suckered me into investing right away?

Next thing you know, we're good friends. We started talking about our dreams and goals. Come to find out, we had a lot in common. Even though on paper, we seemed like the odd couple. We both had big dreams and believed in ourselves. She was crazy though so I tried to ditch her in Atlanta. I moved to the DMV only to find out she was moving there too. She got married to some dude and then I got married. In the DMV I met so many smart business people that expanded my ideas. However she definitely was the building block.

"Were you and this woman intimate? It sounds like you liked her more than just as a mentor;" Angel said. "No, it wasn't an intimate relationship at all; Christopher said. We never thought about crossing that line, at least I didn't. I know it had to be killing her. Not being able to touch all this sexy, dark chocolate woman candy though. They both laughed at the joke. "Anyway; he continued. I think we had the purest friendship you could ask for. I never thought about her in a sexual way, until that night we had hell of a heated argument.

Although she had pissed me off to the highest of pisstivity, as Robin Harris use to say. I wanted her so bad that night." "Good evening, my name is Lashelle. I will be your server tonight. Can I start you off with a drink?" "Yes you can Lashelle; Angel said. Do you want some tea or are you getting something else Christopher?" "Tea is fine with me;" Christopher said. "Okay, I will be right back with your drinks. Then I'll take your order, or are you ready now;" Lashelle asked? "Do you know what you want to eat ma'am;" Christopher asked? "Yes, I think I will go with The President Barack Obama, baked please. What about you;" Angel asked? "I think I will have The Honorable Bill Perkins." "Excellent choices; Lashelle said.

I will get that baked chicken and salmon right out." "Thank you very much Lashelle;" Christopher said. "So, you really wanted your Accountant really bad that night, huh;" Angel asked? "I sure did, but not as bad as I want her right now;" Christopher said. "Well, as an owner of an Investment and Accounting firm. I would never get involved with one of my clients; Angel said. Especially if he were a good friend. When you cross that line it tends to ruin the friendship;" Angel said. "Well, I don't know about that; Christopher said. My Accountant and I are still really close. In fact, I love her and would marry her.

"Generally speaking and of course there are exceptions to every rule; Angel said. I think when friends cross the line things get cloudy. Inevitably, someone is going to catch feelings. Maybe they start acting crazy because things are not progressing the way they want them. Or on the timetable they want them to. Then, they try to force things and a big mess ensues. "Well that's for those weak guys, because I am not trying to force anything;" Christopher said.

Another way to look at it; he continued. Friends have a better chance to build a relationship from the ground up. They bond with each other without sex clouding their judgement;" Christopher said. Angel replied; "If you and this woman didn't have any technical issues. Do you think you two could get along?" Being you're both such perfectionist and so opinionated? I mean, that kind of woman is not going to be silent, from what I hear. If she has something to say, then she is going to say it.

I mean she's not disrespectful and is not going to try and berate or belittle you. She however doesn't like to be ignored." "That's perfect for me; Christopher responded. I like a woman who has an opinion. Especially if she has some brains in her head and can produce good ideas. I don't want a woman who says, you go out and hustle boo. I'll be here watching Hollywood Divas. You just let me know when it's time to live it up. I could marry any one of those women tonight, if I wanted to. I want a woman I can brainstorm with. A woman who can come up with good ideas.

A woman who knows how to make those ideas work. I also want one that will listen to my ideas as well. For instance, I respect your business Angel. I am very proud of all your accomplishments. I just think you work too damn hard. If I were your man, I would help you restructure your business. Put more responsibility on your staff. So we could spend more time making love and traveling." "So, you're one of those guys that wants a stay- at- home wife? So you can come home and get your freak on all the time;" Angel asked? "No, not at all;" Christopher said. I want a woman who works and makes the kind of money you make. I just don't want you working such long days."

"How do you propose that I cut my hours; Angel asked? I have so many clients and so much business to take care of, Mr. Man." "That's easy; Christopher said. You promote your assistant to do all the stuff you do. Have her hire somebody to do what she does now. Then, you just have weekly meetings with them. Make sure your vision and your standards are being met. Occasionally, you call or meet your clients at random. Just to make sure they verify what you're being told by your folks. Then you join my investment group." "What would I need to join your investment group? What makes you think I could be an asset to the group;" Angel asked?

"Well normally, we ask that anyone who joins the group start off with $25,000. For you I think, I can get that fee down to about $1.50; Christopher said. I will make you the vice president of operations who gets no salary. You will get an even split of every investment we make going forward." "Hmmm, that sounds like a deal, but I don't take charity from people. Unless I really needed it;" Angel said. "It's not charity baby. Sometimes we make a little money off of investments and sometimes we make a lot. When we make a lot, we'd would want to shield some of our tax liability;" Christopher said.

"Ah, like tax sheltered investments. With an in house Accountant who wouldn't charge for services;" Angel asked? "Yeah, there is a method to my madness;" Christopher said. "Not to mention the personal benefits to me." "Like what for instance;" Angel asked? "Well for one, I get to see you more when we have our meetings; he said. I think everybody, I mean erriebody, would get the things they want;" Christopher said. "How do you know everybody doesn't already have everything they want;" Angel asked?

"That's one Honorable Bill Perkins for you sir, and one President Obama for you, ma'am. I will get you a refill on your teas. Is there anything else I can get you;" Lashelle asked? "No ma'am, I think we are good; Christopher said. I know everybody doesn't have everything they want. Some of us work too damn hard; he said. They work hard because they have to be superwoman all the time. Although she knows her current Clark Kent tries. She's just afraid he will let the house burn down, if she ever took off her cape for a day or two.

I think she knows that she'd do better with a Superman. He would not only keep the house from burning down. He would be adding rooms on to it. Then expanding the land by 40 acres and a mule." "Is that right; Angel said. I'm black, you'll tell me anything. When you don't actually have to provide any proof of insurance. I wouldn't want to cancel my policy and then get into an accident." "Precisely why I am offering you the investment group policy; Christopher said. At a deeply discounted rate, so that you will have coverage effective immediately. As a matter of fact, I can have my attorney draw up a contract. Making you a full partner effective last week."

"Interesting Mr. Man, you certainly provide some tempting offers; Angel said. It gives one a lot to think about. However you do know I am a cautiously optimistic person. I have to fully analyze and process this information. Just like with you sir, that won't happen until I'm laying down trying to go to sleep. "Yes the curse of being thinkers; Christopher said. Now eat your food, before it gets cold." "Let me get a piece of your salmon please sir; Angel asked? That looks really good." "Go ahead and cut it with your fork, woman. If you have the flu or Ebola, I've already got it too; Christopher said.

# I want what I want when I want it

"Thank you, now can I have some of your greens too;" Angel asked? "Damn, woman why don't you just pull out a gun and take my plate;" Christopher asked? "I don't need a gun to take anything from you man. I will just take it; Angel said. Then look at you like, what you gonna do?" "Well if you take all my food I will have nothing to eat; Christopher said. I will have no choice but to crawl under this table and eat you. Right here in front of all these people." "You ain't got the kind of nerve to do no such thing;" Angel dared.

Christopher pushed back his chair and began to crawl under the table. Angel whispered in a loud voice; "Man GET UP FROM THERE! I swear you're so crazy." "Just for that, I am taking your chicken leg;" Christopher said. "You can have anything of mine you want;" Angel answered. "Likewise; Christopher said. Do you want the keys to my Escalade? The keys to my safe deposit box? You already know the combination to my safe. You have keys to my house. So I don't know what else I could give you;" he said. "A ring would be nice; Angel uttered. Oops, did I say that out loud?"

"Yes, I think you did; Christopher said. I was thinking this Tuesday I will be back in Maryland. I was going to go by Glover's Jewelry store. I was going to buy a two carat certified diamond ring. One that is about a size….. What size do you wear;" Christopher asked? "I wear a size 7, but I can't take a two carat diamond ring from you;" Angel said. "It's not for you;" Christopher said. "I am buying it for my great, great, great grandmother. She's dead now but in case she comes back I will give it to her. I just want you to hold it for me, until she comes by."

"I know you're joking about that but why are you buying a ring;" Angel asked? "Look woman, you do my taxes, not tell me how to spend my money; Christopher said. I think you're getting too big for your britches. Starting to smell your pee;" he said. "That must be your grandmother talking; Angel laughed. "You just hold on to the ring for me in a safe place. I will pick it up from you if I need it;" Christopher said. "Your great grandmother might come back when she finds out you're spending $16,000;" Angel said. "I am making an investment in something or someone very valuable;" Christopher said.

Maybe I'll end up with what I am investing in. Then no amount of money would have been too much to spend. I believe some treasures are priceless. I personally have traveled many places in this world. Yet I have not seen anything more precious. More valuable than this particular gem;" Christopher said. "So do you think you will ever get what it is you're after; Angel asked? Or do you think fate will keep it just within the tip of your outstretched fingers? Maybe swinging in and out of your grasp. Not letting you hold it forever, like you want?" "Well, fate is a funny dude sometimes and it drives me nuts; Christopher said. I hate chances.

Usually I want what I want when I want it. For the most part, I get it. This gem however can't just be walked up to and purchased;" Christopher added. Angel replied; "Well in that case, you make sure you weigh all the risk. The pros and cons of your investment. Don't try to time the market, I would recommend. You just have to be patient until those dividends pay off. Of course in the market, investments don't guarantee a rate of return. You want to pick your stocks carefully as I would;" she said.

"I am willing to take every risk in the book;" Christopher said. Plus some written down on scratch paper that didn't make the book. Whatever to get this gem to be called solely mine. Anyway you ate all my damn Salmon and half my greens. I guess we have had a delicious dinner. You can tell me about it on the way back to midtown;" Christopher said. "Oh, you ordered that plate for you. How was I to know that;" Angel asked sarcastically? "Whatever; Christopher said. Excuse me, Lashelle. Can we get the check, please?" "No problem sir; said Lashelle. How was everything?"

"You have to ask her Lashelle. Do you take police reports for stolen property;" Christopher asked? "No, I'm afraid not sir. I can bring you out something else if you like;" Lashelle said. "No I did get to eat half of my food, and I ate some of hers;" Christopher said. Christopher handed her back the signed receipt. "Well thank you sir for your generous tip;" Lashelle said. "No problem ma'am; Christopher said. The service was excellent." "Well you two come back and see us again soon;"Lashelle said. "We will do that;" Christopher said. He gave Angel the guest copy receipt and said; "I need this taken off my taxes. This was a business meal. I was trying to get you in bed to take care of business." "I don't think it works like that;" Angel said.

They arrived back into midtown. They parked the car in the garage and decided to go for a walk. "This has been a beautiful weekend I have had; Angel said. Thank you so very much for bringing me up here. For taking me to see Denzel and for all the beautiful things we've done. I really wish this weekend could last a little bit longer." "Anytime you wish to come back up here. You just let me know; he said. I will bring you back. Maybe next time, I will get to eat my own food;" Christopher laughed.

"I will give you something to eat when we get back inside;" Angel said. "Then I am good to go;" Christopher said. "Here take a picture across from the Empire State Building. If I see King Kong falling over your head, I will tell you to move;" Christopher said. "Ha Ha, Mr. Funny man. If you see King Kong, you better come and rescue me without hesitation or delay;" Angel said. "You got that baby; Christopher said. I will run right over to fight a big three story tall gorilla. Even if he could crush me with his pinky finger. As soon as he grabs you I'm going to run around the corner. Then I can sneak up on him from the back.

So when you see me run after King Kong grabs you, don't panic Angel. I'm coming right back." "Let me understand this because I need clarity; Angel said. You told me you loved me and now you won't stand and fight an ape for me." "Well everybody has to draw the line somewhere; Christopher replied. I draw mine at fighting a big ass giant gorilla that's pissed off;" Christopher said. I won't forget you though, woman." "Is that what we're doing now; Angel asked? Letting me get killed because you're scared?"

"Anyhow woman, let's go back towards Times Square. Do you want to catch a movie or something;" Christopher asked? "No, we already sat through a play today; Angel said. We can go back to the hotel and see what's on T.V. Or order a movie. What time are we leaving out tomorrow?" "We have to get up and go uptown to get your movie; Christopher said. Then drop the car off at the rental place. Hopefully get them to take us back to Penn Station. So we need to be up at least by 8a.m. We can get that done and catch our train at 1:45p.m. We'll just grab something to eat at the train station, until we get home."

"Okay sounds like a plan;" Angel said. "Why don't you run into this pharmacy store and get some popcorn? In case we find a good movie on T.V." "I am going to call Jamal. Make sure he is back home and ready for school tomorrow. Then make sure my sister knows what time he has to be out the door." "How about you wait until we get back to the hotel to make that phone call. Or at least until I come back out the store;" Christopher said. "Why? I'm going to just be standing right out here while you're inside;" Angel said.

"Cell phone snatching is a big issue here, just like in Baltimore. I don't want you pulling out your phone without me being here. So like I said, wait or wait, those are your two options woman;" Christopher said. "Alright Mr. Man I love it when you take charge." They exited the store moments later. "Now may I use my phone to call my son sir, or will you arrest me;" Angel asked?" "I might put you in handcuffs soon enough. You'll probably like it though, now make your phone call;" Christopher said. After talking on the phone for about 15 minutes, Angel hung up. "Now we can go watch that movie;" she said.

"Well, first I am going to take a shower real quick; Christopher said. Then I can get comfortable and lay in bed." "Oh I will take a shower first; Angel said. While you shower, I can pack our things. Then see if you're trying to do something tonight;" Angel said. "I'm trying make it do what it do;" Christopher said. After he showered Christopher began brushing and flossing his teeth. He found Angel in bed with the T.V. remote in hand fast asleep. He helped her out of her slippers. He tried to figure out a way to get her under the covers without waking her. Of course he was unsuccessful. Angel mumbled; "What time is it?"

"It's 10:45p.m dear. I just want to get you under the sheets so that you can sleep comfortable;" Christopher said. "Did I fall asleep;" Angel asked? "Yes, but that's fine. You had a long weekend. We didn't exactly sleep all night last night;" Christopher said. "Let me get up and put some water on my face. I will be as good as new; Angel said. Then I'll be ready." "Ready for what;" Christopher asked? "You're tired so go to sleep." "You won't be mad;" Angel asked?

"Mad about what? I'm spending time with the most beautiful woman in the world. What would I possibly be mad about;" Christopher asked? Angel dragged herself to the sink to brush her teeth. Christopher checked the locks on the door and packed their clothes away. Angel finished rinsing and she strolled back to bed. She kissed Christopher on the mouth. "Good night sweetie;" she said. She made a valiant attempt to try and watch television with Christopher. In a matter of minutes she succumbed to sleep.

Christopher stayed up and watched another 30 minutes of television. He too was overcome by sleep. He turned on his side to watch Angel dreaming. She instinctively turned onto her side and pushed her back into his chest. He ran his fingers lightly across her forehead and into her hair. He then kissed her arm and shoulder. Angel smiled as if to say she feels safe and secure at this moment. Christopher then laid his head down on the pillow and fell asleep as well. Hours later Christopher thinks he's dreaming. He sees Angel get up from bed and go over to the sink to rinse her mouth. She is wearing no clothes. His mind is trying to orient him to his surroundings. He looks for the familiarity of his home but realizes this is not it. Then he remembers Angel and he are 30 flights up in New York City.

"What are you doing woman;" Christopher mumbled? "It's 6:30am and I'm about to have breakfast;" she replied. "Did you order room service or something;" Christopher asked? "No, I am about to have you;" Angel said. She hands him a cup of mouth rinse and he goes over to the sink. He washes his face and Angel stood behind him with her arms folded. Patting her foot she says; "I am waiting Mr." He turns around and they walk back over to the bed. "You do know it's the break of dawn and people are not up yet; Christopher said. Looks like you're up to me; Angel replied.

Angel grabbed his penis and turned him to her. She kissed him with that magical kiss that makes him so weak for her. She removed his shirt and pulled his pajama pants down to his ankle. He quickly took them all the way off. She then pushed him gently to lay back in the bed. He asked; "Am I in trouble?" "You could say that;" Angel replied. She kissed his legs and worked her way up to his inner thighs. She kissed both thighs while letting her natural hair brush up against his genitalia. She gently nibbled his left inner thigh and then his right. Sensuously running her tongue across his testicles as she moved to each thigh.

"Do you like me licking your balls;" she asked? "Ooooh, yes baby, I love it when you do that to me. You make it feel so good;" he answered. Angel then climbed onto the bed and laid next to him. She lay in an angle where she had complete access to his naked body. She sucked his penis and shifted it so that she can lick his testicles which drove him crazy. She stroked his penis with her soft hand and moistened it with her mouth. Alternating back to licking his balls. The moans he made let her know that he really liked that. Christopher was literally tearing the sheets off the bed.

She decides to take some time and spend licking and kissing his testicles. Her gorgeous full lips and her sweet tongue were heavenly to him. "Angel, I love you, I love you, I love you baby;" Christopher moaned. Angel wouldn't stop to respond. He didn't know whether to close his eyes, do sit ups or shake, rattle and roll. Angel was pulling him deeper and deeper into her spell. She was adamant in her pleasing him. She begins to write her name with the tip of her tongue across his balls. Christopher shook almost as if he caught the Holy Ghost.

# The Sunlight Rushed In

Christopher's hips moved wildly trying to catch the sweetness of her touch. Angel took him on a journey to paradise where only gods must be allowed. His hands caressed the back of her neck and massaged her scalp. Her shiny, curly, natural hair looked so beautiful in the morning light. Her lips and tongue continued to send shivers of riveting pleasure pulsing through his body. With the force of what seemed like laser light radiated energy. He knew in this moment, how black men had been motivated to build the Pyramids. He was as high as any man had ever been off of cocaine or PCP.

The only side effect he was suffering from, was falling deeper in love with this woman. Angel gently kissed his balls as if she were making love to them. She ran her fingernails gently across his tight stomach. All Christopher wanted to do at this point was scream her name. He wanted life in another galaxy to know of this goddess. Her chocolate kisses had every part of him ready to explode. His eyes closed tightly and he just enjoyed the journey. Then he was given one kiss on his inner left thigh. Suddenly he no longer felt her touch.

Although he had no complaints about the service, he still felt like there was some unfinished business. Apprehensive about opening his eyes, he slowly did. Only to see Angel crawling on all fours from the bed over to the window. She pulled the curtains open with the rod. She then turned to him. As the sunlight rushed in she motioned with her index finger. She summoned for him to come to her. He walked over with a raging hard dick. He met her on her knees with her mouth open ready to receive him.

Those luscious full lips of hers felt beyond heavenly belief. She wrapped them around his shaft and sucked him deep into her mouth. Deep enough until she could tickle his balls with her tongue. Christopher briefly looked down at all the people hustling through the city. Then at some of the buildings that surrounded them. He and Angel knew somebody in one of those buildings were watching them. Neither of them cared as he pumped his penis in and out of her mouth.

The world belonged to them. They were standing high on top of it like the god and goddess that they were. Sharing the true expressions of love so that all the world may take note. He watched her glowing beautiful skin and gorgeous face. He watched those incredible lips make love to him and was ready to faint. Angel had complete and total control of Christopher and she knew it. She knew exactly how to push all of his buttons. How to bring him the most exquisite of pleasure. She opened her eyes and looked up at him. Inviting him with her look to work his penis deeper into her mouth.

He became intoxicated from her eyes and the sight of those beautiful full lips. The sweet humming sound she was making was too intense for his resistance. He stroked into her deeper, so that his testicles tapped on her chin. Then he felt her tongue beseeching him. Urging him to the pending volcanic eruption boiling inside of him. Angel didn't flinch. She took her hands and grabbed his hips pulling him in to her completely. He released warm gushers of sweet creamy icing into her mouth. Christopher's body seemed to implode. He may have fallen if Angel hadn't held him up. Angel unmistakably was Christopher's weakness. It was like she was taking his breath away and giving him life. All in the same moment. She was able to choose either one at her whim.

Angel kept him inside of her, until he had ceased convulsing. She chose to grant him life. He looked at her and knew, he was more in love with her than he was an hour ago. He took her hand to help her to her feet. He kissed her eyes and wrapped his arms around her. "You're the most precious woman ever;" he whispered in her ear. She kissed his neck. She kissed both sides of his chocolate face and then she kissed his lips. Holding him tightly, as if to tell him without words how precious he was to her as well.

With the curtains still open and both of them completely naked, they kissed. They kissed as if they knew God and all of New York City were watching with approval. Christopher then led her to the side of the bed. Her back was facing the window and she faced the bed. He pushed her gently to get on the bed. He positioned her on all fours and he slid his upper body under her. Like an automobile mechanic working on a car he went to work. Angel knew exactly what to do as she sat on his face while he licked and sucked her pussy. He spread her cheeks apart and licked her up and down. Her melanin rich areas he made sure he sucked and licked with a vengeance.

She took her right hand and pressed against his forehead. Now she could control the angle of his mouth. She was spreading her sweet nectar all over his face. "I'm going mark you with my scent baby; Angel said. So that any woman that meets you will know you belong to me. They will know that you bear the scent of this goddess. I'm going to spread it all over you face, neck and body. Oooh yes drink from the Queen's cup;" she said. Angel closed her legs tightly against the side of his face. She pushed her hips forward and her clitoris down into his waiting mouth. While her vaginal lips were kissing his lips and chin.

"Yes, that's it baby. Eat this pussy like you really want it;" Angel said. You do really want it, don't you;" she asked? When Christopher tried to answer, she brought her weight down. Grinding her clitoris up against his nose. Pouring her juices from her vagina into his mouth. "Ooooh you make me feel so good Christopher, so damn good;" she moaned. Christopher maneuvered his hands under her body. He then spread her labia apart and licked her clitoris without any impediment.

He lifted his head off the mattress and sucked it in his mouth. Followed by jamming his tongue inside of her and swirling it all around. His hands and fingers were roaming in a multitude of directions on her body. Angel was grinding her hips on his face as if she were on a mission. When Angel moaned louder, he slid his body from under hers and stood behind her. He pushed her head down onto a pillow. With her still kneeling he drove his face into her wetness with fierceness. He ran his tongue up and down her slit. Licking everything before sucking on her vagina. She made him drink as much of her juice as he could get.

"Ahhhhh Daaayyyaaaammm;" Angel moaned. His mouth seemed to be all over her. All over her most sensitive erogenous zones at the same time. He licked her cheeks as if he were a painter applying a coat of paint. Then returning back to that beautiful slit and pushing his tongue inside her. Once again he was flicking his tongue like a snake. As far as he could get it to go in her. "Ummmm your pussy tastes so good Angel; he said. I could just lick you all day and all night. You beautiful, sexy, chocolate Queen." Christopher kissed her at the base of her spine. Running his tongue from there until her reached her clitoris. His tongue was followed by his fingers that probed inside of her.

He then kissed her pussy like it was her mouth. That began to excite Angel intently. Ooooh, you're going to make me cummmmmmm. You're going to make me…" She gasped as he grabbed her cheeks and spread them wide, licking her up and down ferociously. Ramming his tongue in her pussy meeting her river flow. Angel began to feverishly grind her hips into his eager face. Her hands clenched the bed sheets while her face dug into the pillow. Angel glanced out the window and saw window washers at the lipstick building. One appeared to have binoculars watching them but she didn't care.

"Cum for me Angel; Christopher pleaded. Say my name when you cum baby. Say my motherfucking name." He kissed her pussy once again and rammed his tongue in and out of her. Until he heard that now familiar breathing of her inevitable climax. He pushed even harder into her with his face buried inside her pussy. Her breathing slowed warning Christopher that he had lost the spot. He desperately searched for the right place to lick and brought her back. Angel began panting and moaning uncontrollably.

Her orgasm had immense viscosity. Passion forced out her waterfall onto his face and into his mouth. The thought of knowing she was being watched heightened Angel's climax. Her lava eruptions came out in squirts and a high pitched scream. She almost knocked him onto the floor. Like the committed lover he was, he grabbed her hips even tighter. He held firm as she shook out every delicious drop of her love. She then fell forward onto the bed depleted from the exertion. Angel was only vaguely aware of her name for a few seconds. Christopher slowly kissed her back as she began to grasp reality.

Her perspiration even tasted good as he kissed her from side to side. Making his way to her shoulder blades and then the back of her neck. Angel still breathing heavy, struggled to speak. "Oh my God that was so good. You are trying to wear me out up in here. I think you've succeeded. I need a nap;" she said. "You can take about a thirty minute nap;" Christopher replied. We have to get up soon and go take care of a few things before we leave. "I can sleep on the train when we leave; Angel said. Right now, I want you inside of me."

They kissed and caressed each other. Angel's hand found his penis and stroked it. His penis awakened and Angel pulled him to her as they continued to kiss. "Are those people watching us over at that building;" Angel asked? "Do you want me to close the curtains; Christopher asked? No not at all; Angel said. They will have to explain to their boss. Why it took them so long on one window; she smile." "Okay;" Christopher responded. He bit the left side of her neck with passion.

Angel gasped at the intensity of his bite. His fingers masterfully rubbed her pussy and clitoris. His mouth moved all over her shoulders, breast and neck. She took her free left hand and drove her nails into his back. Firmly planting her marks on this man that belonged to her. His fingers digging deeper and harder into her wet pussy. Hers were digging harder into his back. The sweetest pain hurt so damn good for both of them. Christopher shifted his hips over hers. He removed his fingers out of her wet hole. Sucking all the juice off of his middle finger. He then took his remaining fingers and smeared her scent on her breast. He kissed them sweetly alternating from left to right.

His hands groped her breasts and his mouth followed them. He vacuum sucked her right nipple and then ran his tongue around it. He then kissed her left nipple doing the same. He lifted her right breast, so he could lick the underside of it. From her chest up to the nipple then the same with the left breast. Now he just dove in sucking her right breast tenaciously. Fondling it and suckling at much of it as he could get in his mouth. Angel took her right hand and she cupped the back of his head and held him as a newborn while he feasted on her tits.

His mouth went back and forth from sucking her right to left breast. Like a child that had missed his last feeding time. Occasionally, he would swoop down and kiss her glistening stomach. Probing the tip of his tongue into her navel and gently biting her sides. The way Angel's legs opened he knew exactly what she wanted at this moment. He carefully slid down her body. Placing his hands under her thighs lifting her knees to her chest. Her genitals were covered already in her cream. Christopher insatiably began to lick it up. Her scent was so powerful and seductive now. He couldn't stop, even if he wanted to.

He spread her slightly more, so that his tongue could paint her inner thighs. He let her legs down on the bed as he was kneeling between them. He stood and took his erect penis, smacking it down on her clitoris. Angel jumped as it sent a pleasant jolt through her body. Then Christopher tapped her clitoris again with his rod. He teased her pussy as if he might enter her. Only to strike her clitoris again with his meaty tool. Repeatedly he smacked her clitoris with his shaft, toying with her. Rubbing the head of his dick over her entrance only to smack her clitoris again.

Christopher licked and sucked Angel's clit to get it more aroused. Then he smacked it with his penis again mercilessly teasing her. He turned her over onto her stomach. Then positioned himself between her legs once more. Spreading her round soft cheeks with one hand he then smacked his dick down on her anus. He continued as if he were a parent giving a spanking. The head of his dick kept spanking her asshole driving her to insanity.

# I Was Just Laying Here Minding My Own Business

"You want me to fuck you don't you Angel;" he asked? "Yes I want you to fuck me Christopher;" she begged. He turned her back face up and leaned to kiss her. "Do you really want this dick in your pussy Angel;" he asked? "Yes I really want that dick all inside of me Christopher;" she responded. He stuck his dick balls deep inside of her. "Is this what you want Angel; he asked? He lay on top of her without moving and talked in her ear. "I love sucking this nice, juicy swollen clit of yours, Angel. I sucked your little woman dick on top of the world. For all to see as you came in my face baby.

He suddenly pulled Angel's legs over his arms and began to wear her pussy out. "Oh this dick is so addicted to you Angel; he said. I want to fuck you so bad beautiful lady. I need to fuck you Angel. Do you need this dick to fuck you?" Yes, YES I NEEEEED this dick to fuck me; Angel cried. Angel started panting and breathing faster, harder and heavier. Christopher knew she was approaching an intense climax. Just when she was only seconds away, he pushed her legs higher crossing her ankles over her head.

He started to grind his pubic bone against her already excited clitoris. His arms locked under her shoulder blades and his mouth bit her lips gently. He wanted her to tell the world this was his pussy. Already close to orgasm, Angel's geysers released like steam from a boiling teapot. She held Christopher with a force that was resolute as her body convulsed.

She mashed his face to her right side and bit down on his neck like a viper. She was marking him so that would be violators could now detect by scent or sight. This man was hers. Just as her body began to calm down from her massive orgasm, Christopher lowered her legs. Leaving his shaft inside. He wrapped his right leg under her left one. He then stiffened his body and began to grind his pubic bone directly on her clitoris. She came in a matter of seconds. He then allowed her to take over the grinding. He held his body achingly stiff, so that she could use it to get herself off at will.

Angel detonated in one powerful orgasm after another. She was almost to the point where she couldn't catch her breath. Her clitoris had become so sensitive that the slightest touch would set it off. So she released Christopher and grabbed his face kissing him. He lifted her legs and plowed his dick deep into her pussy. Making sure to strike her super sensitive clitoris with the pubic bone and base of his dick. Angel came again as she was blabbering his name. He quickly moved her onto all fours and pressed his love inside. He rocketed faster and faster inside of her. He slammed his balls up against her swollen clitoris with each stroke.

Angel uttered; "Oh goddamn, fuck you making me cum, I can't stop, I can't stop, I can't stop ca, cu, cum cummminnggg OOOOh fuck CHRISTOPHER! Oh it's your pussy, baby, it's yours, take it, take it, fuck me with that good dick. Ooooh that dick is sooooooooo gooood. It's so good baby. I love that dick. I love you, Christopher. I love you, I love you, damn oh, fuck I love you!" Christopher leaned down and kissed her cheeks before continuing his pounding. He held her hips firm and was unwavering in ramming into her from behind. He took his hands off her hips and grabbed her swaying breast.

Christopher then took his moist dick out and beat it over her asshole. He did this to her for about two minutes. Then without warning he shoved his dick back into her pussy. His balls dropped and tapped over her exposed clitoris like bombs dropping in a war zone. Angel's body was super sensitive to touch. His dick was firing into her pussy and his balls were battering her clitoris. A Hurricane force orgasm was building very quickly inside of her. Christopher looking down at this beautiful specimen making love to him, also began to detonate. They both screamed each other's names as gravity and time appeared to be suspended.

I'm going to cum inside your pussy baby. Oooh fuck I want to cum in you so bad woman." "Yes! Angel yelled; I'm coming all over that chocolate dick. Christopher began stamping his dick inside of her. He was determined to fill her with every drop of cum inside of him. Angel was bucking wildly like a horse in a rodeo as she climaxed. "Aoh, Ooo, Ummm, Ahhhhhh, Christopher grunted as he released his hot creamy fluid inside of her. They climax simultaneously feeling on fire. Angel collapsed on the bed and Christopher fell next to her. They were both panting heavily out of breath.

Once his movement stopped, Angel would not let him touch her. Her body was too sensitive to touch and she was in a zone. They lay there trying to catch their breath and staring at each other. Both of their bodies were drenched in sweat. Christopher softly wiped her forehead with the back of his hand. "You're a nasty somebody;" Angel mumbled. "Let me get you a bottle water out of the refrigerator;" Christopher said. "Yes please, I could really use that; Angel said. May I have a towel with some cool water on it too?" "Who are you calling nasty; Christopher asked? He handed her the water and towel.

"I was just laying here minding my own business. You violently attacked me. You made me do things I don't do;" Angel said. "I'm black, you'll tell me anything; Christopher said. Is that your story that you're going to stick with woman?" "Oh so let me get some clarity here because you know I like clarity. So you don't believe me;" Angel asked? "I don't care who you tell that lie to; Christopher said. Erriebody over there in that building saw who attacked whom. Hell, I don't know if Pastor will let me sing in the choir this week because of you woman." "Oooh, somebody needs a shower in here; Angel said.

You have made me break a sweat and I'm usually too cool for that; she said. "Well, let's take a shower together. We need to get out of here and make it uptown;" Christopher said. "Okay, you go turn on the water, I'll be right there; Angel said. I'm just going to lay here on this side that's dry for a moment. I need to finish catching my breath." Once the water was running, Christopher did his oral hygiene and put on some face wash. Angel bumped him out of the way as she brushed her teeth and rinsed. He then stepped in the shower and Angel soon joined. She stood behind him and wrapped her arms around him. She kissed the back of his head and neck.

He faced her and they kissed. The water ran over their faces and down their bodies. Christopher turned her to soap up her back really well and then she did his. After their shower, they got dressed. Christopher took their belongings down to the lobby. He sent for the car and when it arrived Angel stepped off the elevator. They were off to 125th street, where Angel got her movie. Running late they dashed back across town to turn in the rental car. "Can we drop you folks off anywhere;" the rental agent asked. "Yes, we need to get to Penn Station;" Angel replied.

Someone is then assigned to take them to the train station. The driver took them in the car they had. They didn't have to unload their things. They arrived at Penn Station 45 minutes before their train departed. Christopher carried most of their belongings inside. Angel carried the lighter things. Once she was seated, Christopher went on a quest to find them something to eat. He found a pastry stand and purchased them two crème cheese pastries. He also got them a bottle of apple juice. "Not the healthiest breakfast I know; Christopher said.

I promise to cook you a better one next time you're at my house. I also hope that is soon." "I am going to hold you to that;" Angel said. "You have some filling around your lips;" Angel said. As Christopher went to wipe it, she stopped his hand. "I'll get it;" she said. She kissed the corner of his mouth and kissed him fully on the lips. Christopher took his pastry rubbing it all over his lips and Angel laughed. "I'm not getting all of that nasty stuff off of you Mr. Funny man;" she said. "Damn, it was worth a try anyway;" Christopher said.

Moments later they boarded the train back to Maryland and very soon were moving. Angel laid her head on Christopher's shoulder and fell asleep. Christopher took her hand and kissed her forehead. He closed his eyes remaining semi- conscious of movement around him. Once back in Maryland, Christopher awakened her. He told her to ensure they had their things. They exited the train and made their way outside to his truck. Are you going to sleep at my house woman, because you still look tired;" Christopher asked? "I am tired, but I need to get home and check on Jamal;" said Angel. "Awww, does that mean you're going to leave me all alone tonight;" asked Christopher?

"I do have to spend some time at home Mr. Man; Angel replied. You know that whole family thing I have to deal with. Everybody's child isn't off in college yet. Hopefully in three more years, mine will be. "Oh, so in three more years, I will get you to spend the night over here. Or wherever I may have a home at that time;" asked Christopher? "I've spent the night over at your place before Christopher, and I had a wonderful time. Now can you just drive, so I can get my car;" Angel demanded? "Okay pushy woman, you don't have to be talking to me like I work for your ass.

Last I checked, I was self-employed and don't need no woman to take care of me;" Christopher smiled. They placed all their items in the truck. Christopher drove them to his house in a few minutes. He pulled inside the garage next to Angel's car. She waited for him to open her door. He held her hand as she exited and kissed her quickly on the lips. She thanked him for helping her out the vehicle. He placed her items into her car. "May I come in and use your restroom;" Angel asked? "Why are you asking me that woman; Christopher asked? You know anything I have in this house is yours. As a matter of fact, I can make this house yours. "I just need to use the restroom for now dear. Thank you for the offer;" Angel said.

She walked into his house and into the half bath where she checked herself in the mirror. "Man, what did you do to my neck; Angel yelled! You know I cannot have you marking me up like this." "I didn't do that to you; Christopher yelled back. "I saw when you went to the bathroom at the Play. Denzel wasn't on stage. You were gone about five minutes. You're not fooling anybody." "Whatever;" Angel replied. "I am going to have to put some heavy makeup on around my neck.

Just in case any of my neighbors are out when I get home. I can't have Jamal asking any questions either." "Just tell them you got bit by a big ass mosquito;" Christopher said. "I'm going to give you a big ass whipping; Angel said. I can't believe I let you do this man. You know this is a foul ball, a 15 yard penalty and a back court violation;" she said. "Damn, I guess it will be hard to win this game. I don't even know which one I am playing;" Christopher said. Angel exited the bathroom and walked over to him and kissed him.

"Well, it doesn't matter; she said. No matter which game we play, I will always win. I got it like that brother man." "Oh, you can get it woman; Christopher said. Keep playing with me. I'm going to give it to you right here on this floor." "Ooops, you lose; Angel replied. I have to go so we will have to pick this game up some other time. Next time, I may spot you 69 points before we play." They walked to the garage and she got in her car. Christopher opened his garage door and she backed out. They waved goodbye as she drove off. Angel turned on her mp3 player and the first song that comes on was "Feel like Making Love" by Bob James. It was a Jazz interpretation of Roberta Flack's classic. Angel turned up the volume and flowed with the music.

How wonderful it was to get away if only for a short time. I love New York City, she smiled. Now, she was back home and ready to refocus, regroup. Maybe realign her company. "Christopher may have been right; she thought. Why should I work this hard when I have people working for me? Do I really need to Micro-manage? Maybe I can free up my time and spend it with Christopher. While my husband is on one of his many business trips. I know he doesn't need his secretary to tag along on all those jobs. She's doing more than keeping paperwork up I bet.

# Are You Serious Right Now?

*"I'll be in Denver for a week. Then we're flying out to Chicago on a job for a month;"* Angel mocked her husband. Probably doing more than working on buildings. Why do you take contracts that send you all over the country in the first place? When you have a family right here. Plus a Governor that will keep you working near home? I know that new secretary takes your dictation. You probably told her you couldn't afford separate rooms for you and her. With your cheap self;" Angel said out loud.

She exited the highway and proceeded down the main road into her neighborhood. Next on her playlist was "Forthenight" by Musiq Soulchild. She really cranked up the volume. Her premium speakers were serenading the neighborhood. *"I know you're not my man and you know, I'm not your girl but we can hang, like it's that way tonight;"* she sang. She turned onto her street singing like nobody's business. *"Would you do that baby?"* "WHAT THE FUCK….. is he doing home?" As she approached her home, she could see that her garage door was open. David's car was inside.

"He was supposed to be gone for a month. It's only been two weeks. "What is he doing here and how long has he been here; she wondered? Damn my neck! Damn you Christopher! I knew I shouldn't have let…" She stopped at the stop sign one block from her house. I need to back out of here. Go somewhere and get myself together;" she thought. Just then David walked out of the house and he saw her car. "Think fast, think fast;" she said to herself. I'll put my purse on my shoulder and push my collar up on my left side.

I'll carry my clothing bag over my left shoulder. I'll say I just came from the dry cleaners. Shit that is not going to work. He hasn't seen me in weeks. He is going to want a kiss and probably be standing all in my face. This is not good! This is not fucking good! She rolled up her tinted windows and began to let the roof up on her car. This would provide her temporary cover from David as he stood outside. He was waiting and looking down the street at his wife. Angel put on her sunshades, in hopes he can't read her eyes.

"Maybe I ate some shellfish and it broke me out. He might buy it, she thought. Then again, I have to get in the bathroom. I need to see if I have marks down on my inner thighs. What were you thinking Angel? Letting this man that is not your husband mark you up like this? I may as well pack my bags right now and go over to Christopher's. Then again if I'm single, he may not want me. He was just having fun when he knew he didn't have to commit. FUCK! FUCK! FUCK! FUCK! Damn this is not good! Okay pull yourself together and get out of the car." She drives into her garage.

She carefully puts her purse on her left shoulder and lifts her collar up covering that side. She turned to the back seat grabbing her clothing bag. She put it over her right shoulder, as she opened her door with her right hand. "Hey baby; David said. Honey I'm home!" "I see that, Angel replied. What a pleasant surprise but what are you doing here?" "Well, there was a police shooting of a black kid a few days ago. People started to protest. It was getting ugly. Basically, we had to get out of town because it wasn't safe for us. I'm surprised you didn't see it on the news. I don't want to talk about that baby. Come here and give me a kiss; David commanded. Why were you sitting at the stop sign so long, did you think I was a burglar?"

"I've been eating onions;" Angel explained. She gave him a peck on the lips. "Baby, I haven't seen you in over two weeks; David said. That's all I get is a peck?" "Let me get inside and brush my teeth baby; Angel said. Then I will give you all the kisses you want. Where's Jamal, is he home;" Angel asked? "No, he was here when I got in about two hours ago; David said. He asked me could he go down to somebody's house. I was like yeah, just be home by 7 o'clock. "Somebody's house;" Angel questioned? You mean you don't know whose house?

That is pretty bad man;" Angel said. Desperately she tried to keep the conversation away from affection. She walked briskly upstairs to their master bedroom and her speed was not unnoticed by David. "Do you have to go pee baby; he asked? You're moving awfully fast up those stairs." "Yes lord, I have to get to the bathroom; Angel said. I will be out with fresh breath to kiss my baby real soon." "Well hurry up, baby; David shouted. I'm starving for your kiss and what are you making for dinner? I'm starving for that too."

"Oh, I was thinking about making some Hawaiian meatballs; Angel said. I forgot to stop at the store and get some ground meat. What we have is frozen. Do you mind going to get us some, baby?" "I already stopped at the store on the way home; David said. We have steak, ground turkey, salmon, shrimp, fish, chicken and all kinds of fresh vegetables down here;" David said. "In that case, why didn't you start dinner;" Angel asked? "Baby, you know I don't cook like you; David replied. I just wanted to taste some of your food tonight." "Well, I'll get started on that in a minute; Angel replied. Give me a second in the bathroom." She unbuttoned her blouse and looked at the marks on her neck. Two marks are very small and one is very noticeable.

"I can cover these small ones up with a little makeup. Think Angel; she said. I will put on this Hampton University sweatshirt with a hoodie. David must have just bought this. Hell, he probably won't notice me anyway. He only tends to focus on what he wants." She pulled down her pants and looked at her thighs. "Look at that mark on my inner right thigh; she thought. It's high enough up that he would never see it if I wear shorts. Okay get it together, just keep him off of you until…. Once we get in the bedroom together I'll make sure the lights are off. Or turned down real low."

She darted into her master bedroom adjoined with her bathroom. Frantic in her closet she tried to find shorts to match her hoodie. "Bitch, what the fuck are you doing up here all this time; David yelled. I told your ass I was hungry. You're taking all motherfucking day." He walked into the room as he spoke. "I know you done lost your damn mind calling me a bitch; Angel said. You think I will cook for your sorry ass now?" "I didn't mean it like that baby; David said. You were just taking a long time, and I'm hungry." "Well, that's not the way to get fed, especially not from me; Angel said.

You might want to take that bullshit to your secretary. Or whomever lets you talk to her like that. I'm not the one." David walked over to where Angel was. "Look. I said I didn't mean it old evil ass woman; he said. Why do you always have to make a big ass deal over bullshit;" David asked? "You're calling your wife a bitch. Are you serious right now;" Angel asked? That's where the bullshit is. "Motherfucker, I said I was just playing; David griped. Why don't you just go downstairs and start dinner;" David demanded! "I'm not cooking a damn thing;" Angel replied. "Bitch, as long as I've been away from home and you wanna act a fool?

You better get your ass downstairs and cook something before I"...." "Before you what?" Angel cut him off and asked? He grabbed her arm as if he was going to drag her down to the kitchen. "Get your damn hands off of me;" Angel screamed! David shoved her with intense force across the bedroom. She fell over an accent chair and onto the floor. "Now get your ass up. Stop playing and go fix us something to eat woman;" David repeated. "I'm not fixing you shit but an open door to get out of my house;" Angel yelled! "Bitch this is my house; David taunted. I pay for this motherfucker, just like you do. I'm not going anywhere."

He grabbed Angel's arm again to lift her up. She stood, pulled away and slapped his face. David returned a back hand slap like Serena Williams across Angel's face. He knocked her once again to the floor. "Now look baby, I haven't had to do that in a long time. Why do you want to go acting up now? Bringing out my ugly side;" David chided. I can't bring out the ugly side of someone already ugly inside and out;" Angel said. David moved in with his hand drawn back. Angel quickly grabbed the nightstand lamp and threw it at him. She then grabbed her cell phone and ran and locked herself in the bathroom. "You better not be calling no police over no petty shit like this;" David barked!

"I'm not calling any police; Angel said. I'm calling my friend, Christopher." "What the fuck are you calling that faggot motherfucker for; David responded? He's not a cop anymore, he can't arrest anybody." "No, but he can whip your sorry ass for putting your hands on me;" Angel said. "Oh is this your boyfriend or something? Are you and him fucking;" David quizzed? "I wish I were with him fucking. Instead of being here with your sorry, violent ass;" Angel answered.

David began to bang on the door with ferocity. "I will show your ass violence. When I get in this bathroom bitch;" he warned. Angel quickly scrolled to her recent calls. In a hurry to find Christopher's number. She dialed and it began to ring. David was banging harder and harder on the door and then he began to kick the door. "Come on pick up the phone Christopher;" she whispered. After several rings it went to voicemail. "Fuck;" Angel exclaimed! David kicked the door a little harder. Just as Angel was about to dial 911, Christopher called her back.

"Hello;" Angel said with a shaking voice. "Hey sweetie, I'm sorry the phone was in my bedroom; Christopher said. I was in my office. How are you doing, pretty lady?" Angel was silent, until she let out a quick sniffle. Christopher listened intently. He could hear David banging on the door and yelling in the background. "Where are you;" Christopher asked? Angel was still silent not wanting to talk and further anger David. "Angel, talk to me. Where are you;" Christopher demanded? "Home," Angel said softly. "I'm on the way;" Christopher replied and hung up. Angel thought of each step that Christopher was taking to get to her.

How he was distraughtly grabbing his car keys. How he checked to make sure he hadn't left his stove on. How even in crisis mode, he was going to make sure he was being safe. He was going to make sure he left nothing dangerous on at the house. Christopher always checked on everything to make sure it was safe at his house. Hopefully now safe for her she thought. If only long enough for her to stay and get her thoughts and plans together. Meanwhile, she has noticed that David was no longer banging on the door. It didn't sound like he was right outside of it anymore. She listened carefully to find out what he might be up to.

She estimated that Christopher must be about 35 minutes away. That's if he took the tunnel. Her mind worried about what David may do in that amount of time. She ran to the window to see if he may possibly be outside. She thought; "if I have to escape out the window how will I get down. The fire escape ladder is in the bedroom area under that window." She had a small ledge outside the bathroom window. She could possibly climb down but still would have about 16 feet to the ground from there. There was a tree she could jump to she thought. Will she be able to get enough leverage from the ledge to make it? Her attention was then redrawn to the sound of footsteps in the bedroom.

David said; "I'm gonna get your ass out of this bathroom, one way or the other. Now you can open the door. Or I'll use this butter knife to press in the lock and let myself in." Angel was terrified, she knew David was angry. She still had very vivid memories of a beating he gave her months ago. He blamed her for not awaking him to catch a flight. "I should have left you then; she thought. I should call 911 now." Yet in the back of her mind, she wanted Christopher to get there. She wanted him to be the one to save her from this mad man.

She just hoped she didn't press her luck and end up hurt badly, or worse waiting on her hero. The sound of the bathroom door beginning to rattle shook her to her core. David was working the dull butter knife between the frame and the door, trying to pry it open. Quickly, she sat on the floor. Pressing her feet firmly against the bottom of the door to hold it closed when he succeeded. She was well aware he could get in this way. They had done it before when she inadvertently locked them out several years ago.

Never did she think she'd be now hiding in this bathroom and fearing for her life. "Bitch, get your ass from behind this door. I have to use the bathroom;" David yelled! "There are four other bathrooms in the house you can use;" she yelled back. Finally, he got the knife where it needed to be. He pressed back the lock and tried to push the door open. Angel's feet prevented it from opening more than a sliver. David stuck his arm through the upper portion as he pushed the knob with his left arm.

Angel pressed both feet against the door as if it were a matter of life and death. It very well just may be. David could only get his arm down towards the mid-section of the door. So he squatted down. He took the butter knife and stabbed the top of Angel's left leg pressed against the door. Thankfully he didn't have leverage when he stabbed her to do real damage. She screamed in pain, her wound was not deep but it was painful as he broke skin. Angel tried to slide her feet over to the right. Too far over right and he could push the door open. Too far to the left and she could be cut again.

Just as she tried to readjust her hold, David got his arm in up to his elbow. He brought the dull blade down on her leg swelling a painful wound. Angel screamed in pain and agony. She knew she couldn't let this door open or it would be worse. She took her right leg that wasn't injured and she stomped the door. Smashing David's arm and causing him to drop the knife. "Fucking bitch, I will kill your ass up in here;" David yelled. "Hurry up Christopher;" is all Angel could think. She imagined where he was and how close he might be. David went over to the bed where Angel left her purse. He knew she carried pepper spray. He intended to spray it under the door to flush her out. He dumped all the contents of her purse out on the bed to look for the canister.

Angel could hear him, but she dared not open the door. Then there was a pause in David's movement. "BITCH, WHO THE FUCK DID YOU HAVE LUNCH WITH IN NEW YORK!!!??? GET YOUR MOTHERFUCKING ASS OUT HERE AND EXPLAIN THIS SHIT!!!" David walked briskly back to the door and began kicking it! "Open this door, you retarded ass woman. I want you to tell me who the fuck you went to New York with, and why I shouldn't beat the hell out of your ass." Just then, she heard a car screeching into range and it seemed to stop at her house. The car door slammed and seconds later the doorbell rang. It rang again and again.

"Who the fuck did you call over here bitch; David asked? I'm going to tell you the Police you hit me too. We both go to jail." The doorbell rang again. Christopher yelled for Angel to open the door. "Oh, that's your boyfriend out there; David asked? Is that the nigga you went to New York with bitch? That motherfucker, a washed up cop? A nigga who I've been fixing his cars for him? He better not be the nigga you went to New York with." The doorbell rang several times. "Fuck you nigga, stay outside;" David yelled! We're having a husband and wife conversation in here."

Angel quietly got up. She didn't want David to notice that she was no longer holding the door. Slowly she opened the window. She knew Christopher like a book. Soon he would begin to walk around the house, looking for signs of trouble. Almost like clockwork, she saw him turn the corner on the side of her house. "Use your key and hurry;" Angel yelled down to Christopher! Suddenly, David busted open the door and said; "This nigga has a key to my house? Bitch, have you lost your motherfucking mind?" He forcefully pulled Angel from the window and threw her to the floor.

He stepped on the wound on her leg and drove his weight into it causing severe pain. He knelt and began choking her. Christopher ran into their bedroom. Christopher drew his gun and pointed it at David. "Motherfucker, if you don't get your bitch made ass off of her in half a second; Christopher commanded. You will die in this motherfucker right fucking now!" David slowly stood up with his feet on either side of Angel's face. "Nigga, this is my house you're standing in. Pointing a gun at me; David said. You need to get the fuck out of here before...."

"You're not going to do shit but what I say, you punk bitch; Christopher said. First thing you're going to do is move from over her. Before I drop your ass like the trash you are. Angel, sweetie, are you okay;" he asked? "He stabbed my leg with a butter knife and it hurts badly, but I think I will be okay;" Angel replied. "Oh, you like to play with knives huh; Christopher said. You simple minded motherfucker. I tell you what, pick that knife up now! I dare you, punk motherfucker;" Christopher taunted. "Man, get the fuck out of my house before I call the police;" David said.

"Somehow, I really don't think you will, you little bitch; Christopher said. In case you do, here's my phone. The number is 911. Christopher tossed the phone to David, who let it fall on the floor. "Angel, can you stand up and come over here to me, baby;" Christopher asked? He then said to David; "You need to move out of her way. If you touch her again, I will whip your motherfucking ass from now until Jesus comes back." Angel struggled to stand and when she stepped down on her left leg, the pain was stinging. Christopher held out his left hand, while keeping the gun pointed at David with his right. Christopher looked at her leg and it did not appear to be seriously injured.

# Do Yourself A Favor

When she reached Christopher he gently guided her to stand behind him. "You call this being a man, you little sissy ass bitch;" Christopher asked? I should stab your ass a few dozen times in your fucking face. Unlike your dumb ass, I have some brains though. If you don't do exactly what I say, I'm going to blow your brains all over this goddamn bathroom. We'll just call it self-defense. I mean, you did attack her with a knife, I thought I was next. Now, get down on your knees, motherfucker."

David stood there staring at Christopher with a look of rage. Wishing he could kill this man standing in his house. "I said, get your punk ass on your knees;" Christopher repeated. He kicked David in his crotch and then pushed him to the floor. "Nigga, I will stomp a mud hole in your ass if I have to tell you again. Now get up on your fucking knees." David got on his knees and Christopher walked behind him and placed the gun to the back of his head.

"What, are you going to execute me in my own house;" David asked? "Only if I have to; Christopher replied. For right now, I just need you to tell Angel you're sorry you ever hit her." David repeated the words he was told. "Now crawl your bitch ass out this bathroom; Christopher said. Grab a few clothing items. You're about to go stay at a hotel, motel or your bitches house. Hell you can sleep on a park bench for all I care. You just won't be here tonight." "Nigga you can't throw me out of my own house; David protested. Who the fuck do you think you are?" "I'm that nigga that kicked your ass; Christopher said. He then kicks David in his ass while he's crawling.

"Now stand your sorry ass up and start packing clothes; Christopher demanded. "Angel can we talk about this, just me and you;" David asked? "You can talk to my Attorney when the divorce papers come;" Angel said. "Divorce; David said. Now you're going to try to take my house and half of everything I've worked for?" "She doesn't need this house nigga; Christopher interrupted. She doesn't need half of you shit either. She's going to walk out of here with 100% of her company. All she and Jamal will need are personal items out of here. I will give her everything else she could possibly want or need.

So you can keep this house. If there is a something she is really fond of in here we're taking it. Or I will buy it newer and better for her." "Why would I let my wife move out of here and into your house;" David asked? "Do yourself a favor brother; Christopher responded. Shut the fuck up, before you get beat the fuck up, then locked the fuck up. I can make all that shit happen right now. "So, you just going to come into my house and steal my wife from me;" David asked? Christopher replied; "I didn't steal her, you gave her away. When she fell in love with you, it wasn't because she liked being hit.

Even after you were beating on her she still wanted to love you. Each mark on her body you gave her showed you didn't love her back. "Man, what are you talking about; David asked? I still love my wife. You know that I still love you, don't you Angel? "No, you don't nigga; Christopher said. If you did, you wouldn't have ever hit her. I know she didn't hit you first. You certainly wouldn't have stabbed her with no damn butter knife. You're like a little high school girl. Angel, are you able to write up a list? Everything you want to take out of here so we don't forget it?

"Yeah, I can start a list right now; Angel said. I have a lot of clothes and shoes that may take some time. "No, it won't; Christopher replied. I'm going to call my regional manager Carnell Weatherspoon. He'll get some security guards over here. He'll offer them time and a half to pack your things for us." "So, you're going to just come in here and destroy my life;" David said. "On the contrary you idiot. I'm doing you a favor. I could easily pick up this phone and have police come here and arrest your ass. That will probably go public and mess up some of your business. Particularly your business with the Governor's office.

I'm not going to even take her to the hospital to get her leg looked at. That will raise questions." "I do need to get my leg checked out;" Angel said. "I know baby, I got you; Christopher said. My boy Torrence Stepteau is the best doctor in the area. He will come over to the house and fix you right up. "So, you're her knight in shining armor; David asked? You have all the motherfucking answers. "Nope; Christopher responded. I don't have all the answers, not even close. Angel and I started out as dear friends. From what I knew her life was good with you.

Never in a million years, did I think about being her knight in shining armor. Or anything along those lines. However you started drinking and acting such a fool. Beating on her, talking to her like she's some motherfucker on the street. You have anger issues and need to go talk to somebody. That shit might get you hurt real bad. In fact here's a card from my therapist, Dr. Thomas L. Watson. No relation, motherfucker! Christopher threw the card at David. It hit him in the head before falling to the floor.

"She clearly tried for years; Christopher continued. To hang in there and put up with you. You flipped that script and drove her to another man." "What the hell does that mean;" David asked? "It means, he knows how to love me without all the sanctimonious bullshit; Angel yelled. When he puts his hands on me I like it." David tried to lunge and go toward Angel. Christopher pushed him down on the floor. He then said; "Like Nino Brown told G-money, you better sit your five dollar ass down before I make change!" Are you done with that list baby;" he asked Angel?

"Let me think, I know I'm forgetting something;" Angel said. "Okay, whatever it is, don't worry about it; Christopher replied. I'm sure Mr. dick head here is going to cancel the cards on your joint account. I have $10,000 in my safe that is your start over money. You go get anything you and Jamal need. Make sure you're comfortable at the house. I mean your new house." "Actually, you only have about $9,200 in there; Angel said. I borrowed $800.00, because I needed some boots for winter. They were on sale for $400.00 each pair. I was going to put it back when my invoices came in." "Don't worry about it; Christopher said.

I may really have to start selling aluminum cans. Maybe I can get a job at a construction company; he said. Alright David, go get a toothbrush and your car keys, then get the fuck out. Oh and one more thing. If you ever put your hands on her again, I will kill you. Got it?" "Yeah;" David said. Tomorrow around 7p.m. we should have everything she wants out by then. Tonight, however, I wouldn't come back, if I were you. Some of my guards are going to be sitting out on this street in an unmarked car. If they see you anywhere near here, they will escort you into the woods. You probably won't like it out there; Christopher said.

"Big mean guys, these employees of mine. They were in infantry in the Marines and they love to play." David went to the bathroom and grabbed his toiletries. On his way out he stared at Angel, as if seeking some help. Christopher called his manager Carnell. He told him to find three guards to come to this address. He asked him to get a box truck and some boxes. He told him he also needed Officers Sanchez and Brandenburg. He wanted them off the post they worked tonight. Have them get the blue GMC truck and sit outside this address overnight.

He texted a picture of David with additional instructions. Once David pulled off, Angel called Jamal home so they could all talk. After they spoke with Jamal he understood the situation. Christopher's guards showed up shortly thereafter. Once they got the box truck parked, he handed them the list. Angel showed them the closets and items she wanted packed. The paintings on the list Christopher instructed them to wrap real well. Be very careful with those; he said. An hour later his guys Sanchez and Brandenburg arrived. Christopher instructed them on what to do. The clock approached midnight and everyone was tired. Angel was finally certain that most of the things she wanted were packed and ready to go.

"What about all the food in the freezer here;" Angel asked? "Woman you have $10,000. I mean $9,000 at home; Christopher said. I will give you whatever you need for the rest of your life. I promise you won't ever starve, not for food, not for love and not for anything." Upon arrival at their new home, Angel directed Jamal to his room. The room was more than familiar with Jamal. He had slept over a few times in the past. Christopher reminded him that he is no longer a visitor.

He will be expected to keep his bathroom and bedroom clean. His mother will not be allowed to wash his clothes any longer. Jamal was told he will have to iron his own clothes. He would learn to sew a button on a shirt. "Why do I have to learn to do all of that woman's stuff Mr. Christopher; asked Jamal? I will have a girlfriend that can do all of that." "You won't have a girlfriend every day for the rest of your life boy; Christopher said. You're going to learn to take care of yourself because life doesn't work like that.

Two, you're going to learn to do it, because I said so, end of discussion." Jamal looked at Angel and she said; "Don't look at me. You better get to sewing, when it's time." Jamal asked; "Mr. Christopher, can you tell me again why my television in my room doesn't have satellite T.V? Can I get it now that I'm older?" "It doesn't have satellite for the same reason you won't have a smart phone; Christopher said. There's too much trash on T.V. and the internet. Too many black folks are being paid to act like niggaz. You don't need to see that garbage.

"No smartphone; Jamal asked? I'm almost 16. How is that going to look, if I don't have a smartphone? "It's going to look like you're 15; Christopher said. Where your body is going through significant changes. Your friends, who know less than you do, are pressuring you to be grown. More grown than you can handle right now. That phone can give you unlimited access to video and images. Things that should be very limited at your age. I know you've seen pornography before on that phone of yours. I know even without a Smartphone your friends will show you stuff. I just want to make sure you develop a healthy understanding about sex. In those videos online, sex rarely has any consequences other than fun. In real life nothing could be further from the truth.

We don't need you getting an unhealthy perception of how men and women should interact." "Man, this will be like living in prison;" Jamal whined. "Negro, you live in a house most people can only dream of. I didn't say you can't watch satellite television. I just said I want to know what you're watching. If you balance it out with some reading and explain the book that you've read. Then you can watch more stuff on T.V. Instead of sitting in a room staring at a phone, we're going to go out and see some of the world.

This summer, we're going to go on an African Safari. Maybe, go see the Great Wall of China." "Are we going to be out there with the elephants and lions; Jamal asked? Wow that would be cool!" "Yes, elephants, lions, tigers and bears;" Angel said. "Oh my;" Jamal chimed in. "We'll stay in luxurious hotels in Kenya or South Africa;" Christopher said. "Wow I'm going to take a million pictures when we get there;" Jamal said. "We'll also go to Egypt and go visit London too;" Angel said. "Not to mention all the places here in America we'll go see; Christopher added. I really would love to go back to New York for some reason." He smiled at Angel and she winked back at him. "Then visit my sister out in the Bay area of California. I know you both will love it out there;" Christopher continued.

# What, You Set Tripping?

"Now, finish unpacking and straightening up your room;" Angel said. "First room inspection at zero dark thirty in the morning;" Christopher added.  "What;" Jamal yelled! "I'm just kidding dude; Christopher said. You don't have to get up until zero dark thirty one." "Tomorrow there's no school; Jamal said. Why do I have to get up? "No school; Christopher said. Then we should be up milking the cows, churning butter and all that stuff." "Your house is big Mr. Christopher, but you don't have any cows or any butter to churn;" Jamal replied. "Oh, you're one of them smart Negroes huh boy; Christopher joked.

We'll see how smart you are. When I trade your ass in for a Latino or Indian kid." "You can't trade kids in, we're not property;" Jamal said laughingly. "Did you see any kids when you got here tonight;" Christopher asked? "No;" Jamal said. "I traded them for some magic beans; Christopher said. Don't make me go back and get some rice boy." "Mr. Christopher you're a little psycho;" Jamal responded.

"What are you set tripping, Lil homie; Christopher taunted. I bet I will make you break yourself and run your jewels up in here." "Let this boy get his room together; Angel said. You come help me get my stuff situated." "Oh Oh, looks like your mother is making me break myself;" Christopher joked. Angel grabbed Christopher's hand. She walked with a slight limped out of Jamal's room towards their bedroom. "Look at all these boxes; Angel said exasperated. Are we sure this is what we want to do?"

"I mean I know we've always been great friends. Living together is a whole different step; she said." "Angel, I have loved you more and more as I got to know you; Christopher said. There is nothing more I am sure of. I'm wanting to be around you every day and night. We will be more than fine. How much liquid cash do you have in your personal accounts;" Christopher asked? "A little over $200,000;" Angel said. "Okay and I have about $400,000 cash in my accounts; he said. So I'm going to give you $100,000 and then we'll both have about $300,000.

We start this off even right down the middle. That way you can buy me some cereal. "I think I can help you out with that; Angel said. I'll buy you the generic brand of corn fluffs." "What the hell; Christopher exclaimed! Corn fluffs, I don't even get some smacks?" "I'll smack you alright;" Angel said. "What, do you think I'm scared of you;" Christopher asked? "No, you don't have to be scared; Angel said. Not right now. I'm going to go run us some water in the Jacuzzi. Then you may want to be scared. I might hurt you boy." He helped Angel walk towards the bathroom. He watched as Angel bent over to run the water.

Christopher turned on the radio and walked behind her. He stared at her body swaying as she swirled her hand in the water. "How does your leg feel woman;" Christopher asked? "It stings like hell, but I think he just scraped it real bad;" Angel responded. Christopher got some antiseptic and cleansed it for her. He then covered it with a Band-aid and gauze. He tried to tape it to make it water tight but they both knew that wouldn't hold. "I texted my boy Torrence; Christopher said. He said he can be here around 8a.m. before he goes to work.

Of course, if you think you need to see a doctor before then. Just let me know sweetie; Christopher said. I will call and find out what time the next bus comes up the street. You'll just have to limp your cripple ass up there to the bus stop that's all;" Christopher joked. "Oh, that's how you're going to treat me; Angel asked? Now that you got me all to yourself. I guess neither of us can get a ride from the other." "Wait, what! I said wherever you need to go, I will take you right now;" Christopher said. She wrapped her arms around him and put her face close to his. "That's what I thought you said;" Angel replied.

"If you stay like this, we won't make it into the water;" Christopher promised. "So what do you want to do Mr. Man; Angel asked?" "I've got this rich, smooth chocolate bar; Christopher answered. I want to give to you love. First I want to let these warm bubbles blow on our bodies." He undressed her, letting her clothes fall carelessly to the floor. She did the same for him. Once they were undressed, she turned to the Jacuzzi and slowly stepped in. The water burned her injured leg. She took it and hung it outside the tub as she sat. Christopher placed his hand in the water.

"Damn woman! Are you trying to clean me or cook me; he asked? This water is hot!" "Oh, you big cry baby; Angel teased. Get in here and I will blow on you to cool you off." "Okay; Christopher said. Boiled Negro it is." He entered the tub sitting behind her. Angel turned on the bubbles and laid her head back into his chest. He laid his head back on the bath pillow and they just closed their eyes. Letting the warm water caress them from all angles in the tub. "This is nice;" Angel said. "Yes it is; Christopher replied. Never imagined when we became friends we'd end up like this but damn I'm glad."

Page 268 of 280

"Fate found a way to make this happen;" Angel said. "If I had only known about David, it would have happened sooner; Christopher said. I should have picked up on things. When we were supposed to hang out and you would cancel. I figured it was because of your husband but damn. Angel tilted her head back to kiss him. "Honestly, I've always thought you were the only one who gets me. I know there were times you could sense I was really having feelings for you. When I'd let you massage my shoulders. Or I'd call you at wee hours of the morning waking you out of bed. I wanted to talk to only you. Then I had to tell myself, Chris is just my friend.

Something inside of me was saying you were where my happiness would be. Sometimes you made me mad being silly. Or you dating all those random women. You even had to the nerve to bring some of those skanks to my house for dinner;" Angel said. "Wait a minute; Christopher said. I only brought them by so that I wouldn't be the oddball out with no date. I didn't want your husband to think I was there for you. I really wasn't at the time. I was trying to see if any of your friends were like you. None of them were Angel. As a matter of fact you tried to pass me off to a few women your damn self.

You should have just manned up and said what you were feeling woman." Angel threw some suds from the bubble bath at his face. "You should have manned up; she said. Maybe, we could have had this life a long time ago." "Oh, my man is definitely up woman; Christopher said. Let me wash your neck and back, so we can a get a move on." Christopher took the peppermint soap, squeezed some into his hands. He massaged it across her neck and shoulders. "Ummm;" Angel moaned. His hands glided across her arms, back and shoulders.

Christopher firmly, but gently massaged her back. His hands worked their way around to her breast. He lathered his hands really well. Then he cupped and massaged her breast. Covering them in soapy warm suds. He kissed her neck and ran his hands all over her breasts. He whispered in her ear. "Angel you are so beautiful and I love you;" he said. "I love you too;" she replied. He guided his hands under the water to wash her legs and thighs. "Turn around and let me wash your back Chris;" she said.

Christopher turned around and she contorted to face him. The movement stirred a little sting on her leg wound. However she wouldn't let that ruin this moment. Christopher handed her the bath pillow. He then lay his head up against her soapy breast. She poured globs of peppermint soap on his chest. She then rubbed it in, letting her fingernails gently slide across his body. Alternating with slow sensual rubs from the palms of her hands. "Damn woman, you're going to make me call my Pastor over here. I'll marry you right in this bathroom right now. Your touch is so damn good to me;" Christopher said.

Angel lets her caresses go further down his body, as she rubbed his inner thighs. Teasing him as she let the back of her hands touch his penis. "Stand up for me;" she said. Christopher complied. She poured the peppermint soap in her hand and cleaned his genitals. The soap had an extreme cooling sensation. Mixed with the heat from the water it was immensely pleasing to him. Angel could see he was enjoying this cleansing process. She stroked his manhood almost as if she was stretching it out. Watching it grow bigger with each stroke of her hand. She then took a washcloth and held it over him. Squeezing the water out to rinse him off.

Once he was rinsed, she kissed the head of his shaft. Allowing just the tip in her mouth and flicking her tongue on the underside. "Now, you stand;" he ordered. He helped her up and lathered her hips and vaginal area. He then sat down so that her golden treasure was at his eye level. He gently rubbed her body. Making sure to rub the peppermint over her labia and clitoris. He reached around and washed her firm round ass. Spreading her cheeks apart, he let the warm bath sponge provide lots of soap in between them. He then repeated her action and squeezed water out of the sponge to rinse her off.

He then motioned for her to put her injured leg up out the water. He moved his face under her body and began to lick her nectar. Angel was washed in multiple sensations. She looked down and saw Christopher gliding his tongue across her moist lips. Consuming all the juices she knew were flowing out of her. Damn this is turning her on and she wants to fuck his brains out. The mood was set. The Original Quiet Storm on WHUR was playing "Anticipation" by a group called Guiltypleasures. Angel pushed his head back from her and she turned her back to him.

She then lowered herself carefully into the water. Reaching to find his shaft, she sat as her vagina swallowed it. She began to ride him up and down and he was matching her thrusts. Driving himself deeper into her. The sounds of the bubbles percolating in the water were sensual. Their bodies splashing into each other. His hands were all over her. Angel pressed down on his thighs to steady him and herself. All she wanted from this position was to work her body to get herself off. The bubbles were blowing on her clitoris as she rode him. In a matter of minutes, her explosion ripped through her. Christopher thought she may nail his thighs to the base of the tub.

The heat from the water and their movements had them both sweating profusely in the tub. They exited the tub and drained the water. Then moved to the shower to rinse the soap and perspiration off. They toweled themselves off and Christopher led her into the bedroom. The radio was playing "Angel" by Anita Baker. After the song's opening line "If I could, I'd give you the world" Christopher takes her hand. "Yes, you do deserve the world; he said. I promise I will never stop trying to give it all to you."

Angel wrapped her arms around him. "I love you Mr. Man;" she said. She kissed him with those lips that made him weak. He carefully laid her down on the bed and lit some candles in the room. In a very dimly lit room, he kneeled down and disappeared from her view. "One step closer" by R. Kelly was the next song played. She could hear him moving, taking steps toward her. About to do what she wanted him to do so badly. He kissed her feet, her ankles and worked his way up her legs. Once he arrived at her injury, he kissed softly around her bandage. He worked his way up to her thighs.

He bit softly on her inner thigh flesh in various spots. Switching from left to right and back again. Then he took his tongue and traced over those imaginary bite wounds. As if healing any wounds he caused before sealing them with a kiss. He then moved up to her very warm and moist box. In the background R. Kelly sang; "girl I'm about to do it, get ready, get ready." Christopher pushed her legs apart and then he did it. He jabbed his tongue at her clitoris, taking drops of moistness. He kissed her labia like the lips on her face forcing his tongue inside. He then paused, breathed heavily on her and buried his face into her. Her hips moved to his rhythm. He licked her up, down, left, right, diagonally, in and out and all the way around.

Angel moaned in approval under the sounds of music. She worked her hips all over his face. Christopher gave her a severe tongue lashing. His fingers touched and probed her inside and out. His mouth never lost contact with her sweet vagina as he willed her to cum. The warm juices began to flow from her and poured down his chin. "Oooo Fuck; Angel screamed! Damn I can't hold this cum from exploding in your face." Christopher paused one second to say; "Don't hold it." He quickly went back to consuming her pussy.

# I Love How You Look

"Damn, you're going to make me cum; Angel said. Eat my pussy baby, eat your pussy just like that. Just like that;" she demanded! She closed her legs to keep his head right where she wanted. Grabbing the top of his head to hold him still. She grinded her pussy all over his face. She closed her legs tighter and sat up. Readjusting her grip to the back of his head. Her pussy ruptured like a volcano. Spraying hot lava all over his dark glistening face. After her heart rate slowed, she pulled him onto the bed. She lay him down and sat on his face. Her hands pressed into his chest.

"Do you mind if I sit right here; she asked? I want you to lick my pussy some more. I love how you look with my juices all over your face." Christopher held her hips and tried to guide her body where he wanted to lick her. Angel quickly took over and rubbed her labia across his nose. She rammed her clit onto his lips which he gladly nibbled. "Oh, yes, she moaned, suck that clit for me. Suck it like you want to fuck me. Oooooh yes, suck this Cliiiiiiiiiiiiit!!!" Christopher slurped and licked everything he could. He protruded his tongue, so she could grind her pussy over it and get herself off once more.

With his tongue out and stiffened, Angel moved her body up and down. She was moving as if riding his dick and soon experienced another intense orgasm. She fell forward with her pussy still on his face and took his dick in her mouth. Christopher can feel she's not just sucking him. She was sensuously loving his dick with her mouth. Her tongue ran up and down the underside of him and then licked his balls. She had him feeling so good, his toes curled almost into a fist.

Wanting so much to return the pleasure, he spread her apart and licked all of her. He paused to talk dirty to her. "Do you like that chocolate dick in your mouth Angel; he asked?" "Ummm, I love it;" Angel replied. "Suck it like you want this chocolate to melt in your mouth; he said. Do you know how bad I've wanted you all night? How much I wanted to put my dick in your beautiful mouth? "Angel;" he moaned as she licked his balls. I want to cum inside of you so bad. In your pussy, in your mouth and on that pretty face of yours Angel."

He then resumed licking her honey and swirling his tongue inside of her. "I need to have you inside of me; Angel whispered. I want you inside of me Christopher." At her command, he slid from under her body. Keeping her kneeling on all fours he got behind her. Forcefully he pressed her face into the pillows. He pushed his dick wet with her saliva into her. He grabbed her hips and there was no beginning slow pace. He just pounded away inside of her with the intensity of a jackhammer. He took total control of her pussy for this moment. Angel made muffled moans as her mouth bit the pillows. Christopher pounded without mitigation inside of her. Forceful enough to shake her vertebrae loose. Angel screamed for him not to stop.

He banged into her several moments more then paused. He got her mini bullet out of his nightstand and turned it on high. He slipped it in her backdoor, then he continued to bang away in her. When he felt the intensity was getting too great, he stopped. He wanted to spend quality time inside of her. Once the wave passed, he went back to his intense pounding in her pussy. Her muffled screams into the pillow only coerced him. Angel was being moved off the bed by the force of his jarring impacts. He pulled her by her curly hair back to him.

She can feel the full throttle of his love plowing furiously into her. The look on her face and the sounds of her moans were extremely beautiful. They told him he was doing the right thing. He had no intentions of disappointing her. He banged into her from behind for almost half an hour. He pulled out and sat behind her. Taking her hand and he turned her to him. Now she could sit on his dick with her legs wrapped around him and their arms around each other. He kissed her madly letting her taste her pussy off his lips. She rammed her tongue in his mouth to reciprocate. "You're my music" by Brian Culbertson was playing on the radio and it seemed so perfect.

He thrusted upward into her while they continued to kiss. Angel grinded her clitoris deeper and deeper onto his body. At that moment, they were not making love. They were two wild creatures doing anything. Anything to please one another and themselves. Angel pushed him back, so that he was now lying in the bed. She leaned forward to ride him like a woman on horseback. She was literally slamming her body into his. With the intensity he did her only moments ago. At this second Christopher thought, she may not have been playing when she said she might hurt him.

Angel pinned his arms above his head as she rode him. "Whose dick is this; she asked?" "It's yours Angel;" Christopher replied. "Whose fucking dick is it; she demanded again? "It's yours; Angel. All I've ever wanted it to be was yours;" he said. Angel continued to grind her clit on his pubic bone as her pussy consumed his shaft. Quickly working herself up to an intense orgasm. Her body ramming into his as she watched the look on his face. Her orgasm was building with the bullet inside her to hydrogen bomb pressure. She swirled her pussy on him just right and she erupted.

She climbed his body and sat before his face. Rubbing her clit and squirting a waterfall of liquid onto him. All over his face and neck. She muffled her scream as she lets out tidal waves of orgasm. She made sure his handsome face caught as much of it as she could give him. Out of breath and extremely satisfied, she looked to dissolve on the bed. Christopher was quick to climb on top of her and pin her legs up over his arms. He lifted her ass up off the mattress with his hands under her body. He once again was wailing away inside of her. He knew her pussy was super sensitive now. He would love nothing more than to get her off once again.

He kissed her all over her gorgeous face mixing her juices and perspiration onto her. He buried his mouth on the side of her right ear and talked to her. "You think you can just come in my face like that and not get fucked; he asked? I got this pussy now, stranded up in the air. I'm going to drive my dick in you until I cum inside this pussy. I'm going to write my motherfucking name on your pussy walls Angel. Tell me I can have this pussy baby." Give it to me Angel." "Take it, TAKE IT, Angel screamed! Take that pussy and do what you want to it. "What I want to do is cum inside of your sweet pussy Angel; he grunted. May I do that baby? Can I cum inside of your pussy Angel?"

"YES, YES, OH FUCK YES!!! she screamed! Cum for me baby, cum for me Christopher. Oh yes give me that dick!" "Oh fuck, here it comes Angel! Ooooh Goddamn, here it cummms!!!" He lifted her ass and body up a little higher and he slammed his dick deep into her. Letting his milk and cream blast into her like a fire hose. They both moaned in pleasure as his body convulses while the remaining drops of his love seep into her. "Angel, I am so in love with you;" he said as he gasped for breath.

"I am so in love with you too Christopher;" she said back breathlessly. "That was so good. I'm going to go fix you a sandwich;" Christopher said. "I hope we stay this perfect;" Angel said. "I don't see why we can't;" Christopher replied. "To think all those years, I saw you as nothing more than my friend. Now this is the best love I have ever had;" Angel responded. "I thought you were my ideal woman, but how was I supposed to tell you that; Christopher asked? You started dating that idiot back in Atlanta. By the time I realized how perfect you were, you had married him.

However you're here now. All those years we should have been making love together. We have to make up for them." "Is that right; Angel asked? First thing tomorrow we need to set up your home office in that spare room. Then get your people prepared for your absence. I will get mine group prepared for my absence. We're going on vacation together. "Oh you're just going to put me on vacation from my business; Angel asked? Anything you say, Mr. Man. Where are we going?" "Well Jamal is out of school for summer next week; Christopher said. We can go to South Africa, Jamaica or Niagara Falls. "Oh that sounds wonderful; Angel said. My friend Jennifer and her husband just returned from South Africa.

They stayed at a really nice place and posted some awesome pictures on Facebook." "Okay then, we'll be there in two weeks; Christopher said. Anyplace else you want to go?" Anything you want for the rest of your life Angel. I will make sure it happens. "For now let's get in the shower and change these sheets; Angel said. We can lay in the bed talking about everything and nothing." "Yes we can; Christopher agreed. We can talk about when your divorce is final. Then someday after that we can get married."

At that moment, Angel reflected on all that had transpired over the last few months. All of her life she had strong convictions. About loving her husband until death parted them. That was not that long ago. Even though she was not nearly as happy as she wanted to be. Now, she was with her best friend. Someone that cherished and loved her. One societal conditioning told her she should have never gotten involved with. What she was now sure of is that Christopher had seen all of her. On her good days and her bad days and he still loved her. Through her triumphs and failures, and he still loved her.

When she was a sweetheart and not so nice, he still loved her. He was just like the joy of going home again. After being gone from your loved ones for a long time. She had never been so happy before in all of her life. Christopher was that friend she never saw this way. Now she can't see him being anything less. They had both convinced themselves that this love shouldn't be. They worked hard to assure that this love wouldn't be. Love just worked harder. Sometimes, love makes things happen that you just can't predict.

*There is a difference between whom we love, whom we settle for and whom we were meant to be with.-Unknown*

# THE END!

# Also Available From:
# The Black House Publishing Inc.

www.jonathanpmance.com

http://a.co/8sXiGjU

www.Amazon.com/Kindle

## God Has Given

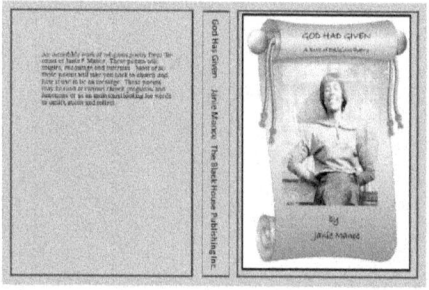

An incredible of collection of religious poetry from the mind of Janie Mance.

Also

Romance & Spice (For The Lady In Black)

(A book of poetry dedicated to the black woman)

by: Jonathan P. Mance

## Coming Soon From:

## The Black House Publishing Presents

## Are We African-Americans or Euro-Centric Niggaz?

www.jonathanpmance.com

www.Amazon.com

BlackHousePublish@gmail.com

## Love Makes Things Happen

2016 Copyright©

## About the Author

That's him right there.

Join us on Facebook for news about *The Black House Publishing Inc.* Upcoming Contest and Projects.

# Christopher's and Angel's Soundtrack

## (In case you know the song)

1. Borrow You-Eric Roberson

2. Breathless-Corinne Bailey Rae

3. Forthenight-Musiq Soulchild

4. He's Not Good Enough-Solo

5. I Can Make You Feel Good-Shalamar

6. Love Makes Things Happen-Pebbles ft. Babyface

7. More Than Friends-Jonathan Butler

8. Next Lifetime-Erykah Badu

9. Secret Lovers-Atlantic Star

10. Seven Days-Mary J. Blige

11. What About You And Me-Conya Doss

12. Until You Get Enough Of Me-The Revelations ft. Tre' Williams

13. Wish That You Were Mine-The Manhattans

14. You Were Meant Just For Me-Will Downing ft. Avery Sunshine

15. You're My Music-Brian Culbertson ft. Noel Gourdin

16. Anticipation-GuiltyPleasures

17. If Only You Knew-Patti LaBelle

18. Lover And Friend-Minnie Ripperton

19.      What If-Babyface

20.      Saving All My Love For You-Whitney Houston

21.      Let's Just Run Away-Johnny Gill

# Thank you!

*To my EFIL4ZAGGIN Thomas (T-Cat) Watson, Carnell (Spoon)
Weatherspoon and Dr. Torrence (Steprock) Stepteau, I am so proud of you
brothers but not surprised. We came out of that mighty Capitol Senior
High. My other home boy from Capitol High holding it down in the DMV
with me Mr. Corey Grant, My Devil Dog. Semper Fi. Deidre Sanderford,
(Baton Rouge) My childhood sweetheart and lifelong friend. Even if you
always back the wrong team. Harry and Almonda Allen Fort Washington,
MD, Thank you, two finer humans I do not know. Ms. Shameika Rhymes-
(Charlotte, NC), Another show sometime? My treat. Hi Tracey K. Sikes-
Boston, MA, I love your sense of humor. Raushanah Butler-Atlanta GA,
The epitome of a classy lady. Turner probably won't let me stop by now.
Smile. Pauline-Abby Lovelace-Queens NY, My conscious sister.
Conversation with you is always deep and I love that. Moureka Forbes-
Brooklyn NY. Maybe we can do Brooklyn Loves MJ together. Katalin
Sekeres, My home-girl from Budapest, Hungary. What a sweetheart you
are. Thank you for looking out for me and the house, Smile. Ms.
Marcelline McMath-Birmingham Al, Ms. Caren Richard you two let me
know when our next trip to Canada is. Ms. Jennifer Watson, Nedra
Weatherspoon, Kristi Stepteau. Thank you for taking care of my boys. Ms.
Nina Hollis (Norcross, Ga.) I told you back at Cookies in the Plaza I was
bad. (Smile) Jane Jackson-Walker, (Baton Rouge, La) where's my Kool-
aid woman? Hi Lakia Nicole, (Baltimore, Md) Roslyn Mickens
(Washington DC) working on business together is overdue. Joycetta
Baines (Raleigh NC) how are you lady? Paula Verrett my other homegirl
in the DMV, I love you lady. Melissa Ann??? It broke, you should try to
fix it. HQBN 2nd MarDiv Comm Co. and 26th MAU/MEU-look me up.
David Cipriani where you at bro? Ms. Jess Bastidas, thank you for amazing
work. Charisse Williams, thank you. Percentages was a better deal. Hi
Charmin Dawns (Dallas Tx.) Can we catch a game? Cynthia Fontenot,*

*Sulphur, La. My Facebook home-girl. Maybe we'll get to see them marching in together. Brittnie Broach, Jackson, Ms. I haven't forgot the plan. For anyone I may have forgotten I do apologize. The bosses I work for at the label have been sweating me to get this book done.*

# The Black House

Baltimore, Md.

Contact: For Book Signings and Appearances. Also if you'd like to write and be published by The Black House. No matter where you are in the world you may contact us here.

BlackHousePublish@gmail.com

www.jonathanpmance.com

(443) 904-0649

# We Say It Loud!

# We're Black And Proud!!!